THE LAST THROW

A BLACK BEACONS MURDER MYSTERY

DCI EVAN WARLOW CRIME THRILLER # 13

RHYS DYLAN

WYRMWOOD
BOOKS

COPYRIGHT

Print ISBN 978-1-915185-25-9
eBook ISBN 978-1-915185-24-2

Published by Wyrmwood Books.
An imprint of Wyrmwood Media.

EXCLUSIVE OFFER

Please look out for the link near the end of the book for your chance to sign up to the no-spam guaranteed VIP Reader's Club and receive a FREE DCI Warlow novella as well as news of upcoming releases.

Or you can go direct to my website: https://rhysdylan.com and sign up now.
Remember, you can unsubscribe at any time and I promise I won't send you any spam. Ever.

OTHER DCI WARLOW NOVELS

THE ENGINE HOUSE
CAUTION DEATH AT WORK
ICE COLD MALICE
SUFFER THE DEAD
GRAVELY CONCERNED
A MARK OF IMPERFECTION
BURNT ECHO
A BODY OF WATER
LINES OF INQUIRY
NO ONE NEAR

THE LIGHT REMAINS
A MATTER OF EVIDENCE

CHAPTER ONE

<small>MONDAY</small>

The roads north of the university town of Lampeter split apart like the arms of a V. North-west, the way led to the coast and Aberaeron. North-east, there was the old market town of Tregaron. Directly east there was no main road. To head that way meant going further south, because directly east lay the Cambrian Hills and vast acres of emptiness. Of course, heading north on these byways linked the two diverging A-roads like the silk of a spider's web, but they crossed a hinterland dotted with villages, most, if not all, with names full of those cursed double l's and f's and n's, and not forgetting the throat-clearing ch's that flummoxed non-Welsh speakers so. But that could not be helped. After all, this was a Welsh-speaking, rural heartland.

The village of Ffynnon Fach—Welsh for "Little Fountain" —was home to a combination post office and convenience store. While many similar businesses across the country had been forced to shut down due to recent government policies, this one had managed to stay open. Now, as summer arrived and tourists began to flock to the area, the store was seeing an uptick in business.

When post office closures loomed, the store's owners volunteered to incorporate a post office counter within their shop. Fortunately, they avoided the scandal that engulfed many sub-postmasters across the country. Unlike those wrongly accused of fraud due to a faulty IT system, these proprietors emerged unscathed from the widespread investigation that unfairly tarnished so many reputations.

Despite competition from a nearby petrol station that offered a range of essentials for drivers, the shop continued to flourish. It stayed open during lockdown for a start, supplied by one of the country's grocery wholesalers. And over the years, it expanded, knocking through to an attached garage area to accommodate more fridges and shelves, a toy section and cards for all occasions. Van drivers called to buy the fresh rolls made daily. eBay entrepreneurs called to post their flotsam to whoever wanted to add to their own collection of jetsam somewhere else in the world.

Its success largely came down to the commitment of its owners.

What was more, the shop bucked the stereotypical trend. The owners were immigrants, but only from across the Severn. Jan and Mick Semple had worked in Bristol for some big insurance company. Jan had Welsh roots and wanted their kids to embrace the culture. That chance came with the death of her parents at a tragically young age. Her inheritance, via the sale of a big house on the Downs, meant that Jan and Mick could up sticks, thumb their noses at the insurance company, and buy a business in Wales.

Mick liked to fish, and Jan attended a Welsh immersion course to keep up with their kids who, after five years of education, were now completely bilingual. The shop and post office were hard work, but the Semples were now very much a part of the community and had found staff to help, which meant Mick only worked three days and Jan only two. That gave them a lot of time for the kids and the dogs and… living. Time they'd had none of in Bristol. They considered themselves very lucky.

Unfortunately, on this fine June morning, their luck was about to run out.

Mick was busy behind the post office counter. Behind the shop counter stood Libby, a twenty-eight-year-old humanities graduate from the University of Trinity Saint David just down the road who'd fallen for the area, and an electrician called Karl. At the back of the shop, where a step led up in an L-shaped arrangement to a section where the toys and cards, fishing tackle, buckets and spades, and local area maps were displayed, a sixty-seven-year-old employee by the name of Denzil Williams checked inventory.

The queue at the post office counter had four people in it. Three more buyers were browsing along the three aisles separated by floor-to-ceiling shelving, and two people stood at the till waiting to pay. The man next in line had a small basket with a six-pack of lager and a family pack of crisps. Mick had seen him come in wearing a baseball cap and sunglasses. He had a very dark stubble and an olive-green shacket done up over a black t-shirt and jeans. Not local, but then it was holiday season, and they got all sorts calling in.

At the desk, Shacket Man asked for a scratch card. Libby, an all smiles, twenty-something shop assistant, asked the man for his preference and he muttered, 'Don't matter,' in response.

Libby turned to a separate till and as she did, Shacket Man grabbed the six-pack and made for the door.

From behind the post office counter, screened by rigid acrylic panels, Mick Semple yelled a warning.

But Shacket Man was already through the door.

Libby stood in shock and watched the door swing slowly shut.

From the back, Denzil Williams ran forward, triggered by the unusual noises.

'We've got a runner,' Mick yelled.

Denzil, a wiry ex plasterer, half ran towards the door and out.

Mick called over to Libby.

'What did he get, Libby?'

'Just the six-pack.'

'No scratch cards?'

'No, I never gave him any.'

Mick lifted the countertop flap opening and swung it upward after locking the till.

'Sorry,' he blurted to the customer in front of him as he hurried around and through the store to the front door and pulled it open to step out onto the pavement of the Main Street. He shielded his eyes from the dazzling sunlight.

A quick glance up and down told Mick that the thief and Denzil had not run that way. Quickly, he hurried past the garage, painted bright orange like the rest of the shop, to the side road leading to the car park at the rear. It could not have been more than two minutes since Denzil had left the shop, but as Mick rounded the corner, what he saw brought him up short.

There, on the ground thirty yards away, lay a figure instantly recognisable, because of the navy shop waistcoat and the shock of white hair, as Denzil Williams.

Mick sprinted forwards. Denzil was unmoving, his face turned to one side, his mouth open. Mick noticed that the gravel ground looked stained with dark smudges in a halo around Denzil's head. Three feet away, the six-pack lay on its side, the cans displaced and splayed open but held together by the plastic rings. Mick took this in as he fell to his knees next to the prostrate man.

'Denzil, Denzil.' Mick put his hands on the unmoving form.

He felt for a pulse but didn't really know what he was doing. He pushed Denzil onto his back and saw right away how the colour was draining away from his face. A slight cut on his temple had bled, but nothing ran down the pale skin. It looked as if the bleeding might have stopped. But from clotting? Or because there was nothing pumping the red stuff around? That new thought sent an unwelcome jolt of fear down his spine. He leant in and put his face close to Denzil's open mouth. He felt no breath.

'Denzil, shit… Denzil. Come on, Denz… come on.'

A dozen thoughts rushed through Mick's head.

Denzil had a head injury, and it didn't look as if he was breathing. Should he move him? Should he try CPR? Was that the wrong thing to do?

'Shit, shit.'

Mick fumbled for his phone and called Libby.

'Libby, listen carefully,' Mick said urgently. 'I didn't catch him, and Denzil's hurt badly.'

'What happened?' Libby gasped.

'I'm calling an ambulance now. I need you to shut the shop immediately and get everyone out.'

'But the queue—'

'Forget the queue,' Mick cut her off. 'This is an emergency. They'll have to come back later.'

'Are you doing CPR? There's a defibrillator at the community hall—'

Mick latched on to that. 'Yeah, good idea. Shut the shop and get that.'

'Okay. I'll do all that. What'll I say to—'

'Libby. Christ's sake. Lock up the shop and grab the defibrillator.'

Mick's hands shook as he dialled the emergency number as the sun beat down.

'Yes, police and ambulance. We've had a robbery. A man has been hurt. I don't think he's breathing… yes, I'm with him… no, I can't feel a pulse… I can try CPR and someone's fetching a defibrillator. But please, get here, for God's sake… what… you can talk me through CPR? Okay… okay… I'll try.'

CHAPTER TWO

Evan Warlow, like most people, or at least most normal people, considered paperwork a necessary evil.

Okay, evil might be stretching things a bit, though, now and again, as the predictive text in his grammar checker persisted in swapping in the word "trot" for "true". It made him wonder if his PC had been possessed by a demon tasked with frustrating the hell out of him.

Paperwork was something that needed to be done, like visits to the dentist or the barber. You did them because, unless you pitched up, you'd end up worse off in the long run.

They were still in the aftermath of the investigation into the horrific killing of Mark Morgan, a man wrongfully convicted of attempted rape, murdered after being released from prison by the very man who'd actually committed that crime. The case had led the team on a tortuous journey full of dark revelations and harrowing deception.

Now they were meticulously preparing and checking up on the evidence that the CPS needed to prosecute the killer.

Most of that involved… paperwork.

Witness statements needed checking. Phone records needed going over. It had all been done once. But it did no harm to recheck these things.

DI Jess Allanby knocked on the partly open door of the

SIO room. When she poked her head in, her striking grey eyes meeting Warlow's, he felt a sense of relief at the interruption.

'Sorry to disturb,' Jess said.

'Don't be.' Warlow looked up from his screen and slid his glasses off. Tom had convinced him to get some "computer glasses", a halfway house prescription between his readers and his driving glasses… which he kept in the drawer at work. Functional and not in any way stylish, Jess had once commented that they made him look like he'd stepped out of a '60s industrial safety film. And she was right, given that he'd bought them online for fifteen quid.

'Hard to believe, but we've just had a shout.'

'Another one? Christ, is it the hot weather, you think?'

June had arrived and brought with it a dry and hot spell. In temperate climates, the stats were stark. Warm weather came with an increase in the level of crime. Someone had even looked into it and come up with two main reasons. People, especially younger people who were the main perpetrators of crime in the broadest sense, were more likely to be out and about, gathering in groups, and drinking alcohol. As they said in the States, more perps and potential victims in proximity was an explosive mix. But there was also the theory that heat itself, somehow or other, made people more antsy and aggressive.

They were entering, if not already in, the 'silly season' - regardless of the real reason.

'What have we got?'

'A robbery in a village supermarket north of Lampeter. A shopkeeper gave chase and is now dead.'

'That's all we have?'

'Response vehicles are there. Ambulance on the way, but the first on scene reports a fatality.'

Warlow pushed back from his desk. 'We've still got the Mark Morgan case up on the Gallery and the Job Centre, haven't we?'

'I'm getting DC Harries to tidy that up.'

'Of course, Catrin's gone up to meet with that bloody journalist.'

DS Catrin Richards, the acknowledged expert in organising the boards, had indeed left a good hour ago to travel up to the site of the previous murder to complete a set of interviews with a journalist by the name of Geraint Lane. Normally an activity Warlow and everyone else on his team would rather crawl across broken glass than pursue. But Catrin was fulfilling a promise made by the higher-ups in an attempt – misguided in Warlow's, as well as Catrin's, opinions – at improving the Force's public image. Catrin's involvement stemmed from her starring role in a recent documentary about the team's success in clearing another murder case involving a Welsh sporting icon. Chief Superintendent Bleddyn Drinkwater, a man wearing a corporate communications strategy hat, ably "assisted" by Superintendent Pamela Goodey, whose hat had an agenda far less easily labelled, thought allowing Lane a fly-on-the-wall access to Catrin, a splendid idea.

Catrin, meanwhile, considered Lane more of a creepy-crawly than a fly – with emphasis on the creepy – and considered it about as much a good idea as walking through a nest of Komodo dragons with a bleeding wound. And everyone knew how Komodo dragons killed their prey. Well, everyone on the team did now that Rhys had explained it to them on hearing Catrin's metaphor.

'They have so many bacteria in their mouths that their saliva is like uber toxic. One bite and you'd die from septicaemia in a couple of days max. And that's when they come back for your corpse, when you begin to stink.'

That brief explanation had earned him a silent clap from Sergeant Gil Jones along with a comment. 'Congratulations, Rhys. *Iesu*, that one tops even your blow-fly-maggots-dating-the-time-of-death explanation. Have you ever toyed with doing children's parties?'

'That is a common misconception. A Komodo dragon's bite contain venom,' Warlow said.

'One of us ought to go out there.' Jess's comment brought Warlow's mind back to the room.

Warlow slapped his palms gently down on the desk. 'Tell you what, let's all go. We'll get a Uniform to clear the boards while we're out. Come back to clean sheets. It'll do us all good to get out.'

'Catrin will be miffed she's missed it,' Jess said.

'Well, that's what comes of being a media personality. Your time is never your own once they get their teeth sunk into you.'

'She'd swap looking at a corpse in a murder case for talking to Lane any day.'

Warlow grinned at the truth of that.

'Right, you go with Gil. I'll take Rhys. What's the name of the village?'

'Ffynnon Fach.' Jess's pronunciation was flawless.

Warlow raised one eyebrow. 'You are definitely beginning to sound like a native.'

'Tidy,' Jess said and disappeared into the Incident Room.

'God forbid, not that one,' Warlow shouted after her. He heard a chortled, 'Hah,' by reply. 'Tidy' was a Gil trademark word.

They both appreciated the irony.

————

JESS TOOK HER GOLF. With Gil adjusting the passenger seat back to get comfortable, she asked a question that had been nagging at her.

'I don't suppose there is any way to avoid going through Lampeter, is there?' They were on the A485. A single carriageway plagued with farm traffic because of the season.

'No. Best to bite the bullet.'

'I think I've driven through it once when the road was half-flooded,' Jess mused, memories of that soggy journey resurfacing.

'That happens. Prone to flash flooding up there.'

'I did not know it was a university town until a few months ago,' Jess admitted. 'I'm still learning a lot.'

'It is an unlikely spot, I'll admit, so I will forgive you. Has its origins in the church, which I suppose explains its relative seclusion. Pretty old, mind. One of the oldest. If I remember rightly, it was set up by a bishop to provide higher education for the clergy. So, everything up there is humanities-based. Lots of ologies.'

Jess frowned, intrigued. 'Never appeared on Molly's radar.'

'Psychology and criminology are not the ologies I was referring to.'

'You remember what Molly is going to study? I'm impressed.'

'She's an impressive girl. On the odd occasion we've chatted, I got the feeling she knows what she wants.'

'I won't argue with that. And you'd know.'

Gil was the father of two daughters and the grandfather of three granddaughters. Whenever topics like feminism or gender roles came up in their circle – an inevitability given the age ranges of the team with Rhys being the most "sensitive" as a result of his exposure to the balanced arguments that were the hallmark of social media – one of Gil's favourite quotes was: "Well, it's not so much a patriarchy in our house as a pastryarchy now that the little ones are into baking."

'She finished her exams yet?' Gil asked, reverting the conversation to Molly.

'She has a biology paper this week. After that she's a free agent.'

'Does she have a boyf… a partner?' Gil caught himself.

'No. Not at the moment. She's resigned herself to waiting for uni. No one takes her fancy at college since Bryn. Oh, and boyfriend still works for me, Gil. I'm open-minded about it, but it looks like that's where Molly's preferences lie.'

'Yes. Best to keep an open mind, ma'am. You never know these days. Well, you do. At least most of us do. And even if you don't, it's best to wait until you're able to think for yourself before seeing a surgeon. But the Lady Anwen wisely reminds me half a dozen times a day to shut up and keep my thoughts to myself. These things have a way of working themselves out.'

'Molly sees the world for what it is. Of course, university is going to expose her to a lot of ideas. Some, I don't entirely agree with.'

'All you can do is offer them the opportunity to experience a dose of common sense whenever they come home. That was my philosophy. What they do with it is up to them. Very underrated commodity, common sense. That and letting them all understand that not everyone can be a brain surgeon or be on Love Island because everyone is different in all sorts of ways.'

'That's very philosophical of you, Gil.'

'It's called hard-headedness. All very well wanting to make everyone the same, but dictates are very overrated, in my humble opinion. I'm not saying that things couldn't be better, but I realise they could be a lot worse.'

'Are we straying into politics and ideology here?' Jess threw him a glance.

'We are. I feel the waves of contention lapping, so I'd better get out of these choppy waters before I drown. But all I know is that my girls have turned out pretty well. They've got good jobs. They're married to some good men who they're good friends with. I couldn't ask for more. But they ended up there without either me or Anwen being heavy-handed.'

'Maybe they liked the model you provided.'

'That's very kind of you. I realise how unfashionable staying married is as a concept – no offence intended. But my daughter tells me I shouldn't worry too much about luxury beliefs because I don't have any. And I have a sneaking suspicion it was a compliment. All I ever told them is that it's fine finding yourself and your own energy, whatever the hell that is, but it's twice as important to find people to share that energy with.'

Jess didn't answer.

'I realise that's not everyone's take on modern living,' Gil said after a while. 'I probably wouldn't have passed the audition for the Barbie film.'

'No, you're alright. Every man is not a bastard, despite the zeitgeist. I was never happier than early in my marriage, where Rick and I had a bond. That changed, so I know one man who is a bastard. But I also know one or two aren't. Molly needs to find her own way, and though I'd never say this to her – she's Gen Z for God's sake – but one day, I'd like to have a grandchild or two. And see Molly and a non-bastard raising them. Meeting your Eleri did that for me.'

'She is a charmer, that one.' Gil beamed, his eyes shining at the mention of his granddaughter. From the pocket of his shirt, the Banana Phone ringtone sang out.

'Excuse me.' Gil listened for sixty seconds to whoever was on the line. 'No. Make them stay. We'll be there in twenty minutes.' He ended the call and turned to Jess. 'One of the Uniforms at the scene. They're holding the people who were in the shop at the time of the robbery, but one of them says she has to get back to her kids and the others are getting antsy.'

'Right, hold on, I'm going to overtake this tractor if it's the last thing I do.'

Gil put his hand forward to the dash. 'I think you could have phrased that better. In my humble opinion,' he said, as Jess pulled out and accelerated.

CHAPTER THREE

In Warlow's Jeep, the conversation took a very different turn.

'Are you going back out to Australia this summer, sir?' Rhys asked.

'No immediate plans.' Warlow had been out to Perth to visit his son and daughter-in-law and their two children in January. 'Besides, it's winter there now.'

'But are their winters cold, sir?'

'In Perth, no. I mean, no snow or anything. But I've seen Alun wear a coat in July.'

'Always fancied Australia. Bondi Beach and all that. I could see myself as a lifeguard.'

'In those red shorts and a swimming cap? Or is that California?'

'Exactly that, sir.'

'What does Gina say?'

Rhys shrugged. 'She's up for a visit. Not so keen on emigrating.'

'You've discussed emigrating?' Warlow's question emerged with a hint of surprise.

'Only, like, in theory, sir,' Rhys explained. 'When one of those programmes comes on the telly. You know, when someone ups sticks and just goes for it.'

Warlow understood the attraction since Alun, his eldest, had done exactly that.

'But I wouldn't, sir. Not now that my dad has been ill.'

'I thought you said he was good since the stents?'

'He is. But if something else happened, and we were that far away, it would be difficult.'

Warlow couldn't agree more. When his daughter-in-law suffered complications during the delivery of his grand-daughter six months ago, having to hear about it second-hand via a video call left him feeling deeply helpless and useless separated by so many miles.

'Never mind,' Warlow said. 'You'll have to put up with us lot.'

'Yeah. Flights are expensive. Everything is expensive. Not just in Australia. And we're trying to save for a deposit on a house. Cutting back where we can. Doesn't help when the landlord threatens to put the rent up, either.' Rhys sounded despondent.

For once, Warlow did not know what to say. The news was full of the same lament: inflation, food banks, the economy and productivity in the toilet. He realised he was one of the lucky ones. He had his own place and didn't owe anyone a penny for it. But for the youngsters coming up, the prospect of being in the same position someday seemed about as likely as colonising Mars. His own sons were renting. Tom was in London and tearing his hair out at the cost of a two-bedroom flat with his partner Jodie in a less than salubrious neighbour-hood. A couple of years ago, a mortgage might have been affordable, but now there was no chance.

People were suffering. Even in a country like the UK with supposedly a top ten world economy ranking. There was something wrong somewhere and though it was easy to blame politicians, after Covid, the world was in a post-war state. The common misconception persisted that, because the pandemic was over, everything could go back to normal at the flick of a switch. But it didn't work like that. Giving people free money to cope with an existential crisis might have seemed like a good idea. But someone needed to pay the piper, or so Alun, Warlow's eldest, who understood more about these things than he did, opined.

But what could you do other than tighten your belt and wait for things to get better? The effects were visible everywhere - shops now only put out dummy packages, there were security tags on £2 bars of chocolate and formula milk, and in towns and cities, big retailers lived in fear of gangs turning up and running off with armfuls of goods. Warlow read the stats. In areas of high population, shoplifting had gone up seventy-five percent. Some of the bigger retailers now encouraged their staff to wear body cameras. But a village store north of Lampeter was hardly a bloody Westfield shopping centre.

'What do we know about this shop?' Warlow asked, bringing them both back to the job in hand.

Rhys scrolled through notes on his phone. 'Looks like any other shop, sir. And it's a post office too. I had a quick look back at HQ. There were no reports of any trouble or previous thefts.'

'How close to Lampeter?'

'Six miles.'

Warlow grunted. 'Too far for the Townies, then.'

Lampeter, like any town, had its share of crime and seen it rise. Mostly minor offences. Even though theft and abusive behaviour were never minor incidents for the victims. Lampeter's drug problem wasn't rampant. But it also had its share of troublesome areas. Like most towns, the vulnerability of tenants and the social mix of communities sometimes took a back seat when supporting drug treatment and rehabilitation.

'You think this might be drug related, sir?'

'It's something to consider given the age of the thief.'

'Isn't that a bit cart before the horse, sir?'

'Might be. Let's find out.'

The June sun blazed in the sky, beating down on Ffynnon Fach as Warlow drove his Jeep Renegade through the cordoned-off entrance of Mick Semple's store. The dark-blue car glistened in the oppressive sunshine, and Warlow waited until the last moment before flicking off the air-con. Rhys Harries stepped out first, stretching his long limbs and not bothering with his jacket. As usual, he towered over everyone present.

Warlow followed, inspecting their surroundings with distrustful eyes, moisture already seeping through pores on his weathered face within seconds of exiting the vehicle. Traffic still drove along the road that was also the Main Street.

A crime scene manager greeted them, and Warlow took in the little gaggle of people standing in the shadow of the orange walls of the store ahead, out of the sun. To their right, a CSI tent had been erected, shrouding its contents. But it held no surprises for Warlow nor anyone else here. Everyone knew inside was a lifeless body.

Alison Povey, Chief CSI Technician, her Tyvek snowsuit glistening in the sun, waved and met Warlow halfway across the few yards between tent and car.

'It's a scorcher today,' she said, wiping her perspiring forehead for once not covered by the Tyvek suit's hood.

Warlow grunted, 'Tiernon been?'

'He's on his way,' she responded with an apprehensive frown. 'I don't think he likes this kind of weather.'

'I don't think he likes anything, or anyone, never mind the weather. Is he in a relationship, do you know?'

'He is. Nice woman. Forensic psychiatrist.'

'Jesus. That must be a fun dinner table to be sitting at.'

At that moment, Jess's Golf pulled in and parked next to Warlow's Jeep. The DI and DS Gil Jones got out.

'We ought to send Gil to supper with them. That would cheer them up,' Povey muttered.

'Bloody hell. Gil and a forensic trick cyclist? Now that is something I'd pay to see.'

Tiernon's reputation as a misanthrope went before him. And well deserved. But Warlow had to acknowledge the man's expertise. 'Right, well, hopefully I can be away before the jester arrives. Let's have a look at our corpse.'

Povey led Warlow to the tent and unzipped it to reveal Denzil Williams. The deceased lay sprawled on the floor – a wiry man in his late sixties, clean shaven and face up, head to one side. Povey moved around the floor on the metallic anti-contamination stepping plates. She bent at the waist and pointed to the large gash on the dead man's temple.

'Fall or bludgeon?' Warlow asked.

'Could be either.'

The tent flap opened, and Jess Allanby stood on the threshold. 'What have I missed?'

'Not much.' Warlow walked back to allow Jess a chance to see what Povey wanted to show him.

'See what you mean by not much,' Jess said.

'His hands show no bruising or scuff marks suggesting a fight,' Povey added.

'That his blood on the floor?' Jess retraced her steps and was now looking at the little indicator flags placed on the ground in a rough half circle.

'Not a hundred percent. But this close to the body, I'd say highly likely.'

'Want to see what all the fuss was about?' Povey asked and exited the tent, only to walk a few yards on to a different tent with the detectives close behind. On a trestle table inside, a laptop and some bagged items had been set out, including a six-pack of cheap lager.

Povey, wearing nitrile gloves, went to the laptop and pressed some buttons. The screensaver disappeared and, in its place, a photograph of the car park came into view. This time showing the six-pack of lager in the foreground as found.

'That's what was stolen,' Povey said.

'What's that even worth?' Jess asked.

'Less than a tenner,' Povey answered. 'It's the cheapest lager available from the shop.'

Warlow could only shake his head. 'Where are the others?'

'Gil went to the shop. He and Rhys are going to talk to the shoppers there at the time that this,' she glanced at the beer, 'was stolen.'

'Okay. You happy to talk to the shop owner? I want to have a wander around.'

As Warlow exited the tent, the warm air prompted him to remove his jacket and drape it over his shoulder. After surveying his surroundings, he quickly returned to his Jeep, tossed the jacket inside, and retrieved sunglasses from the driver's side door. Putting them on, he felt immediate relief from the bright sunlight.

He began to circle the car park, studying the area. To his right, a private driveway led to a property concealed by hedges. Beyond that, he observed fields and a stream that flowed under a bridge on the road. He reasoned that if the victim had been in the car park, the thief must have been there too.

He wandered along the lane towards the hidden property. Just before the gated entrance, a path led into a field of rough pasture beyond. Warlow jumped over a locked metal gate and got some inquisitive stares from half a dozen sheep. Following his nose, he kept close to the trees bordering the left side of the field until he came to a stile under a green public footpath sign. Over the stile, a short path led back, through a gap between houses, to a curving street with modest properties on both sides, each with a bit of garden front and back. He took a left along the street and emerged on the main road they'd driven in on, but a hundred yards further back.

Warlow was a big advocate of the Countryside and Rights of Way Act, allowing people to ramble where it was sensible and safe. But it didn't help when it came to tracing criminals, that was for sure. Lots of ins and outs in this spot. Assuming, of course, the thief had no transport.

But somehow, a man who stole a six-pack of lager did not strike the DCI as someone likely to have a fast car as a getaway vehicle.

CHAPTER FOUR

WHILE THE DCI completed his walkabout, Jess spoke to Mr Semple in the relative cool of the shop. They stood just beside the post office counter. Semple kept his hair short and his beard trim. The rest of him looked compact, and Jess decided that running this business agreed with him. But now he appeared pale and harassed, swallowing frequently, as if he might throw up at any moment.

'Denzil had only been working with us for six months. He came in three times a week to help with deliveries and restocking the shelves. He does one late session on the tills on a Wednesday so that me and the Mrs could take the kids to gym…' Semple paused as the present caught up with the past in a bitter flash. '… Did one late session.' Semple turned away and cursed, his voice low enough for the word he used not to be heard. He looked back up at Jess in appeal. 'He was only doing it because he was bored at home. Retirement gets some people that way.'

Jess listened, letting him vent. 'And you've checked? Nothing of value missing?'

'I haven't checked thoroughly, but no booze has gone, and we don't have any high price stuff. We keep the ciggies behind the main counter and locked up. We must.'

'But there's CCTV?'

'There is.'

'We'll need a copy.'

'But Jesus, a six-pack of Dan's lager? I mean, bloody hell. If he was that desperate, I'd have given him a can. I know it's a hot day but…' Semple ran a hand across the hair on the back of his head. 'It's hard to take in, it really is.'

'Denzil was first out of the door after the thief bolted, right?'

Semple nodded unhappily. 'I've told all of them a dozen times not to confront if someone threatens them. But when I saw him run out, I couldn't help myself. I shouted and Denzil… he was old school. Reflex reaction, I suppose.'

'How long after he left did you follow?'

Semple grimaced. 'I had the post office till open and the safe. I had to shut them both. I was halfway through a transaction as well. Mrs Reynolds was posting to her son in Germany…' He frowned. 'God knows what's happened to that. I'll have to ring Horizon. That'll be joyful. I don't know… maybe two minutes tops?'

'And there was no sign of the thief?'

'None. The street was dead quiet… oh God, I didn't mean that. I didn't mean to say that.' Semple winced.

'Where did you look? For the thief, I mean?'

'I stopped outside the shop and looked up and down the main road. I guess whoever did it had some transport. But I didn't hear a car or see one. Or a motorbike. We get a lot of them come through on a weekend. Though I know it isn't a weekend.' Semple was rambling, his nervous thoughts running through his mouth on high revs.

'So, you saw and heard nothing?' Jess reminded him again.

'No. As I say, it was quiet. I turned into the car park and that's when I saw him. Denzil, I mean.'

Jess had her phone recording the conversation. Much better than taking notes, though sometimes, with suspects, she liked to jot down points as a meaningful beat. It concentrated the mind wonderfully. Both hers and the interviewees. But not today. Semple was a man in shock.

'Do you think…' Semple attempted another swallow. 'Do you think that bastard hit Denzil? I saw the cut on his head…'

'Too early to say, Mr Semple.'

'I've advised them against getting involved,' Semple reiterated. 'If someone causes a ruckus or is violent, I've told my staff repeatedly, it's not worth it. And this place is such a close community. Hard to believe that someone…'

'Did Denzil live alone?'

'He was a widower. But there is a daughter and grandchildren and… oh God, I have to ring her.'

'It's okay, Mr Semple. Give me the number. I'll do that.'

Semple's expression relaxed into relief and gratitude. Jess then moved on to talk to Libby.

———

CATRIN HADN'T BEEN to Cân-y-barcud for almost five months. The isolated cottage had become infamous after a murder took place there half a year ago. Then she'd been a part of Warlow's investigative team looking into the killing of Royston Moyles, the property's owner who'd been found at the address by a renting honeymoon couple.

Their investigation had led them to Roger Hunt, an ex-broadcaster and wildlife photographer who had once rented that cottage to meet with a woman in an illicit liaison. The last thing that Hunt had expected was that his assignation would end up on record. Moyles had set up hidden cameras in *Cân-y-barcud* to film unsuspecting people in unguarded moments. Predominantly sexual unguarded moments. His footage of Hunt with his secret partner, doing what people did in such circumstances, ended up online. The partner's identification had so far not been made public, though that revelation would no doubt emerge when the case eventually went to trial.

Hunt had found out, and so had his wife. His marriage

disintegrated. He'd been made unwelcome in his own home. He'd resigned his broadcasting job before being pushed and took murderous revenge on Moyles, as well as his alleged partners in the hidden camera circle.

His attempts at killing the other two people he'd identified as co-conspirators of Moyles had resulted in one being still in a coma, and the other, John Napier, in hiding after narrowly avoiding being burned alive.

Catrin was involved in protecting Napier, and Hunt was still in the wind.

It was this that formed the kernel of Geraint Lane's fascination with all things Hunt-related. A pitch he'd sold to Drinkwater and Goodey as the basis of his in-depth interviews with DS Richards. A direct consequence of that was Lane's desire, if not insistence, on visiting the scene of the crime with Catrin there to provide a narrative. Or so she assumed.

Superintendent Drinkwater had a lot to answer for in her book.

Cân-y-barcud, a crogloft cottage, so described because of its ancient design where a sleeping area was allocated to a loft over the half of the cottage furthest from the cooking area and fire, sat isolated amidst the wilds of Carmarthenshire. It took Catrin some time to get there.

At the conclusion of the investigation of the last case the team had run, she'd announced that she was now pregnant after several rounds, and months, of IVF. Her concern over that revelation had evaporated within three seconds with the genuine cheers and congratulations that she'd received. And even though he already knew, Warlow's congratulations in that revelatory moment had been the warmest.

Lane's Renault Captur sat in the little parking area as Catrin pulled up in her Mazda. He'd obviously done a ten-point turn in the narrow space so that the bonnet faced the entrance, ready for his exit. It left little room for Catrin to do anything other than poke her car's nose into the remaining space.

She opened the door and stepped out. The scene that greeted her was nothing short of spectacular. The white-washed walls of the cottage threw a blaze of reflected light back into her eyes. She reached for her sunglasses before contemplating the landscape. The Carmarthenshire country-side had transformed itself into a picturesque masterpiece under the warm embrace of summer. A vivid tableau of lush green fields undulating to the horizon. The trees in a nearby copse, now adorned in leafy finery, whispered secrets to the breeze. Sunlight bathed everything in a golden glow, almost too bright even with her shades.

The sweet scent of blooming flowers mixed with the earthy aroma of freshly cut grass greeted her. She couldn't help but marvel at the stark contrast to her previous visit, when winter's icy grip had rendered this place desolate and haunting, chilling her bones. Now, the countryside was a testament to the beauty of nature's cycles, and she almost bought into the effusive descriptions she had once regarded as hyperbole on the NON website. The "No One Near" website, specifically worded to attract people who wanted some peace in their chosen rental property. Just like the honeymoon couple, who had found Royston Moyles suspended from the rafters and asphyxiated by his own weight via an elaborate arrangement of ropes, had hoped for but sadly never found. Her gaze drifted across the distant hills with no sign of another property within sight or earshot. Peace is exactly what one would get here were they to stay.

But her copper's head was never far away. A place as isolated as this had also made an ideal venue for the murderous attack on Moyles. Just like in space, at *Cân-y-barcud*, no one would hear your screams either.

She had to pass the tiny window letting light into the kitchen. Within, Lane sat on a stool, his eyes—which always seemed slightly undersized for his face—gleaming with antici-pation as he spotted her. He'd even shed his waxed jacket and had opted, sensibly, for a short-sleeved shirt.

Catrin returned Lane's wave with a brief, acknowledging

smile. She swallowed her misgivings and took a deep breath before opening the front door. As she joined the journalist inside, she searched her repertoire for a professional game face. The smile she managed was barely adequate, but it would have to do.

CHAPTER FIVE

GIL AND RHYS were in the shop having a quick Look around to see if anything had been disturbed. Gil rounded the bottom of one of the aisles to find Rhys staring at the biscuit array.

'Are you able to speak, Rhys? Or is your mouth too full of saliva?'

'Seen this selection, Sarge? Puts the Human Tissue For Transplant box to shame. They've got pink wafers here, and jammy dodgers. Some things I haven't seen for years. The sweet section is even better. White mice, rhubarb and custard boiled sweets, pink shrimps, coconut mushrooms.' His eyes fell on a jar. 'Chocolate limes! I'm definitely going to get some of those for Cai.'

Rhys's cousin was a big confectionary fan who had Down's. 'Did I tell you they've started putting jokes on iced lollipop sticks?'

'Started to?' Gil couldn't hold back the scorn. 'That was a tradition when I grew up. A joke on a stick. The ultimate crock of gold at the end of the brain-freeze rainbow. They were inevitably rubbish, mind. So, more a crock of something else, usually.'

'Oh, no, sarge. They're good ones now. Cai's favourite is, "what does a lollipop do when it gets a cold?"'

'Go on, then,' Gil said.

'It self ice-o-lates.' Rhys spread out the syllables for emphasis.

'One for the post-Covid age, there. I love kids' jokes. My granddaughter came out with one last week. Why have I got a stepladder?'

Rhys, grinning already in anticipation, played the game. 'I dunno, sarge. Why have you got a stepladder?'

'Because my real ladder left when I was a baby.'

Rhys's mouth dropped open. 'Ooh, bit dark, sarge.'

'Tell me about it. And this from a seven-year-old who has only ever known the love and support of the extended nuclear family. She found it hilarious. *Argwlydd mawr*, I'm telling you. The TV cartoon universe is a very different place from when I was a kid. But I'll tell you what, I'll stump up for a bag of pick and mix so you can munch as you walk about.'

'Will you, sarge?' Rhys's delight was genuine.

'No, I bloody well will not. There is a time and place for levity, detective constable, and this is not it. Do I have to remind you that someone has died here?'

'Sorry, sarge.'

'I should think so. But when you ask the shopkeeper for your bag, get one for me. Easy on the bubble gum. I am not ten years old. Floral gums and toffee bon bons should make up the vast majority.'

'Think it'll be okay, sarge?'

'Once we've seen to the witnesses, I'm sure the owner will be happy to accommodate you. Seen the other section, toys and cards?'

'Not yet.'

'Well, have a peep and take some photos of how the shop is set out and where the thief got the lager from. The till area, etcetera. Detective Sergeant Richards will want to decorate the Gallery, no doubt.'

'Got you, sarge.' But Rhys made no effort to move.

'Before the end of this month would be good,' Gil said. 'We need statements from everyone in the shop, too. I'll do the people at the post office counter; you do the people on the tills.'

'They've even got Fizzers.' Rhys pointed to a little white and lilac tube with paper twisted ends.

Gil gave him a chin-down glare. Reluctantly, but with a grin still plastered on his face, Rhys moved on towards the fridges.

———

GIL'S INTERVIEW with Mrs Lounds, the witness to the thief's escape, was an exercise in patience. They stood near the shop's back entrance, uncomfortably close to the bins, which occasionally reminded them of their presence with wafts of an unidentifiable, yet distinctly unpleasant odor.

Mrs Lounds, seemingly oblivious to both the smell and the purpose of their conversation, embarked on an unsolicited travelogue about Bavaria. She extolled its virtues with the enthusiasm of a part-time resident, given her biannual visits to her son. Her eyes sparkled as she urged Gil not to miss the *kaffee und kuchen* should he ever find himself there.

Judging from the way her summer dress literally strained at the seams, *kaffee und kuchen* were something Mrs Lounds applied herself to with commendable vigour whenever she visited.

'So, you were getting a parcel weighed, am I right, Mrs Lounds?'

'Indeed. Mick knows what to do. He's done it lots of times before.'

'And then what happened?'

'Very little drama. I'd noticed the man. Not very broad in the shoulders, so I would say quite young. My Adam is late thirties, and he is strapping. This man looked thinner.'

'Did he yell, or make a fuss?'

'No, that's the thing. I couldn't hear because I was concentrating on Mick. He was telling me about his daughter going to secondary school in September. She's been on a visit, like an open day sort of thing.' Mrs Lounds glanced across at the bins, from where a fresh waft of something eye-wateringly rotten arrived on the breeze.

'What about the thief, though?'

Mrs Lounds shrugged. 'Libby had her back to him when I looked across. He picked something up—'

'The lagers?'

'Yes, that's it. Picked them up, grabbed the front door and left. Didn't bolt. First I knew something was up was Libby shouting, "Oy, you can't do that". Or words to that effect. Mick looked over and asked her what was wrong. She shouted back that he was stealing the lager. Then Denzil comes from the back and goes after him.'

'What did he look like? The thief?'

'I didn't take much notice. I think he wore jeans. Dark jeans. And one of those baseball cap things on top of sunglasses.'

'Did you hear him speak?'

'No,' Mrs Lounds whispered, leaning in conspiratorially. 'Mick's quite the chatterbox. We were just having a good old natter.'

She paused, a mischievous smile playing on her lips, before abruptly switching gears back to her travelogue mode.

'Oh, and when you visit Bavaria, you simply must see Hitler's Eagle's Nest,' she gushed, as if recommending a quaint café rather than a Nazi stronghold. 'It's where he spent his summers, you know. Tunnels through the mountains and everything. Absolutely fascinating place,' she added. 'I mean, for a dictator's holiday home, it's really quite spectacular.'

'I've been to the Spread Eagle in Carmarthen. Is it anything like that?'

'No.' Mrs Lounds's confusion added a touch of impatience to the denial. 'This is near Berchtesgaden—' It was when she noted the blank expression on Gil's face that her own expression cleared, and she gave him a toothless smile. 'You're a bit of a joker. I can see that, sergeant.'

'*Jawohl*. We'll be needing your telephone number, Mrs Lounds. In case of a follow-up.'

———

RHYS'S LINE of questioning was almost identical to Gil's. But the woman he was currently directing them at was a very different entity. He'd already spoken to a retired plumber by the name of Iolo, who'd been choosing a birthday card for his niece when the robbery took place. A man with an excellent memory, but who'd seen and heard nothing because of his alcove positioning. Rhys had also taken the details of Betty Vaughan, who had just arrived at the till when Libby shouted out the 'Oy, you can't do that' warning. Her glimpse of the thief was fleeting and unhelpful.

But now, standing next to the orange wall of the side of the shop, sheltering from the merciless sun, Rhys looked down at a young face and its eye-catching piercings. One in the right nostril and one in the eyebrow. Her name was Kaylee Francis, and she gave her age as twenty-eight. She stood a foot shorter than Rhys, despite the chunky wedges that she wore at the end of her shapely but pale legs. Kaylee had dressed for the warm weather in cut-off jeans and a sleeveless t-shirt. She told Rhys that she lived on Bryn Road in Lampeter and had come to Ffynnon Fach to visit a friend. She explained that she had traveled by bus and had decided to do some shopping before returning home, to avoid having to go out again later. 'But that didn't happen, did it? Talk about bad timing.'

'You were next in line at the till?' Rhys asked.

'Yeah. My stuff was ready to be scanned. And then all this happened.'

'The man in front of you. Can you describe him?'

'Older than me,' Kaylee said.

'How old would you say?'

Kaylee stuck out her lower lip as she thought. 'Fortyish. Stubble but not grey."

'What about his clothes?'

'Black jeans, cheap ones. Cheap trainers too. The baseball cap looked old. I couldn't make out the logo. But his shades were expensive. Unless they were rip-offs. Hard to say, but they were Pilot, I think.'

Rhys noted all this down in his notebook. 'What happened exactly?'

'He took the chips and booze out of his basket. Crisps and booze. Then he asked for a scratch card and the girl behind the till turned away to get it. As she did that, he picked up the lager and left.'

'Remember anything else about him? Car keys in his pocket? Tattoos?'

'He had gloves on.'

Rhys glanced up. 'Gloves?'

'Yeah. Pale. Same colour as his skin. Like what doctors wear.'

Rhys's expression shifted from neutral to curious. 'Wow. That's... interesting.'

'Yeah, I thought so too.'

'Did he say anything? Did he seem jumpy to you?'

'Jumpy?'

'Did he seem... agitated?'

'Was he high, you mean?'

'That, or drunk?'

Kaylee frowned. 'He wasn't drunk. And I wouldn't say high. Just... normal.'

'So, calm?'

Kaylee nodded.

'Okay.' Rhys read over what he'd written. 'That's all very useful.' He tried a reassuring smile, but Kaylee looked unhappy.

'The bloke who went after him. He's dead, isn't he?'

'Yes.'

Tears sprang to Kaylee's eyes, and she turned away. 'That's awful,' she whispered. She wiped moisture away from her cheeks with her fingers, sniffed, and looked back up at

Rhys. 'My bus is due in ten minutes. Okay if I go? There isn't another one for hours.'

'Of course. I'll just need your phone number in case we have to contact you. I'd offer you a lift, but we might be out here all afternoon.'

'It's okay.' She picked up a backpack from where it sat against the wall and slung it over one shoulder. 'Do you have a card? I can text you my number.'

Rhys handed one over. 'Thanks for your help,' he said as she walked away.

With one glance back over her shoulder at the DC, Kaylee crossed the road and hurried down to her bus stop.

CHAPTER SIX

DENZIL WILLIAMS's daughter worked in an administration office at the University in Lampeter. When Jess offered to break the news to her, Warlow volunteered his support. Jess drove. Warlow, as always, wondered how she got the car to smell so fresh and said as much.

'For a start, I don't have a Cadi,' Jess explained.

'There is that. Even on her wettest days, I don't suppose Molly smells anything remotely like a wet dog.'

That got him a "you'd be surprised" look from Jess. 'Oh, she has her moments. Many a black plastic bag brought home from a festival has needed gloves and a mask because of the funk.'

Warlow snickered. 'Rhys and Gil still doing a sweep of the shop?'

'And the street. They're looking for any likely CCTV. Doorbells, all the retail properties. You know the drill.'

'That's assuming he left that way. If he went to the car park, there is no surveillance. There's nothing but open coun-tryside behind.' Warlow glanced out at the traffic.

Lampeter was in Ceredigion. Cardiganshire in old money. The county next to Carmarthenshire that stretched as far north-west as Aberdyfi, though of course, the Dyfed Powys patch spread further north than that to the English border at

Oswestry and the bottom end of Gwynedd. But Lampeter was referred to as being in Mid-Wales.

'It is odd, I have to admit,' Jess agreed. 'Who the hell steals a six-pack of lager?'

Warlow found no answer to Jess's rhetorical question. Instead, he opened another avenue. 'So, how was your weekend?'

'Nice to see some old mates. Worrying that they haven't changed much. Or that I've changed so much.' She added the last sentence with a wistful half smile.

'I don't know Manchester that well.'

'It is buzzing. First, to a Tiki bar for drinks, then a meal that was 80% Prosecco. Then to a club and ended up doing K2 karaoke until 3am.' Jess grimaced.

'Wow.'

'Yeah. Most of yesterday morning was spent in bed. I can't hack it. Hard to believe those girls do it every weekend.'

'A fortieth, did you say?'

'Yeah. They're a close-knit bunch. I worked with most of 'em. The trouble is when I was with Rick, I excluded myself. Half of the girls are divorced, so now I fit right in.' Jess said all of this without rancour. 'I had to give Molly an Instagram guided account of events, of course. So that I could exchange her FOMO with JOMO.'

Until Molly and Jess moved in with him after Tricky-Ricky's – Molly's dad's – extraction from undercover work in an organised crime gang for his own safety, and the two women had been advised to remain hyper-vigilant for fear of reprisals, he would have had no clue what these acronyms meant. But Molly had schooled him well. Fear of missing out and joy of missing out. One word but a world of difference.

'But Molly misses Manchester, I bet,' Warlow said.

'She does. But she's quite focused now.'

He couldn't argue with that. Molly had knuckled down to her exams with one eye on the university prize.

They drove on in silence. Though it was only six miles to

Lampeter, the late morning traffic meant a good ten-minute journey.

'I met someone you'd like,' Jess said.

'Oh?' Warlow tilted his head.

'Yeah. Really nice bloke. In fact, he's down here on holiday shortly. Always goes to Newport for a week in July, so he said.'

'Right.'

'Name of Mark. We might go out for a drink, so you're included.'

'Surely not.'

'You'd like him. I insist.'

Warlow sat back, wondering why he'd want to be within a mile of a man Jess met and liked at a party. Was she craving his approval? He turned to stare out of the window again, wondering also where such a begrudging, toxic thought had even come from. He had no claims on Jess. Or if he did, they were all in the rusting tinderbox of his own imagination.

'Did Molly behave in my absence?' Jess asked. If she'd noticed any reaction from him, she was good at disguising it.

'She's no trouble. Like you say, she is focused on exams. All I needed to do was stay out of the way. Most nights, I'd end up reading, having given up trying to find something on TV which wasn't some ham-fisted attempt at ideological education masquerading as entertainment. I let Cadi do all the emotional heavy lifting.'

Jess suppressed a giggle. 'Still waging war against the pander-verse, I see.'

'Hollywood I can almost excuse since virtue signalling for them is a religion. But it peeves me when I am legally obliged to pay a licence fee to own a TV in this day and age to watch only what they decide to serve up. I don't have a licence for the microwave and it doesn't force me to only heat up lettuce.'

'Lettuce?' Jess coughed out an easy laugh.

'You know what I mean.'

They fell into a comfortable silence as the countryside gave way to more urban surroundings. Warlow pushed Mark to the back of his mind as they entered the town. He'd taken compartmentalising personal issues to another level over the years. This might come back to bite him, but for now, he had a job to do.

The campus had experienced a decline over the years and now had less than five hundred students. But it was also out-of-term time and the place had a ghost town feel to it.

The office where Nicola Sheedy worked was a low, single-storey brick building just off Station Terrace. They parked right outside and found the door open. Once through it, they entered a six-feet square vestibule with a thick security door in front of them and an intercom system next to a keycard-activated electronic lock.

'The University are security conscious, I'll give them that,' Warlow said.

Jess was more cynical. 'Cheaper to have a system like this installed in the long-term. Probably had a porter at one time.' She pressed the bell marked "ring for attention". A male voice answered, and Jess made verbal introductions. The door clicked open.

Inside, a large room ran the length of the building. Warlow counted six desks behind a glass partition. In front of the wall, a man on the far side of a counter sat staring at a screen desktop computer. He looked up and smiled with teeth the colour of virgin snow. His lanyard read "Edward".

Jess showed him a warrant card and asked for Nicola Sheedy. Edward responded with an anxious grin and then disappeared through a door in the glass partition.

Twenty seconds later, a woman came back through the doors with Edward.

In her late thirties, Nicola Sheedy's slender five-foot-three frame was swallowed by a floral summer frock. She wore spectacles to counteract her short-sightedness, and a nervous smile played over her mouth as she introduced herself.

'Hello?'

Jess offered a hand. 'I'm Detective Inspector Allanby and

this is DCI Evan Warlow. Is there somewhere we can talk in private, Nicola?'

The woman took on the flummoxed look of someone instantly out of her depth. Most people, the majority in fact, had no interaction with law enforcement and were at a loss how to react when it presented at their front door, or, as in this instance, their place of work. Behind the partition, four other curious staff members sent inquisitive looks their way.

'We have an interview room,' Nicola said. 'For the students. Hardship cases and the like.'

'Sounds good,' Warlow said.

Edward fished out a key and gave it to Nicola. She came out from behind the desk, walked to the right, and unlocked a door.

The office was tiny and cramped, with barely enough room for a small desk and four plastic chairs placed opposite each other. Bright June sunlight streamed through the large window, forcing Nicola to hastily close the slatted blinds. She surveyed her surroundings before turning to the officers. Her brow creased in puzzlement.

'What is this all about?' Nicola asked. 'Is it something to do with student complaints?'

'No,' Jess said. 'I'm afraid we have some bad news about your father.'

'What?' The word emerged as a half whisper.

'Denzil Williams is your father, is he not, Nicola?'

'Yes.'

'I'm afraid there's been an incident at the shop in Ffynnon Fach. Your father was involved in that incident and I'm sorry to tell you he passed away this morning.'

By the window, Nicola stood frozen, struggling to comprehend Jess's words. She half slumped against the desk, putting her hand out to steady herself.

'But he…'

'You want to sit down, Nicola?' Warlow asked.

She ignored him.

'How…'

THE LAST THROW   37

'We're trying to find out, Nicola,' Jess said.

'Did he collapse? Was there an accident?'

Warlow zeroed in on that one. 'You said, collapse. Was he well, your father? He was what, sixty-six?'

'Sixty-seven. And yes, he was well. He'd had a few headaches, and I told him he needed to go to see the doctor, but you know what that's like these days. You'd be lucky to get an appointment in three weeks. Meanwhile, keep taking the paracetamol.'

'For his headaches?'

'That's what the pharmacist told him to do. That's who you see first these days. The pharmacists. And his headaches did not come every day. He had a touch of blood pressure and took Ramipril. At least he was supposed to. Even that was a struggle because he didn't believe in pills and such like. Old school was my dad. I can't believe he'd collapse.'

'I'm not saying he collapsed, Nicola.' Jess explained that there had been an altercation in the shop. That her father had run out after a thief. After that, it wasn't clear what had happened.

Nicola looked stunned. 'Typical of him,' she said, with bitter pride between the tears. 'It's not in his nature to sit by and do nothing when something like that happens.'

She pressed them for the details that they didn't have.

'We're treating it as an unnatural death, given the circumstances.'

Nicola confirmed that, apart from the odd headache, he'd been remarkably fit for his age and cycled most weekends.

'Pushbike or motorcycle?' Warlow asked.

'Road bike,' Nicola explained. 'And none of your e-bike nonsense. That's for wusses.' She smiled at remembering his words, but it faded quickly.

The conversation went back and forth between the police officers and Denzil's daughter. They did their best to be kind. But these were unsatisfactory answers from Nicola Sheedy's point of view. The important fact was that her father was dead.

'What am I supposed to tell the kids?' she asked.

Neither Warlow nor Jess had answers for that one.

'There'll be a postmortem. Once we have a clearer idea of what happened, I promise we'll be in touch immediately,' Jess said.

They exchanged numbers.

Warlow wandered outside and spoke to Edward, briefing him on their reason for calling and suggesting that they give Nicola some space until she was ready to talk to them.

As they walked back to the car, both officers were silent, the weight of delivering such news hanging heavily between them. Once they were settled in the Golf, Warlow checked his phone and read a message from Gil.

'Tiernon has been to see the body. They're moving it up to Cardiff. Says he'll do the postmortem this afternoon,' Warlow said.

'Worth going?' Jess asked.

'No. I think we'll be more use here. Get the groundwork done back at HQ. Agreed?'

Jess gave a distracted nod. 'Breaking that news to someone never gets easier. Molly's grandad would have been seventy-five this month.'

'Would be?'

'Yeah. Mum and dad have been gone 20 years. And I have no idea why I'm saying that.'

'So Molly never knew her grandparents?'

'No.'

'I'm sorry to hear that,' Warlow said. 'That''s tough. For you and for her.' He had his own boxset of horror stories when it came to dead relatives. He decided not to probe and instead let it lie with a beat of silence.

Jess did not elaborate. 'Gil would make a joke now,' she said after a few seconds of contemplation.

'He would. And it would be very cheesy, no doubt.'

'Can you think of one?'

'He told me one last week.'

'Go on, I can take it.'

'He said he'd once arrested a schoolboy who maliciously kept changing his classmate's essays. The kid wrote a computer virus and got it on everyone's laptops via email so that any essay they wrote turned into gobbledygook. It swapped around the verbs with the adjectives, changed the commas to full stops. Very disruptive. Anyhow, it ended up in court, but all he got was a reprimand and a school suspension. Gil was furious because he felt the kid didn't get the sentence he deserved.'

'God.' Jess laughed out the word. It sounded a little forced but there was a smile in her voice as she did. 'That's—'

'Dad-joke Gil,' Warlow said.

'Three cheers for that.'

Warlow crinkled his eyes and tried not to think too much about a man called Mark.

CHAPTER SEVEN

AFTER INTERVIEWING KAYLEE, Rhys went back into the shop. He'd taken photos of everything, but then remembered he'd not visited the card and toy section.

It was not a large alcove, but well-stocked with the cards laid out neatly. The usual suspects were all there: birthdays, births, deaths, special occasions, and generic congratulations. He was glad to see a separate section in Welsh and, on a rotating carousel, a range of blank cards which would do, at a push, for just about any occasion. He'd always liked pictogram cards himself, where the message was in images that spelled out a word or a phrase. It appealed to his pub quiz nature. At Christmas time, he'd bought Gina an expensive card. A very tasteful, expensive card, eschewing the crass comedy ones for fear of causing offence. Gina had harboured no such qualms and sent him a card with a not-so-innocent-looking female Christmas elf in a brief tunic standing under some mistletoe with the caption,

"'Tis the season to be naughty or nice. Guess which one I am?"

He'd liked that card very much. He'd liked the sentiment even more.

Apart from the cards, a second wall had an incongruous array of beach-related toys with buckets, spades, balls, fishing nets, and frisbees. On the third wall, a wider shelving unit had an eclectic selection of toys and games. Trivia, board games, party games, often cut-down versions in little boxes. In addition, there were some electronic games, but cheaper versions than you'd normally get on the high street. And in the same vein, some pint-sized remote-control drones and cars. None of them had a price tag of over £30.

The shop owner had been canny here. Holidaymakers on their way to the coast, if they stopped, could pick up the colourful beach toys if the weather was fine. If the forecast was for gloom and rain, the board and party games would draw the eye with promises of hours of family fun… or feuding. And, in between the showers, what better way for a kid to while away the dull hours around the caravan or tent than with a remote-control toy that rolled around on four wheels or buzzed through the air?

A smart cookie, Mick Semple.

'Rhys,' Gil called to him from the entrance.

Rhys stepped back to show himself.

'Tiernon is here. Mr Warlow wanted me to make sure you listened out for any pearls he had to contribute.'

'Great,' Rhys said.

He was too far away to hear Gil's muttered, 'And I know you really mean that, too.'

'You coming, sarge?' Rhys asked as he joined Gil at the tills.

'No. I'll listen to the BBC news if I need a fix of misery and death. I'm going to leave Tiernon in your capable and morbid hands. Finished up in here?'

'Yep. And I've taken loads of photos as instructed.'

Gil glanced over at the tills and the unpaid for contents of a shopping basket still sitting there.

'Povey's lot has finished, too. We could let them re-open. The punters will want their shopping, I daresay.'

Rhys followed Gil's gaze. 'Hmm. I doubt it, sarge. A couple of the people I spoke to just wanted to get away.'

Gil sighed. 'Oh well. Never mind. But if they open up at least you can get the pick and mix sorted.'

'And I fancied a couple of greeting cards.'

'My granddaughters wrote me a get-well card last year when I got the Norovirus. "Thinking thoughts of you today because you're feeling blue. Hurry and get better because we need the loo." Remarkable how poetically adroit they were, considering an average age of five. And of course, the Lady Anwen, who supervised the writing of said card, added the right degree of believability by getting them to write it in their own scrawly hands in crayon, and allowing the misspelling of hurry with just the one r.'

'Devious, sarge… Did you really have norovirus?'

'I did. And I can tell you, it's *norra lorra* laughs. I'm chilled about it now, yes, but at the time, not a laughing matter. More a bowl-for-each-orifice matter.'

Rhys winced. 'Maybe we should forget the pick and mix, then.'

'Maybe we should. I know there are scoops but tell a four-year-old that when they're elbow deep in the jellybeans, despite all the warnings. And, believe me, I know where that four-year-old's hands have been, and it's never pretty.'

———

At *CÁN-Y-BARCUD*, Catrin stood in the tiny cottage, while Lane sat on a stool, using the kitchen work surface as a desk to take notes.

'From what I read of the case, Moyles was found upstairs in the loft area, correct?'

Catrin's gaze strayed to the small match-board wall above her against which the bed head rested, her mind recalling the stark crime scene photographs of the body dangling, oozing, putrefying.

'He was.'

'And is this place still used? To rent, I mean?'

Catrin's answer was noncommittal. 'We've finished with it,

from an investigation perspective, if that's what you mean. Though why anyone would want to stay here, knowing what took place is anyone's guess.'

Lane inhaled sharply. The noise made Catrin's eyes narrow. But barely, not so that anyone, bar her, would notice. But ever since arriving, she thought Lane was on edge. Every brief twitch and affectation seemed just a little more amplified than normal. But perhaps being at the scene of an actual murder might be getting to him. God forbid he was getting a kick out of it. Catrin felt something inside her roil.

'Oh, come on,' Lane said. 'There are people out there who would want to book it *for* that reason.'

Sadly, Catrin knew it to be true. But it hadn't happened yet, at least not to her knowledge.

'Didn't you say that Moyles had hidden cameras in other properties too?' Lane asked.

'Another property, yes.'

'And what about the co-conspirators? The guy who is in a coma, for a start.'

'Daniel Hughes?'

'Yes, him. And Napier, of course. What evidence is there that they were involved?'

'Moyles shared some office space with Napier, and the three of them were hand in glove. Drinking partners, etcetera. We're still looking into that.'

Lane paused. 'Yes, John Napier. I'm intrigued.' He shifted his lower jaw to the side. 'You still haven't told me where he's living?'

Catrin folded her arms. 'And you are well aware of the reason for that, since he's still under police protection.'

'I did some research. His wife is from Pembrokeshire. Her father worked in the oil industry. They had a property in Angle, didn't they?'

'Did they?' Catrin said and watched Lane studying her features. Had she replied a little too quickly there? Damn the man.

Lane grinned. 'Delightful spot, Angle. Well off the beaten

track. And mind if I ask how much protecting John Napier is costing the taxpayer?'

Catrin couldn't help but smile. She'd given nothing away, but Lane read people. And here he was, back on his soapbox. A scruffy old dog with a month-old bone.

'I have no idea,' Catrin said. 'That's the beauty of being a foot soldier. You do as you're told and let someone else worry about the details.'

Lane turned back to scribble on his notepad again. Eventually, he looked back up. 'What about the next steps in this investigation? With a murderer still at large… it remains an open case, doesn't it?'

'It does. And as such, I cannot discuss that operational side of things with you. Chief Superintendent Drinkwater surely made that clear?'

'He did.' Lane's eyebrows shot up half an inch. 'Though, I have been liaising with Superintendent Goodey the last few times I've discussed things. She is very… cooperative.'

'Amongst other things,' Catrin said under her breath, but added a smile to water it down. 'Right, since we're here, would you like me to go through what we found?'

Lane got up from the stool. 'Sounds good. Any idea how long Moyles had been videotaping for?'

'Anyone's guess. But we think four years at least. We found tapes going back that far.'

'Hidden in light fittings?'

'Yes.'

'Are you chasing the people he filmed to let them know?'

'Where we can, yes.'

Lane grinned again. A sly, unpleasant thing. 'Bloody hell. What a rude awakening for some poor punter. Imagine opening the front door to be told that your arse and lots of other bits are all over the internet. Puts Candid Camera on another plane altogether. Enough to put you off your cornflakes.'

The windows in the cottage were all shut for security and the sun had already heated up the small space. From somewhere, the creak and groan of expanding timbers made the cottage sound momentarily alive and echoing Catrin's silent protest at having to be here, listening to this man. She glanced up at the loft. 'Have you looked up there? Where it all happened?'

But Lane turned and put his hand on the front door latch. 'Not yet. Thought I'd leave that until last. Can you take me through the access to the place first? How did the killer escape? It would be good to know what your first impression was when you got here.'

'That won't take long.' Catrin followed him outside. Though the sun was strong, the air, compared to the trapped atmosphere in the cottage, brought a cool and welcome freshness to her lungs and skin. Plus, an opportunity to step a few more feet away from Lane.

She caught herself. In all their meetings, and there had been a few by now, he'd been nothing but professional, albeit unable to suppress a smug superiority that grated. She had not felt threatened in any physical way. And as for any sexual peril... Lane was in a gay partnership, though his previous partner had been a woman. Whatever floated your Lilo, as Gil would have said. Still, she couldn't shake off the sacrificial goat to his Monitor Lizard disquiet that fizzed around the edge of this whole palaver. She didn't like it. Any of it. But then, she reasoned, she didn't have to. She'd leave the shits and giggles to when she was with the team. Here, she would be ice-queen Catrin.

Cherishing that thought, she walked towards the back edge of the property.

CHAPTER EIGHT

WARLOW GAVE Gil a lift back to HQ, but as he walked through the doors, he glanced towards a seating area and stopped.

'Martin?'

A man got up slowly, showing his age. Tall, thin, with the ruddy complexion of a drinker in a craggy face, dressed in raspberry chinos and a crisp white shirt. Martin Foyles was the last person Warlow expected to see anywhere, let alone in his place of work.

'I called in to leave something for you, but they said you were on your way, so I hung on. How are you, Evan?'

Warlow extended his hand. The widower of Denise, Warlow's ex-wife, had aged in the few months since Warlow last saw him, which, he realised, had been at the funeral.

'Come up to the office,' Warlow said.

'No, I will not hinder you.' He pointed to some chairs around a small table. 'This will do.'

Seated, Martin, his face still etched with the weariness of loss, explained his presence. 'Evan, it's about Denise's will.'

The probate process had been a long and arduous one because of arcane processes only understood by the solicitors involved. Warlow had known that this conversation would come, but where legalities were involved, often the wheels, in his experience, moved glacially. In fact, the whole thing had slipped his mind, not that he was invested emotionally. But there were always the boys, his and Denise's sons, to consider.

'I've finally sorted through Denise's papers,' Martin continued, his gaze distant as he retrieved some envelopes from his briefcase. He looked up with an expression of pained apology. 'I wasn't up to it for a long time. Too long. I left the stuff she had in the hospital until last. I just put it all in a spare room and shut the door. Bloody stupid of me. Anyway, I found something she left for you. A letter. And the solicitors asked me to pass on something from them as well.'

Warlow accepted the envelopes. One was addressed to him in Denise's familiar handwriting, three others with typed addresses for him and his sons. The back of the typed envelopes bore a return address which looked official. He ran his fingers over the sealed letters but didn't open them.

Martin explained, his voice soft, tinged with a sense of melancholy. 'I haven't read the one she wrote. She'd sealed it down.' He laughed softly. 'No idea why I even said that. I simply thought you should have it.'

Warlow appreciated the gesture. He felt no rancour towards this man. His feelings had been those of a muted pity, though he sensed that Martin and Denise's relationship centred around their mutual enjoyment of a drink, and, in one sense, he'd been her enabler. But he had no right, having walked away from the marriage, to pass judgement. Now, in the aftermath, there was a sense of closure in this meeting.

'She rewrote her will while she was in hospital. Even dragged one of the solicitors down, and I am glad she did that. In fact, I encouraged her to do it. Necessary evil and all that.'

'Thank you, Martin,' Warlow said and re-examined the deep lines in the man's face. 'How are you holding up?'

Martin's mouth puckered and Warlow feared he was on the brink of tears. 'I miss her. Haven't been to the villa in

Portugal yet. I may go in October. Not the same on my own, though.'

Martin was a good ten years older than Denise, and her death had hit him hard. His gaze drifted to the envelopes in the DCI's hand. 'Denise, you know,' he began, his voice croaky 'she always talked about her sons in the mornings.'

When she was the least drunk, thought Warlow. And though he couldn't help thinking about it, he said nothing.

'She loved them. You're aware of that,' Martin added.

Warlow smiled. Denise had indeed been a complex woman, torn between her love for her children and the demons that haunted her.

'Yes,' he replied, surprised by the mixture of emotions welling up within him. 'But thanks for telling me. And thanks for bringing these.'

'Of course. The solicitor will insist that copies are sent, so don't be surprised if you get duplicates, but I didn't have Tom's or Alun's addresses. If you could let me have those,' Martin said.

In that moment, as Warlow passed over the addresses and they exchanged a few words about the partner they shared, an unspoken understanding of the complexities that had defined her resonated between them. A reminder that life was bloody complicated. And sometimes, closure, when and if it arrived, came in the most unexpected ways.

Upstairs, Warlow put the envelopes in a drawer in the SIO office. Jess and Rhys had already got back, and they were due a catch up. He hadn't eaten since breakfast, and it was now mid-afternoon. Gil insisted they take a five-minute detour to buy a sandwich from the Morrison's garage, justifying the spend with a grumpy, 'You can't think on an empty stomach and with a blood sugar in your boots. If we're traipsing back and forth between here and Lampeter, I will get the Lady Anwen to make us sandwiches from now on.'

Warlow had not objected to either suggestion. The Lady Anwen's sandwiches were a thing of beauty.

At Morrison's, Gil had gone the classic route with prawn

mayonnaise. Warlow had taken the chicken salad sandwich option. All they needed now was a fresh cup of tea and the Human Tissue For Transplant box opened and all would be well with the world.

Tea was already on the desks when Warlow joined the others a few minutes later. He unwrapped his sandwich and sat.

'Catrin not back yet?' he asked just before taking a bite.

'Not yet,' Jess confirmed.

'Okay, we'd better start without her. Rhys, since you've had your lunch—'

'Southern fried chicken wrap times two, McCoy's flamed grill steak crisps and BBQ beef hula hoops, oh, and a Pepsi. Special offer £7.50 with a loyalty voucher.' Rhys sounded well pleased. 'I didn't even go for afters, sarge. I knew there'd be biscuits,' Rhys explained in a plaintive voice.

'Pat yourself on the back, then.' Gil shook his head slowly.

Warlow glanced at his watch, realising they'd spent enough time on lunch. He cleared his throat, drawing everyone's attention back to the case at hand. 'Anyway,' he continued, 'since you've eaten, you have the bridge, Rhys.'

Rhys walked to the Job Centre. 'We have an accurate timeline for a change, sir. Denzil Williams was alive when he left the shop at eleven minutes past ten. We know that because Mr Semple, the shop owner, was running a transaction through the post office computer. He was found at sixteen minutes past ten by Mr Semple in the car park. The 999 call was logged at seventeen minutes past ten and Semple says he spent possibly a minute trying to work out what to do. He phoned his assistant, got her to get everyone out and fetch the defibrillator from the community centre.'

'Defibrillator?' Warlow asked.

'It's not unreasonable for him to assume that Denzil had a heart attack. And I think it was the shop assistant who suggested the defib,' Jess explained.

'It was, ma'am,' Rhys said.

Warlow savoured another bite of his sandwich, relishing

the rare moment of calm and wondering how the damn thing could taste so good. That's what hunger did for you, though. 'Denzil Williams had no pulse by the time Semple got to him, three to four minutes after leaving the shop. Whatever happened must have been catastrophic.'

Gil, always quick to ponder, asked, 'Is this a one-punch incident, you think?'

Warlow let out a weary sigh. 'Possibly.'

'One punch? Is that even a thing?' Rhys chimed in.

Warlow put his sandwich down to explain. 'Unfortunately, yes. Next time you're in the mortuary, you need to ask your friend Tiernon. But I've seen it, so has Gil. Usually, it's inflicted by men on other men, almost always with alcohol involved. And often, they're unprovoked attacks. It's not premeditated and usually ends up being manslaughter. It's worse when it's a coward's punch, delivered from behind.'

Jess interjected, her tone sombre, 'With sickeningly light sentences, too. I was involved in one up in Manchester. A bloke attacked outside a pub after an argument over music. The dead man was fifty-eight, the puncher twenty-six. He'll be out by now, no doubt.'

'Funnily enough, I discussed this with my son in Australia. There, one-punch assaults are also a thing. But it's fifteen years just for the assault there, twenty-five years if it ends up being fatal.'

'But how can one punch…' Rhys began, still bewildered.

'As I say, ask Tiernon. From what I know, the blow causes either a catastrophic bleed or a physiological response that triggers respiratory arrest due to damage to a certain part of the brain. Sometimes, it's the fall and contact with the ground that fractures skulls. But we're speculating here. Let's wait for the PM.'

Rhys appeared genuinely shocked.

'What about the thief? Any further on his motive?' Jess asked.

'I spoke to the customers,' Rhys replied. 'The woman next

to him in the queue said he didn't act like he was under the influence.'

'Could the lager have been a distraction for something else?' Gil suggested.

Jess shrugged. 'The most expensive things in that shop are some handmade soaps and sprays. Maximum value twenty-five quid.'

'Was he going to rob the till and just got cold feet, then?' Rhys offered.

Warlow considered this. 'We'll ask him that when we get him.'

Gil shifted the conversation. 'What about CCTV?'

Jess answered this time. 'There is footage. That's Rhys's job for this afternoon. He's been designated the CCTV coordinator.'

Warlow finished his sandwich, and Gil fetched the Human Tissue For Transplant box. Warlow selected a digestive and dunked it in his tea. 'I did a quick recce. My guess is he scarpered off into the fields behind. I doubt he was expecting anyone to chase him. Seeing Denzil on his tail could have made him take fright, especially if there was an altercation.'

'So, at the very least, we might be looking at manslaughter,' Gil concluded.

Warlow glanced at his watch. 'Any news from Catrin?'

Rhys quipped, 'Probably in the middle of a photoshoot.'

'Now, now.' Warlow chuckled. 'Let's not be catty, just because you didn't make the cut.'

'No way, sir. I've got no interest in swimming with sharks.'

Warlow added with a grin, 'It's the press. Piranhas would be more appropriate. And since Catrin's not here, you're in charge of the boards, Rhys. Let's see if you can get up to Sergeant Richards's standard. She'll be giving you marks out of ten.'

'And not just for effort,' Gil muttered.

'Jess, would you mind giving the Buccaneer a quick catch

up? There are a couple of things I need to do. If Tiernon comes back to us before five, we'll have a quick vesper.'

Warlow watched as his team seamlessly shifted into action. Jess reached for her notes, Rhys moved towards the boards, and Gil cleared away their lunch. No words were needed; each knew their role. Their silent coordination reminded Warlow why they were so effective as a unit.

CHAPTER NINE

WARLOW TOOK what was left of his tea back to the SIO room and sat at his tiny desk. There were things that needed to be done. Things pertinent to the case they'd recently closed as well as the fresh case they'd walked straight into. Instead, he reached into the drawer in his desk and took out two envelopes. Both had his name on them. One typed, with a return address on the rear flap. The second had his name only on the envelope, in Denise's hand.

He opened the latter first.

My Dearest Evan, Alun, and Tom,
*   I'm writing this from a hospital bed. They say my liver is shot and there are veins bleeding in my oesophagus. What a mess. I know there is no one to blame but myself. Ironic that it's taken this to get me to where I'm off the booze for three days and able to think clearly for the first time in years. Those thoughts are dark and painful to me because for the first time in a long time,*

my mind has laid bare all my deepest regrets and sorrows. Regrets and sorrows I buried under a bottle (sometimes two) of vodka every day. And I realise words may never truly capture the weight of my guilt and the pain I've caused, but here I am, putting pen to paper.

My drinking, the fights, the hurtful words - I know they've left scars that might never heal. Evan, you bore the brunt of all that awfulness. We were good once; I know that. But I failed you more than anyone. I regret that our breakup was so bitter, though I knew that love was long gone. I couldn't see beyond my own misery to comprehend the toll it took on our boys.

Alun, I hurt you most. I remember the day you left for Australia, leaving me in a cloud of alcohol-fuelled misery. Your decision to cut ties was survival, not cruelty. I want you to know I understand that now. You had to shield yourself and Reba and Leo from the wreck I'd become.

Tom, you were the peacemaker, caught in the middle of our storms. Your love and patience, that was my lifeline when things got really dark. I can't thank you enough for that.

I need you to know I'm fully aware of all the pain I've caused this family. It eats at me every day. You all deserved better, but I messed it up badly.

When you get this letter, Evan, I will have gone. You may all breathe a sigh of relief. But these last days, my enforced sobriety has been a thousand times worse because of my realisations. I'm not afraid to die. But I'm afraid to die without telling you all how much I regret everything.

In my will, I've left you and our sons what I have. My share of the divorce settlement which I took out of spite, but which is rightly yours. Martin doesn't need any of it. He has his own money, and he knows how I feel. The money will not make up for what I've done. No amount will ever fix that. But it may provide some comfort and stability in the years ahead. It's the very least I can do.

What really weighs heavy on me is knowing I'll never meet my grandchildren in Australia. My greatest regret, Evan, is that I'll never hold Leo, smell his hair, whisper nonsenses, or share those precious moments. Please make sure our grandchild (it may be grandchildren when you read this) knows their grandmother loved them, even from afar. Tell them stories from when I was fun. Show them pictures of before I was possessed. Let them know that I would have given anything to be a part of their life.

There is one more thing that haunts me. After

we split up, some of your lot came digging. They said they were investigating you. They told me their names, but I've forgotten who they were. They were looking for dirt, telling me that if I ever wanted to get even, they could provide evidence. I told them to bugger off. But what they were really after was something else. They wanted to know if you'd ever spoken about an old case. I didn't know what they were talking about. But I remember the name they used. Funny, because I can't remember a lot about what happened over the last five years, but I remember that name because it's a pretty name and one I'd always liked. Fern.

The booze has a lot to answer for, including what it did to my brain. It probably means something to you, Evan, but it meant nothing to me. Now it's like a ghost lingering in my memory. I wish I could offer more clarity, but I don't have all the pieces. What I can say is that these men left me cold. I should have asked for badges. I should have asked for names. I told them nothing because I could remember nothing. Not that there was anything to remember. Evan Warlow, corrupt? So, when did hell freeze over? They didn't like it when I said that. I've lost the contact number they left. I threw it away as soon as they left.

But I remember one of them had a Brummie accent. You know, peaky blinder type.

There's more I could say, but I'm exhausted by it all. I only want you, all my boys, to understand that despite the pain and bitterness, you were the victims of my own failings, and I will carry that guilt to my grave. I hope, one day, you may find it in your hearts to forgive me, not for my sake, but for your own healing.

With all the love I could never express when I had the chance,

Denise

WARLOW READ THE LETTER TWICE, surprised and more touched than he ever thought he would be since he'd never expected to hear or read sentiments like this from Denise. In all the words they'd exchanged over the years since the drink took hold, there'd been little or no contrition on her part. She had been an unpleasant and hateful drunk. A walking paradox, blaming Warlow for all her hangups and not admitting that the booze was even a problem.

He'd discussed all of this at length with the boys. Or, more specifically, with Tom, the doctor, since Alun had always been less prepared to concede that alcoholics were addicts with an altered state of mind. His hard-line attitude was that you always had a choice. Drink or do not drink.

Yet, Warlow had experienced at first-hand Denise's physical addiction and the horror of trying to withdraw. Once, having fallen out with Alun when he was fifteen, she'd tried it. Begged for help.

It had been the worst week of their marriage.

Tom, with the benefit of medical training and hindsight, explained it all to him much later, how the first acute stage of twelve hours caused anxiety and trembling extremities. A state that eased into stage two over the following seventy-two hours with confusion and a galloping heart and then, as had been the case with Denise, the horror of delirium tremens. She'd seen things, cried out at unseen demons, wailed, and screamed, and become a mad thing. In the end, it had been too much for her and she had relapsed within the two hours that she'd found herself alone when Warlow had gone back to work. Relapsed into the cyclical self-preservation mode of alcoholic thinking associated with denial and a firm belief that her problems had their causes in the reality of life around her.

And the core of that reality had been Warlow.

He put the letter down. How ironic that this should arrive – how much better would it have been to have received this before the funeral – on a day when Denzil Williams had become a casualty of alcohol, too. Though in his case, an unopened six-pack of lager as the root cause.

Sighing, Warlow picked up the other letter addressed to him. He read the name on the sealed flap. Doyle Simkins Solicitors and an address in Cardiff.

Doyle Simkins
60 Corporation Road
Cardiff CF1 7MM

Mr. Evan Warlow
    Ffau'r Blaidd, Nevern, Pembrokeshire, SA42
    Dear Mr Warlow,

Re: Estate of Denise Foyles
    I hope this letter finds you in good health. I am writing to you as the solicitor responsible for the administration of the

estate of the late Denise Foyles, regarding her Last Will and Testament.

I am pleased to inform you that the estate has been settled in accordance with her wishes as outlined in her will. As a stated beneficiary, we believe it is imperative to provide you with a comprehensive overview of the settlement.

Firstly, the property, which was granted to Denise Foyles as part of your divorce settlement, has been successfully sold for a total consideration of £478,000. The proceeds from the sale are to be distributed as follows, under the instructions in Mrs Foyles's will and allowing for settlement of tax liabilities:

1. A sum of £239,000 shall be allocated to her son, Alun Warlow.
2. In additional £239,000 shall be allocated to her other son, Tomos Warlow.

In addition to the proceeds from the property sale, Mrs Foyles had accumulated personal savings, ISA accounts, and a share of the pension lump taken at your retirement. The combined total of these assets amounts to approximately £173,000. Denise's wishes, as stipulated in her will, are to return these assets to you.

To facilitate the transfer of the aforementioned funds, we kindly request that you contact our office at your earliest convenience. Once we receive your instructions and the necessary bank account details, we will arrange for the transfer of these funds to your account.

We understand that this may be a challenging time for you, and we are here to offer our support and guidance throughout the process. Please do not hesitate to reach out to us if you have any questions or require further clarification.

Once again, our deepest condolences go out to you during this difficult period. We look forward to assisting you in the expeditious settlement of Denise Foyles's estate.

Yours sincerely,

Richard Doyle

Doyle Simkins

CHAPTER TEN

CATRIN STARED out at the open countryside, stretching away. The heat was now approaching oppressive, shimmering its haze over the moor. You'd need to be a complete philistine not to be struck by the place's desolate beauty, where the lush grasses rustled with the secrets of centuries and the wind whispered tales to the heart of anyone who dared to listen.

'*Get a grip, Cat.*' Craig's voice, imagined but clear in her head, brought a smile that never got to her lips.

Lane stood beside her, his presence still unsettling. She was being silly; she knew that. He was no threat to her. Not physically. That was not what bothered her. Truth was, she didn't know what was bothering her, other than she didn't like Lane. At least she didn't like what he represented; the press and how they delivered information to the world. But at least out here, out of the cottage's claustrophobic confines, he seemed less jumpy, and she was less aware of his eyes darting around as if expecting something to leap out from the shadows at any minute.

'So, here you are. Royston Moyles dead, his car outside, hysterical honeymooners having found the body. What do you do from there?' Lane's words broke the silence that seemed to sit like a weight over the property.

Catrin shifted her gaze from the distant horizon to Lane.

His face betrayed a twisted mix of fascination and provocation. 'As you can see for yourself, the killer could have come on foot from almost any direction.' She kept her voice calm despite the unease that crept over her like a shadow at the memory of that freezing night.

'So, on foot was your working hypothesis?' There was a mocking edge to his voice.

'Obviously, we looked at the nearest roads. Somewhere that might allow access to the moors. There are several, but they all would mean travelling the last leg by foot.'

'The last leg by foot. I like that,' Lane said, a sly grin tugging at the corners of his lips. Catrin winced, sensing his enjoyment of the situation.

'So, your assumption is the killer saw Moyles arrive?' Lane turned three-sixty, taking in the layout, trying to find somewhere the killer might have stayed hidden.

'Lights from a vehicle would have been visible for miles around,' Catrin conceded, her tone betraying frustration at Lane's persistent questioning. She wished he would just stick to his role as a journalist and leave the detective work to the professionals. She swallowed back her irritation. This was why she was here. Superintendent Drinkwater's words echoed in her ear. 'It's important that we're seen to be transparent, Catrin. This is all about optics, as it were.'

'What if he was already here?' Lane asked, his eyes narrowing in thought.

Catrin's own smile twisted into surprise. 'What?'

'Waiting. I mean.'

'There is that possibility. But unless he had a tracker on Moyles's car, how would he know when to expect him? And the night was bitter. We had freezing rain, if you remember.'

Lane's eyes glittered above a snigger. 'I was thinking how this would make a great, true crime book.'

'No one said anything about a book. I thought you were writing a news article?'

'I am. But it would be criminal to let all this research and imagery go to waste, you have to admit.'

'I admit nothing without a lawyer or my union rep,' Catrin retorted.

Lane chuckled, undeterred. 'Oh, very good, sergeant. And what about the man himself, Hunt? What's your assessment of him?'

Catrin's face hardened at the mention of the man. 'Dangerous. Intelligent. Psychologically scarred by what had happened to him. Enough to turn him into a bloody-minded psychopath. He wants revenge. An eye for an eye.'

Lane shrugged. 'Mind if I take a photo of you against the wall with the empty backdrop? I won't use it other than as an *aide-mémoire* for writing the piece.'

Catrin fluttered her hands up in acquiescence, her gaze fixed on the distant horizon as she stood against the stone wall. 'I hope you get a good snap for your "*aide-mémoire*",' she muttered to herself through a closed mouth, adding mental rabbit ears around the affected phrase, though she wanted to follow up with, 'because this is the last time I'm posing for the sake of journalism or anything else.' But she held her tongue as she stepped away to join Lane.

'Okay, why don't I show you the loft area where we found Moyles, and then I'm going to call it a day. We're in the middle of finishing up after our last investigation—'

'Mark Morgan. The wrongful imprisonment guy,' Lane interjected.

'Yes, him. And there's a ton of work to do.'

'Of course. Let's see the killing room, and then we can both be on our way.'

The front door to *Cân-y-barcud* opened inwards, hinged on the left such that its travel took it up against the corner of the steps leading up to the loft. They'd screwed a rubber doorstop into the floor to prevent the door from banging against the newel post. It left a space at the foot of the stairs with the front door open, concealed from the rest of the cottage.

Catrin walked through and around the little kitchen peninsula to let Lane enter. It was as he pulled the door shut behind him that a figure stepped out from behind it, a gun held in its hand.

'Jesus,' Lane yelled.

'No. Not today,' Roger Hunt said. 'Walk over to her and shut up. You've done enough talking for one day.'

'What do you think you're doing?' Catrin asked. Empty words but the best she could muster under the circumstances.

Despite the beard and the hollow, dark eyes, she recognised him from the countless times she'd stared at the various manifestations of his face on her workstation screen. Bearded, clean shaven, smiling for PR shots, rugged out in the countryside, images from over the years. She'd know this man anywhere.

'Closure,' Hunt said, his eyes boring into hers, voice dripping with bitterness.

Trying to keep her voice steady despite the adrenaline coursing through her, Catrin took a small step forward. 'Whatever it is you want, we can talk about this.'

But Hunt's response was anything but rational. Without warning, he raised the gun and fired a deafening shot into the ceiling. Catrin and Lane both flinched into a crouch in response.

'Okay, okay,' Catrin yelled, her heart pounding as the reality of the situation crashed down upon her. This man was desperate, dangerous, and unpredictable.

Hunt gestured at Lane with the gun. 'You. Zip tie her hands behind her back,' he ordered.

Lane hesitated. He was trembling badly.

'Do it,' Hunt said and pointed the gun at Lane's face and nodded once towards the work surface where a scattering of green garden zip ties had been left.

The journalist looked like he was about to throw up.

Catrin didn't resist as Lane bound her with trembling hands.

'Show me,' Hunt insisted, and Catrin half turned.

'Tighter,' Hunt snarled.

A fumbling Lane complied.

'Get her keys and phone from her bag,' Hunt commanded, his voice like steel.

Catrin wore a black Osprey cross-body bag. A Christmas present from Craig. Lane opened it clumsily. He was close enough for her to smell his aftershave. She held her breath while he rummaged. Her keys jangled as he retrieved them and placed them and her phone next to the spare ties on the table.

'Now you,' Hunt said, glancing at Lane. 'One hand zipped to the banister.'

Lane complied. Catrin saw how terrified he was. There'd be no resistance from him as he secured one of his wrists to the wooden banisters. Hunt kept his eyes on Catrin, as if he was more wary of her than what the journalist might try, aware of the way her eyes darted around, searching for any sign of an opening.

With Lane's hand tied to the stair, Hunt stepped closer to Catrin, the muzzle of the gun inches from her face. 'Out to your car, Sergeant. Move.'

Catrin walked toward the door, acutely aware of the gun pressed against her back, its cold metal a harsh and solid reminder of the peril they were in. She prayed for an opportunity to disarm Hunt, but with Lane still at his mercy, she couldn't afford to take the risk.

Outside, morning was heading towards midday. The light made her blink, the warm breeze the only witness to this… whatever it was. Catrin's car sat as she'd left it. She did not want to get in. But Hunt's unrelenting gaze was upon her as he continued to force her forward. She hadn't locked the car. Hunt pushed her aside and pulled open the back door of the Mazda.

'Get in,' he goaded, his voice like an icy blade against her skin.

It wasn't easy with her hands tied behind her, and his presence just feet away provided a constant reminder of her vulnerability. Her mind raced. She had to find a way out of this, not just for her own sake, but for Lane's as well. But what could she do? She watched through the rear-view mirror as Hunt locked the car from the outside and went back to the cottage. Was he going to get Lane? Where the hell was this man going to take them?

The back window of the car was open by an inch. From the direction of the cottage, someone wailed. The first note in a symphony of shouts, screams, and brutal thuds that echoed through the still day. Cracks and slaps landed like a macabre drumbeat, punctuated by cries of pain and desperation.

The gunshot, when it came, split the air and put paid to all the other noises.

'No, no, no,' Catrin moaned, acutely aware that no one would hear her. The silence that followed seemed to stretch on for an eternity.

Her heart galloped as Hunt came back out, calmly, as if nothing had happened, wiping his hands on a paper towel that he scrunched up and discarded onto the floor before inspecting the knuckles of his hands.

Then he turned to the garden and crossed to a hedge from where he retrieved a blue bike hidden behind bracken. He looked up at Catrin only once as he opened the boot and placed the bike with the boot lid closed over it, fastening the arrangement with bungee cords, his expression unreadable.

When he got into the front seat, Catrin whispered, 'What did you do?'

'You don't need to worry about a piece of filth like him,' Hunt said.

Catrin's horror deepened as the unsettling truth washed over her. Geraint Lane had unwittingly become a pawn in this deadly game and had paid the price for their presence here.

Hunt put the key into the ignition, the gun still firmly in his other hand. 'Sit back. We're going somewhere where we won't be disturbed.'

As the car roared to life and pulled away from the cottage, guilt and sorrow clawed at Catrin's insides, threatening to overwhelm her with each passing moment. Why had she gone to such a remote place as *Cân-y-barcud* alone? But she knew the answer. She was there under orders. And Lane, despite his odiousness, had been harmless.

Even so. Craig would say that she should have used her spidey-sense.

She cringed. A stupid, silly thing to think of.

Especially now that it wasn't only her she had to look out for.

Her mind raced, desperate to find a way that this nightmarish journey would not end in further tragedy. The sun had baked the car during the morning. It felt stifling and airless. Sweat ran down her neck. But she steeled herself. She needed to be calm. She needed to think and find out what Hunt wanted.

If there was any consolation in what had happened, and Lane's predicament left little to her imagination, it was that she was still alive.

Which meant Hunt needed her for something.

And while he did, there was a chance she could use that to her advantage.

CHAPTER ELEVEN

WARLOW READ the solicitor's letter twice, too. Both times with equal amounts of surprise. Denise held on to the house that they'd raised the boys in, renting it out for a steady income, though she'd also done some legal chicanery whereby she'd transferred fifty percent of the ownership already to Alun and Tom immediately after the divorce. They'd get the other half of the house sale directly, bringing their share up to just shy of a quarter of a million. All to do with tax mitigation and to not allow the state to purloin the proceeds if Denise ever ended up in a nursing home. That had all been done before she met Martin, of course. And there had always been the possibility that Martin, as her new partner, might have entered the picture somehow. But he'd shown no rancour earlier. As a retired business owner with his own significant personal means, Martin would not miss the money. Even so, the very last thing Warlow had expected was that Denise would even mention him, Evan, the poisonous ex, let alone feel inclined to include him.

He glanced at his watch. He'd need to remember the day and date. Mark it as a day of irony. The alcohol that turned Denise into a monster had also been responsible for the ruptured oesophageal varices that had hospitalised her. Once there, she'd undergone an enforced abstinence and a withdrawal tempered by a cocktail of benzodiazepines to help her through. The irony being that any epiphany she experienced had sprung from that.

Warlow's tea was cold. He ought to let Alun and Tom know as soon as possible. Money like this could be life changing for them.

He stared at the letter on the desk and allowed himself a rueful grin as he whispered, 'You did okay there, girl. For once. And I will tell them, Leo and Eva, about when you were fun. I think Eva has even got your eyes. God help the world.'

He rang the number on the letter and got through to someone in Richard Doyle's office and, having explained who he was and the reason for the call, got an email address and used that to send Tom and Alun's postal addresses. He cc'd them in via their email addresses, too, but experience taught him that the law liked written affirmations. Was it archaic to insist on paper and ink these days, he wondered? He could foresee a time when it might be. But he could also still remember when you had to write letters to people and send them through the post to communicate. An image of the look of confused horror on Molly's face if he tried to explain that to her now floated up in his head. As a teenager, he'd had to walk to a telephone box at a prearranged time to phone a girlfriend. Even thinking about it now made it sound hardly believable.

That is so last century, Evan.

Molly's voice in his head again. But it might just as easily have been Rhys's, though he would have substituted the Evan with a Mr Warlow, no doubt. As he folded the letters back into their envelopes, Jess stuck her head around the door.

'Everything okay?' she asked.

'I've just been visited by a ghost,' Warlow said.

Jess made a show of looking around the space for signs of a spectre.

'A letter from Denise's solicitor,' Warlow explained.

'She suing you from beyond the grave?'

'On the contrary. Postmortem gifts in her will.'

'Oh? Were you expecting that?'

'Not on your elephant, as Rhys likes to say.'

'Do you need a moment?' Jess asked.

'No. She did right by the boys and wrote me a letter from the ICU expressing her… regrets. Not something I ever thought I'd hear.'

'I can come back—'

'No need. What have you got?'

'Rhys has the shop CCTV up. Worth a look.'

Warlow got up and followed Jess out. Gil stood behind Rhys at his desk, studying the screen. Warlow joined them and Rhys ran the relevant part of the tape. On screen, a man in a green overshirt and a black t-shirt and jeans with a black Nike baseball cap and dark glasses emptied his basket.

'He is wearing gloves, sir,' Rhys said.

They saw him remove the contents of the basket and put the six-pack of lager on the counter.

'No watch. The shirt cuff is buttoned up. We can't see his face or his wrist or his skin,' Gil said. Behind him, Kaylee's basket rested on the edge of the counter. Shacket Man then asked Libby something, and she turned to the scratch card display. At that point, Shacket Man grabbed the lager, turned, and left. Everyone stood for several seconds and then Libby must have shouted. Warlow watched the clock. Thirty seconds later, Denzil appeared from inside the store, and then rushed out of the door in pursuit.

'As reported, sir,' Rhys said. 'Nothing about him is remarkable. No labels, jewellery, tattoos.'

'What about other CCTV sources?'

'Yet to be processed, sir.'

'Okay, keep at it. You can have a proper run at things tomorrow morning once Tiernon files his report. Eight-thirty start?'

Everyone agreed.

———

CATRIN PRIDED herself on keeping a level head, but as she sat bound and helpless in the harshly lit space she now found herself in, her heart pounded. They'd driven for an hour, along roads she knew vaguely, through places she'd never stopped at; Pumsaint, Farmers, Llanddewi Brefi, but always heading north towards Tregaron before an abrupt right turn and a long stretch of road across the moors. They'd passed few cars. Twice, Hunt pulled off to park and let cars go by. And then they'd arrived at an isolated telephone box, and they'd veered off the road towards a forestry plantation. He'd driven in, parked the car under the trees away from the track and, as if they were in a dystopian novel, scraped away branches and ferns to reveal a trapdoor in the ground and a shaft leading down.

And now here she was, with Hunt, a man wanted for murder and madness, dragged far from civilisation, and forced, at gunpoint, underground. Her legs ached from the tight bindings that he'd wrapped around her ankles once she'd descended, leaving her helpless to do anything but sit on a rusty old chair in a corner behind the door in the room. Her hands, retied in front of her after being bound behind her back, rested in her lap. The place smelled stale, with a pungent chemical undercurrent of cheap disinfectant.

'Before you ask,' Hunt said as he'd made her climb down the ladder before he'd bound her legs with duct tape, 'it's a Royal Observer Corps outpost. Built in case of nuclear war.'

'Looks like it,' Catrin muttered, taking in the polystyrene tiled walls and the wiring and piping running over them. A bunk in the corner had a sleeping bag on the top, folded clothes on the lower. Two wooden cupboards either side of a desk and a wooden chair made up the only other furniture.

Her captor seemed unfazed by her sarcasm. He pointed to what looked like a clock with a metal pipe running up into the ceiling. The clock had no hands, only a meter. 'That was to measure the strength of any explosion. My father stationed in one of these for a short while.'

'Lovely.' The ties on her legs were not tight but did the

job. If she stood, she'd be unbalanced. The bunker was suffo-
catingly small, only fifteen by seven feet, with concrete floor
and walls visible where the tiles had come loose.

A single ceiling light bulb and some fluorescent strips on
the walls lit up the place. Hunt gave her some water from a
plastic bottle. Now he sat on the one other chair, gun still in
his hand, his eyes glittering above the bushy beard. 'If I'd
wanted you dead, you would be,' Hunt said.

'Like Lane?'

'Forget Lane. He had his uses. Now he's irrelevant. Napier
is who we need to talk about. Where is he?'

Catrin remained resolute, her gaze locked on Hunt's face.
She knew that revealing anything about Napier's whereabouts
would only lead to more chaos. She would protect her witness,
even if it meant enduring whatever Hunt had in store for her.

'I don't know,' she spat back, her voice trembling but
defiant.

A smile crept across Hunt's face. 'Don't lie. But you've
inadvertently saved yourself a lot of unpleasantness. As I say,
Lane wasn't completely useless. But thanks to that little slip of
yours earlier, I now know Napier had some ties to Angle. The
way you clammed up tells me it's important. Care to tell me
more?' His eyes narrowed, and his grip on the gun tightened.

She stayed silent, staring defiantly at the concrete floor.

Hunt seemed to grow impatient. He reached across to a
laptop. 'Signal is crap up here. But there is one provider with
4G, and they do a handy 4G dongle. Now, let's see what we
can find.' Catrin watched as he typed questions into a search
engine. Ten seconds later, he sat back.

'Wow, that was quick. Napier and Angle. There's even an
obituary here for a Henry Napier from twenty years ago.
That'll be his father, I expect.' He read on in silence. 'And
would you look at this? It says there was a small service at
Angle Turn Cottage before the internment.'

Catrin's heart sank. Her earlier slip had given away much
more than she'd intended. Damn Lane. Then she remem-

bered the shouts and screams and thuds, and that final, loud, pistol crack and immediately regretted it.

'I realise you're angry. Who wouldn't be angry after what happened?' Her dry mouth thickened her words.

Hunt hesitated, pondering whether to answer her. He kept his eyes on the screen as he spoke. 'You have no idea. But then being flawed is part of being human.' He grinned, his teeth showing in the middle of his dense beard. 'I had everything. Job, family, fame, but then I found something else. Something I never had before. A little happiness. A bit of contentment. Now, that's a word that's underrated.'

Catrin held back from mentioning the name of the woman Hunt had been having an affair with. The woman whose life would also be destroyed once everything went to court. Saying all that might simply stoke the fire of Hunt's quietly seething anger.

'I get that you want revenge. I get that. But Napier isn't Moyles. All he did was share office space.'

Hunt stared at her. A cold, pitying expression that broke into a mirthless grin. 'The big difference between you and me, sergeant, is that I interviewed Moyles. Admittedly, my techniques were a touch mediaeval compared to yours. You have to take account of some lizard lawyers yelling human rights and slapping your wrists. I had no such constraints. Moyles was very vocal. And I can tell you that Napier and that baker friend of his were not innocent.'

The baker friend Hunt referred to remained in a coma as a result of being thrown off a railway bridge headfirst.

'If you have evidence that Napier—'

'I have Moyles screaming out in minute detail every filthy, disgusting, appalling thing they did in that idyllic cottage.' Hunt squeezed out the word idyllic to make it sound like something disgusting. More abattoir than haven. He tapped his head with his middle finger. 'It's all in here. Every word. Every detail. I can tell you Napier is just as much a monster as Moyles.'

Catrin shifted in her seat and leant forward. 'It doesn't have to be like this, Roger—'

Hunt showed no emotion as he replied to her, writing details on a pad taken from the map he had up on the laptop screen. 'You're good, sergeant. But we do not need a rapport. And you're right. It doesn't have to be like this. I could make you describe what wallpaper Napier has in his bedroom… but that would make a mess.'

Hunt's silence lingered, allowing his unspoken threat to permeate the air. Finally, he spoke again, his voice low and controlled.

'Napier is my target, not you. But make no mistake—I'll do what's necessary.' He turned, fixing her with a glacial stare. His eyes, devoid of warmth, conveyed a chilling promise of violence.

She swallowed hard, realisation dawning. 'You were in the loft waiting for us, weren't you? Listening to everything.'

Hunt's silence stretched, his stillness more telling than any words. His lack of denial hung in the air, as damning as any confession.

CHAPTER TWELVE

GIL WAS WRITING up the morning's interviews and adding them to the local database they always established in a case. In the old days, they called this a murder book. Some people still preferred the old pen and paper approach, but they were few and far between now. Though, any fly on the wall at a briefing would see everyone with a ball-point pen and pad, taking notes. But for sharing this kind of information, the database was king.

The minute hand was approaching three with the hour hand on five when his mobile rang. Still the Banana Phone ringtone put there at the request of his granddaughters.

'Gil Jones,' he said.

'Hey, sarge. It's Craig.'

'Craig, please don't tell me you're reporting a dead body because we're chock-a-block today. You'll just have to find a big freezer and come back tomorrow.'

Craig, well used to Gil's dark sense of humour, let out a snort. 'Is she there?'

'If by she, you mean Catrin, then no, she is not. Phone not working?'

'I can't get any answer.'

'Mind you, she is in the back of beyond. Could be a signal black spot or her battery's gone kaput.'

'Her battery doesn't go kaput, sarge.'

Gil thought about it. This was Catrin Richards they were talking about, and kaput batteries were indeed not something that happened to her. 'She's been up in the wilds today meeting with a vampire, though.'

'Oh yeah, that journalist.'

'That's him. If she looks pale when she comes home, make sure she gets something with iron in it inside her. Steak and eggs are good for that, I hear. But if she takes a chomp of the raw stuff, run for the hills. Get some garlic on the way home, just in case.'

'I didn't know it was an all-day thing,' Craig said. 'I thought she'd be back with you this afternoon. I heard there was a shout in Ffynnon Fach.'

'You heard correctly. Weird one. Someone stole a six-pack of lager and, before you know it, there's a dead man in the car park.'

'Okay, well, if you see her, tell her I rang, and I'll see her at home.'

'Will do.'

Gil turned back to his typing. Fifteen minutes later, he got up and walked through to the SIO room. Warlow was on the phone but ended the call when Gil appeared.

'The Heath,' Warlow explained. 'Crackly Vivaldi on-hold music. Enough to make you weep. Thought I'd try the mortuary and Tiernon, but no joy. You look… troubled.'

'Craig, as of Catrin and Craig, rang me twenty odd minutes ago. Asking about Catrin.'

Warlow frowned. 'I've been expecting her back since lunchtime. But, as you say, she could want to get Lane done and dusted once and for all.'

'There's a pub in Abergorlech. Not always a signal there. A big selling point if you ask me.'

There was a distinct possibility that Catrin and Lane had ended up somewhere like that, Warlow thought. 'Have you tried Lane?' he suggested.

'No. I have his number somewhere, though. Under B for blood-sucking parasite if I remember correctly.'

Warlow allowed himself a grin and found an email from Drinkwater from a couple of weeks before confirming Catrin's secondment as Lane's direct contact for the in-depth piece that the journalist was writing. Lane's mobile had been appended to the document. Warlow read it out as Gil punched in the numbers. The sergeant held the phone to his ear for a long minute.

'No answer. Mind you if his coffin is lead-lined—'

Warlow ignored him. 'Probably means they're out of signal.'

Both men had been up to *Cân-y-barcud* and the surrounding area. Some of the roads were not on any satnav map. 'I'll text her to make sure she lets us know when she's on the way. She'll get that as soon as a signal appears.'

'Good plan,' Warlow said. He could have spoken to Gil about the letters he'd read that afternoon, but there would be a time and a place that would not involve keeping Gil away from a Lady Anwen supper.

Warlow kept his powder dry for now.

———

'How long have you been here?' Catrin asked.

There was no stepping back from what Hunt already knew about Napier. She ran through the conversation she'd had with Lane. What had she said? Nothing specific. But then she had not denied what Lane had surmised either.

Her hands clenched into tight fists, knuckles whitening as frustration coursed through her.

No point trying to negate all of that. But Hunt seemed remarkably focused. Kidnap situations were impossible to prepare for, but she'd had some training and trawled her mind for bullet points. Active listening, maintain communication. Be compliant. If needed, show some vulnerability, and build empathy.

Hunt moved away from the laptop, pacing the cramped length of the bunker in two strides. Catrin's eyes darted around, taking in the surroundings. She noticed a stash of chemicals and equipment in one corner, an ominous collection of materials that sent shivers down her spine.

Hunt picked up a heavy tote bag before turning back to her. 'I'll be away for a while. Don't worry, there's water and food.' He nodded towards a cupboard. 'And plenty of air. These bunkers were built to resist an atomic bomb. No one will hear you if you scream. We have spare batteries and solar power. But I will be back. Once I finish what I need to do. Is he there now, Napier? His office says he's on leave for a few days. Soaking up the sun in Angle, is he?'

Catrin's heart plummeted as Hunt made his intentions clear. She was alone in this dark, dank hole in the ground with a maniac who was determined to find Napier at any cost. The seconds ticked by like hours as she sat there, bound and quelling the shakes in her legs.

Maintain communication.

'Was your dad stationed in this one?' Catrin asked.

'No. Newick in Sussex. It's not in such good nick as this one. They weren't permanently manned either. Three full on exercises a year, training once a week. But the Corps were all volunteers.'

'I had no idea these things existed.'

'Hardly anyone does. Some are more obvious. Most are hidden away. I've changed the above ground to make it unobtrusive and built a dummy site a bit away. Anyone looking will find that and think it's been decommissioned.' Hunt approached her one last time, his eyes boring into hers. 'Now, you're not diabetic or anything, right? You're not going to lapse into a coma while I'm away?'

Show some vulnerability and build empathy.

Hunt was the last person in the world she'd normally discuss her personal life with. But here and now, she had no choice. 'No, I'm not diabetic. But I am pregnant.' It sounded odd, saying it out loud.

Hunt didn't react, but he held her gaze, as if challenging her to look away. Catrin didn't.

'Why am I here?'

Hunt ignored her. 'There's a loo. Chemical, but it does the job.' He picked up her keys. 'Need to borrow your car again.'

'Why am I here?' Catrin asked again.

But Hunt merely turned and walked off. She heard him climb the metallic rungs of the ladder, heard the hatch opening and then shut. She tore off the binding from her legs and stood, hurrying after him up the ladder. But when she got to the hatch, it was sealed firmly shut, not budging an inch as she pushed.

He'd locked her in. She climbed back down, a new thought spurring her on. But when she got to the desk, she saw he'd taken the laptop with him.

'Shit,' she said to herself. She sat back down and sipped water from a litre bottle, knowing that people would wonder where she was. Craig would. Then he'd ask the team. Then they'd start looking.

And soon, hopefully.

But what would bring them to a middle of nowhere spot like this?

She had no answers for that one.

———

JESS GOT BACK to Ffau'r Blaidd to find all the doors and windows open and Cadi stretched out on a patch of slate chippings which, by any measure, must have been uncomfortable but which she, in her canine mind, had chosen as one of her favourite spots. The thermometer hovered around twenty-four degrees. The clock on the dashboard read 6.35pm.

The lawn in front of the cottage looked green, the grass trimmed, decorative thyme and marjoram around the edges intermingled with some heathers and Astilbe. Warlow had a few odd pots near the front door with practical plants like mint, rosemary, and a bay tree. Somewhere in the fields nearby, a tractor droned. After a weekend in Manchester in which no more than half an hour would go by without the sound of a siren, Nevern was a haven of quiet.

Cadi, Warlow's black Labrador, tongue lolling, got up and hurried over to Jess as soon as she got out of the Golf. There was something about Jess's perfume that influenced the dog and acted like an early warning system. Cadi would raise her snout and sniff long before Jess entered a room or exited the car. It happened sometimes with Molly when she was dressed up and scent applied. And of course, it gave Warlow much delight and ammunition to take the Michael.

The dog did the same now. Jess was never sure if it was approval or disgust. But from the wagging, she assumed the former.

'Hey, beautiful. Oh, you must be hot. Why aren't you in the shade?'

Cadi, subdued by the heat, nevertheless did a figure of eight waddle all around Jess.

Through the open living room window, a voice emerged. 'She's got a yo-yo thing going on. Ten minutes in the sun and then fifteen in the shadow of Evan's shed, then back again to the slate chippings. I think she's a Fakir.'

Jess walked across and stood outside, one hand on the windowsill, having a conversation with her daughter through the wide-open window.

'A Faker?'

'K, I, R. Fakir. Like one of those yoga guys that lies on a bed of nails.'

Jess turned and ruffled the dog's head. 'She's hot, poor thing. Has she got enough water?'

'No, Mum. I decided not to give her any water today because I'm an idiot.'

Jess looked up from the dog and gave Molly a silent look.

'Oh, come on, as if,' Molly said with an accompanying eye-roll.

'Studying going well, then, is it?' Jess ventured the question with no holding back on the sarcasm.

'It is thanks. Not that you'd care, judging by the rip-roaring time you had in Manchester.'

'I had a rip-roaring hangover in Manchester.'

'Glad to hear it.' Molly grinned. 'How was Lisa?'

'Mad, as always. Did you see the lip filler?'

'I did. And the immovable forehead. I thought maybe you'd come home with something… done.'

Jess regarded her daughter. 'Thank you very much. Lovely to see you too.'

Molly came away from the table and leant through the open window to give her mother a peck on the cheek and a quick embrace.

'Have you had anything to eat?' Molly asked.

'Not yet.'

'Right. I made a big salad. Lettuce, mushrooms, and some green beans. There's enough for all of us, but you could add some tuna if you wanted a bit of protein. I got some of those little cans with dressings added.'

'Sounds great.'

'Is Evan on the way?'

'He was at his desk when I left. Had a letter about, or even from, Denise.'

'Dead Denise?' Molly made here eyes big ovals.

'The same. But I think he was waiting on a postmortem report.'

'On Denise?'

Jess let Cadi wander back to her spot. 'No, on the dead man that we were investigating this morning.'

'Nice.'

Jess looked around at the tranquil setting. 'It's so quiet here, isn't it?' She turned to look at her daughter. 'How has it been with you two?'

'Hardly seen him. I've been so busy studying.'

Jess scrunched her face up in sympathy. 'Never mind, they're nearly over. Just Biology to go.'

'Can we not mention the "B" word, Mum?'

'I see from the towel on the lawn that you got some sunbathing in.'

'Half an hour lunchtime and fifteen minutes during breaks.' Molly rolled her eyes. Jess had once measured the space between eye rolls. Once Molly had gone forty-five minutes. 'Shall I put the kettle on, or is there more of the Spanish Inquisition left to come?'

Jess grabbed her bag. 'I'll change and get a wash on. If you've got anything, bring it through to the mudroom.'

'Does everyone live the glamorous lifestyle us Allanbys have, Mum?' Molly walked away through to the kitchen.

'If they don't, they do not know what they're missing, do they?'

CHAPTER THIRTEEN

GIL TRIED CATRIN FIRST, and then Lane again on his way home to Llandeilo. The Towy Valley glittered like a green jewel in the summer sun, the river on his left, the Black Mountains ahead. He'd come through Llanarthne and its two watering holes with the thirteenth-century ruin of Dryslwyn Castle like a fractured crown atop a verdant head next to the river no more than a mile away. The grey, crumbling walls stood as a ruinous reminder of the area's past conflicts.

He cut across the valley floor under the shadow of the castle and turned right on to the A40. By the time he got to the bridge at Llandeilo, he'd tried Catrin again. 6.15 by the dashboard clock. With a deep sigh, as he climbed the hill into the town, Gil knew he would not make the Lady Anwen's supper. He gave her a quick call and explained that he would be late. She didn't ask questions. She'd been a detective sergeant's wife for far too long.

Gil drove right through the town and took the left towards Talley. Like Catrin, he had not been back to *Cân-y-barcud* since the winter. He hoped he could remember the way. Several cars were parked outside the Abbey at Talley and the walks up to the woods, but Gil kept going. He remembered Tal Farm and then a left turn along lanes too narrow for anything but the carts they were originally designed for. At least it wasn't dark this time. He got lost only once, backtracked until he found the turning and, two miles later, drove up and down the hill leading to the property.

The first thing that struck him was the absence of any vehicles parked outside. That meant that neither Catrin nor Lane were there. He thought about turning around there and then, but he'd been a copper for too long not to at least look around.

He opened the car door and stepped out into the stillness of an early summer evening. The sun still blazed in the sky behind him, and the hills seemed to sparkle in the light, the leaves on nearby trees silvering in the wind as they twisted to reveal their pale undersides. But these were fleeting observations. The farmhouse was silent and still. The only sound Gil heard was his own breathing as he walked slowly towards it. But within two steps, he could tell something was off.

The door to the property stood ajar. Not enough to show the interior, but open enough to make Gil feel a chill on this summer's afternoon.

'Catrin?' Gil shouted but got only the bleat of a distant sheep by reply. Was it warning him? What had it seen take place here this afternoon? Gil walked in and pushed the door open with his elbow.

His eyes fell immediately on the phone, sitting on the peninsula's work surface.

Gil pulled his out of his pocket. One bar. He adjusted his glasses from where sweat had let them slide forward on his face and dialled Catrin's number and her phone, on silent, buzzed and vibrated its way across the wooden surface until it teetered near the edge, at which point Gil ended the call.

'Shit,' he muttered. The trouble with being used to seeing the worst in people was that you didn't need to go far out of your way to have that mindset reenforced. And Gil was aware of how all sorts of outlandish crap went on every day in busy town centres and in the quietest of corners. And though crime should have no place in this chocolate-box rural retreat, he knew it did not give a tinker's cuss.

His eyes strafed the room. No broken furniture. No bodies. But then his gaze snagged on something on the floor. A long string? No, a zip tie. And next to it, spatters of something dark red. Round droplets and splashes of blood.

He swivelled and had a quick look around the property, mezzanine included, unable to suppress the dread as he took the steps because of what had been found up there in the crogloft previously. He grunted out an exhalation of relief to find the space empty.

Touch nothing, he reminded himself. In case… in case of what, exactly?

No idea.

But from the way his pulse had begun racing away, he didn't like it. Catrin Richards never had a kaput battery. And she didn't leave her phone on a work surface and walk away.

Gil smelled fish.

He brought his phone up again and dialled a different number. Warlow answered after four rings.

'Evan, it's Gil. I'm up at *Cân-y-barcud*. Something isn't right here. Catrin's phone is on a kitchen worktop. The place is deserted, no sign of Lane. But there are zip ties on the floor and definitely blood. Something's happened here. Were you on the way home?'

'I was,' Warlow answered. 'But not anymore. Stay there.'

'Should I ring Craig?'

'Not yet. I'll make some calls first. This may be nothing.'

'Might be Lane. That pasty-faced piece of—'

'We don't know that. See if you can locate his partner. Stay there. I'll be with you as soon as I can.'

Gil almost heard the Jeep screech to a halt and do a U-turn.

————

WARLOW, foot down and heading east, weighed up the options.

Yes, they might have gone somewhere else. Perhaps to see

Moyles's widow, or someone else pertinent to the case. But the phone on the table didn't fit. Craig had once told him and Gil that Catrin had lost her phone, but it was on a night out where other distractions and alcohol had a way of distracting the mind.

But at work, Catrin was a stickler.

This didn't sit well in the scheme of things. He experienced an uncomfortable movement, as if his internal organs were shifting downwards while the rest of him remained in place.

And zip ties? Perhaps there was a good reason, but Warlow couldn't think of any that were not nefarious. That thought came at the same time as his driving sense, on fully automatic by now, made him brake as he came up behind a towed caravan.

Gone were the days when you kept a magnetic blue light under the dash, ready to attach it to the roof when you needed to get somewhere double quick. As a police officer, he had to abide by the highway code, like every other citizen. But he wanted to get to the isolated property double quick because he wanted Gil to tell him they'd found Catrin and that some unlikely reason had made her leave the place, and her phone. Warlow would curse and then they would all laugh about it.

But the heavy feeling in his gut told him otherwise.

It took almost all Warlow's willpower to not honk his horn there and then.

Gil came back to him just as he negotiated the Talley turn off past Llandeilo.

'No luck with Lane. Nor with the partner. A neighbour says he works at the hospital. Might explain why he has his phone off.'

'I'm twenty minutes away. Anything else strike you?'

'Only that someone has been upstairs on the bed. The sheets are rumpled.'

Warlow gritted his teeth. 'If Lane has so much as touched—'

'Whoa, hold on there, sheriff.'

'Okay. I'll be there in fifteen.'

An unsmiling Gil was outside the cottage when he arrived. In silence, the DS showed his DCI exactly what he'd found.

Warlow followed, taking in the rumpled bedclothes, the phone on the work surface, the cut zip ties and the blood on the floor. He grunted and massaged the back of his neck. 'So, how do you see this?'

'The absence of cars makes little sense. And though it's possible Catrin might have forgotten her phone—'

'Possible, but bloody unlikely.'

'Right,' Gil said. 'Suggesting either they left separately and, in a hurry, which might explain Catrin leaving her phone—'

'Or?'

'Or they left together in one car and then someone came back for the other. Possibly on foot, or some other way.'

Warlow considered this. Both were Swiss cheese suggestions: full of holes. 'I don't like either. But of the two, much as I hate to say it, we must assume Catrin left, or was made to leave, with Lane.'

'Agreed. If it's true, if the bastard has been setting Catrin up for this—' Gil didn't finish. He didn't need to. Drinkwater and Goodey would not survive the cluster foxtrot that would follow if one of their own had been abducted while pandering to the media at their request. Warlow and Gil understood the grim reality: predators often targeted victims in situations just like this one. People, most of them women, became victims after being lured into isolated meetings under false pretences. More than one estate agent sprang to mind.

But not a police officer.

Not until now.

Yet, when it came to sexual predators, the rule of law and any connotations it might bring with it never put the hunter off.

'The last time Catrin was seen was when she left HQ this

morning?' Warlow couched it as a question, though he already knew the answer.

Gil nodded.

The DCI walked to the door and turned his face up to the blue evening sky. 'Christ, these are the phone calls you pray you never have to make.'

'Buchannan first?' Gil suggested.

'Yes. He can shoot this up the chain and wait for the fireworks. Then I'll ring Craig. He'll need to stay away, but if I was him, I'd want to be here. Then I'll ring Jess. You tell Rhys. No point in either of them coming up here now. I'll get Povey here and in an hour, it'll be a circus. But we need to see what she can find. Where is the nearest habitation again?'

Gil pointed northwest. 'Couple of miles from here that way.'

'Right. I'll go there now. See if they've seen any activity, and I'll get someone on the traffic cameras. Can you remember what Lane drives?'

'A Renault Captur. One of the new ones.'

'Okay.' Warlow already had his phone in his hand. 'Where is the best signal?'

'Bottom of the garden. Stand on the wall.'

The DCI threw him a look.

'I wish it was a bloody joke,' Gil said.

Warlow did as instructed and dialled Superintendent Buchannan's number as he walked to the end of the garden and stood on a low stone wall, half covered with lichen.

'Sion,' he said before the senior officer could say anything. 'I've got some bad news.'

CHAPTER FOURTEEN

MOLLY HAD TAKEN Cadi out around one of the adjacent fields for her evening ablutions when Jess got the call from Warlow. Without even waiting for him to speak, she said, 'Don't tell me. You want us to carry on without you. You'll have leftovers when you get back.' She said the words with a little trill of accusation in her voice. 'I'm beginning to think that you're avoiding us. Which is a real achievement, considering we live in your house.'

'Jess.' All he did was speak her name, but the absence of any trace of his usual good-natured levity told her instantly something was wrong.

'What is it?' she asked sharply.

'It's Catrin. She hasn't come back from her appointment with Lane. We found her phone at the cottage. Both her car and Lane's are missing. Blood and zip ties on the floor.'

Jess heard the words he spoke, but her pulse pounded in her ears so loudly, she thought that by shaking her head, she might dislodge what she'd heard, and the words might fall away to let better ones in.

'Who have you told?' she asked. There were other noises that wanted to rush out of her mouth. A wail of anguish, or words she hoped Molly didn't think she knew. But she held on and forced out the practicalities. The business of being a copper.

'The Buccaneer, Craig, and you. Gil is on the phone to Rhys.'

'Do you want me to come in?'

'No. It's what, 7:30?'

Jess glanced at Warlow's kitchen clock. 'It's almost 7:45.'

'Right. Povey is on her way. I've spoken to the PolSA, but we won't get that started until the morning. It'll be dark by the time we mobilise tonight. I'll probably hang around here, maybe stay with Gil. We have lots of Uniforms knocking on neighbours' farms—'

'There aren't many of those, if I remember rightly.'

'You do remember rightly. But you never know.'

'Are you sure you don't want me to come—'

'I am,' Warlow cut across her. 'We'll pick up first thing. There's still the Williams's death. I'll probably leave that to you and Rhys.'

'Of course.'

A beat of dead air passed between them until Warlow broke the impasse. 'I was toying with not telling you until tomorrow. No point us both losing sleep. But then I thought about you finding out tomorrow…'

'And you remembered you like your own guts inside you instead of as garters?'

'Something like that.'

'What's your take? You and Gil's?'

Jess heard him sigh. 'For now, Lane is in the frame until proven otherwise. I can't explain the car business, though. Not yet.'

'How has Gil taken it?'

'Badly. As you know, he's not exactly Lane's number one fan.'

Jess asked the questions because it was the right, the decent thing to do, though on one level she did not want to hear the answers. 'Catrin's parents?'

'Craig has spoken to them. But of course, I will too.'

'Okay, but at least let me and Rhys look into Lane properly tomorrow.'

'That would help. It can run parallel with the Williams's enquiry.'

'It'll be my sordid pleasure.'

Another beat until Warlow said, 'I doubt I'll make drinks with your friend now.'

'He's not coming until July, Evan,' Jess admonished him. 'And there is no need to prejudge—'

'Mum?' Molly's voice came through the door before the girl. 'Do we have any—' She saw the phone at her mother's ear and froze with an expression of horrified apology. 'Sorry,' she said in a half whisper.

'Is that Molly?' Warlow asked.

'Yes. Doing her impersonation of the Pembroke to Rosslare ferry foghorn.'

'I said sorry.' Molly sounded put out.

'Say hello from me,' Warlow said. 'Apologise about supper.'

'I will.'

He ended the call, and Jess sent her daughter a pasted-on smile.

'Was that important?' Molly looked abashed.

'It was. But we'd done the important bit. Well, almost.'

'Ring back,' Molly suggested.

'No. There is no point. Evan is busy.'

'Not here for supper, then?'

'Not tonight.'

'All the more for us, then, eh, girl?' Molly bent and ran her fingers up and down the dog's flanks. A move Cadi very much approved of.

'Sit down, Mol. I need to tell you something.'

Molly sent her mother a side-eyed glance. 'It's not about going to Europe again, is it?'

'No. It's about Catrin Richards.'

Molly, her face instantly serious, sat down and listened. It took all of two sentences before she began to cry.

———

Superintendent Sion Buchannan ducked as he stood on the threshold of *Cân-y-barcud* to watch Povey's crime scene investigators do their thing. He did not go inside. Much of the swabbing, scraping, and photography was taking place very near to where the door opened and on the wooden staircase leading up to the crogloft bedroom.

Warlow stood behind the lanky superintendent just outside. Night was falling and with it came respite from the day's intolerable heat. The wind had dropped, and the world waited for the darkness to pass and for dawn to bring meaning back to the dark and shapeless countryside that, beyond the arc lights once more blazing in this quiet corner of the county, stretched away in all directions, dark and secretive.

As Buchannan swivelled his head to talk, Warlow was struck by how the movement made him resemble a kind of prehistoric bird. 'Lane was working alone?' The superintendent asked.

'As far as we know.'

'No one knows he's missing?'

'Gil spoke to Lane's partner. He's just come off shift at the hospital. For now, we're keeping it low-key. He didn't seem too bothered that Lane had not contacted him. He told us that Lane's line of work meant he was often away, chasing a story. We've asked him to let us know as soon as he makes contact. We will have to brief him fully tomorrow if we have nothing by then.'

Buchannan steadied himself with a hand on the door frame. 'Do you think it's likely Lane will just turn up?'

'In all honesty, Sion, I have no bloody idea.'

Povey, a marshmallow vision in her Tyvek snowsuit, appeared from around the edge of the building. 'We have several blood samples. I'll run the first batch as soon as I'm back in Carmarthen.'

'Tell me you still have your rapid access machine.'

Povey gave Warlow a brief smile. 'QuikID? We do. You're lucky.'

Nothing but a turn of phrase. But the lack of response from either of the officers made Povey wince in apology. 'My bad. Lousy choice of words.'

'No, you're alright, Alison.' Buchannan let her off nicely.

'Point is, we will get some results back tomorrow morning, for sure. Maybe by the early hours.'

Warlow looked relieved rather than impressed. Povey's department was assessing a mobile DNA sequencer that had come in very useful in their last case. It would be again if it would give them a DNA profile within three hours.

'We have Catrin's DNA on file, so comparison with that will be easy.' Povey was being pragmatic, as was her way. But there was little solace in her words. Every police officer had their DNA on the system in order to eliminate them from site contamination in investigations.

'Did you find anything else significant?' Buchannan asked.

'Not yet. The place is reasonably clean except for the staircase and bedroom.'

The super turned again to Warlow. 'What about from the neighbours?'

'Nothing.' Warlow's answer was blunt.

'So, where are they? They must be *some*where.'

Warlow stayed silent. Buchannan's frustration echoed that of everyone involved. 'How much longer will your lot be?' This time, the superintendent directed his question back at Povey.

'Another couple of hours.'

'Then, I'm off.' Buchannan fished for his car keys. 'You might as well go, too, Evan. Nothing to do here now.'

Buchannan was correct. But neither he nor Gil had suggested leaving the cottage.

'I could make it an order,' Buchannan said.

Warlow dropped his gaze. Buchannan was right, of course. They were doing no good being here. Warlow gave a reluctant nod in reply.

Once Buchannan had driven off, Warlow found Gil and told him they'd better try getting some rest. He made Povey promise to text him as soon as she had any results. At around 10.10pm, he followed Gil in the Jeep back to the sergeant's home in the market town of Llandeilo.

Warlow had stayed at Gil's house before and would likely do so again. The house was in a quiet cul-de-sac near Llandeilo's rugby field. Such fields were ubiquitous across Wales— a testament to the nation's devotion to the sport. Every village and town in the country had a rugby field. While officially secular, Wales revered rugby with near-religious fervour, the goal posts standing like holy symbols throughout the land.

After a light meal and a cup of tea, he stretched out on the guest bed, still dressed. Warlow closed his eyes to see if sleep might come, only to visualise every horrifying scenario his fraught imagination could dream up play out in a diorama of awfulness behind his eyes.

Bad enough that an officer be embroiled through no fault of her own in the crime she was investigating. Worse that it had happened on his watch. After half an hour, he eventually got up, took his clothes off and found an old t-shirt put out for him by the Lady Anwen. One of his own that he now left in case of situations exactly such as these. He glanced around the guest room with a heavy heart, realising that this had become a familiar place for all the wrong reasons. All very well having a cottage in a quiet rural retreat like Nevern, but when crimes were committed miles away, having a bolt hole in a different county had become a Godsend.

He owed a lot to Gil and his family and now his mind wandered from the grim realities of the investigation to more personal reflections.

Denise had often accused him of being a friendless freak, though she enjoyed adding an extra seven-letter very rude adjective in the middle for alliterative purposes and for emphasis. When he bothered to analyse it, he had to admit she was right, if by "friends" she meant people you had lunch with every other week, or celebrated birthdays with at a spa.

He never saw that as a fault – the only spa he ever visited was the ones you could buy lottery tickets, milk, and bread in – and as clichéd as it might sound, his experiences working with women had reinforced his own observations that female friendships were more fragile. More demanding of intimacy, communication, and frequency.

The men Warlow knew needed none of these things. He could reunite with someone at a watering hole or a game and resume their relationship seamlessly. The psychologists called it side-to-side friendship, bonding over shared activities like the pub or sports. However, that same jokey insult among women friends might be perceived as hurtful and out of place.

His friendship with Gil was built on playful insults and humour, typical of how most men interacted with their close companions.

Warlow sighed. Why the hell was he even thinking about this psychobabble? But he knew the answer. Because thinking about the other stuff, about Catrin Richards, made his insides squirm.

With eyes wide open in the dark room, Warlow stared at the ceiling but found nothing to comfort him there.

Damn Lane. Damn him to hell.

CHAPTER FIFTEEN

TUESDAY

Warlow was still awake at 2.23am when his phone buzzed. A text from Povey.

> No trace of Sgt Richard's DNA

Warlow replied'

> You sure?

He cursed once he'd sent it. Of course she was sure. This was bloody Povey.

> No doubts. I'll know more by morning.

> Thanks, Alison. Much appreciated.

> 'You are welcome. Try and get some sleep

Warlow heard movement on the stairs. He got up and saw Gil with his phone in hand. He followed the sergeant down to the kitchen.

'At least it's not Catrin's,' Gil said, flicking on the light.

Warlow grunted his agreement. Gil had obviously got the same text.

'Anwen has some non-caffeinated tea. Doesn't taste too bad. Not like that herbal rubbish. You want?'

'Love one.'

Gil made the tea while Warlow checked through his phone to review every message he'd had since arriving at the cottage to join Gil that evening. In case he'd missed something. He had not. In terms of useful intel, it was sparse stuff.

Gil handed him the tea.

Warlow stared at it and muttered, 'It's a bloody relief.'

'Lane's, you think?'

Warlow huffed out some air.

'Was there someone else at the cottage, then?'

'That would explain the car situation.'

Gil thought about that, his brows creasing. '*Arglwydd Mawr*, what the hell is going on, Evan?'

Warlow sipped his tea. 'It's a sad state of affairs when a DCI and a DS are glad that a blood sample is unknown.'

'Tell me about it. I've been lying there knackered but about as likely to sleep as a dog in a butcher's shop.'

'We need to, though. Otherwise, we'll be good for bugger all.'

'This will help,' Gil said.

'Why? Is it drugged?'

'I don't mean the tea. I mean Povey's text.'

Gil was right. 'I bloody hope so.'

Gil sent up one eyebrow. 'One of the women in the shop I spoke to today—'

'Shop?'

'Yes. Shop. As in shop, post office… the case we're supposed to be investigating?'

'I've asked Jess and Rhys to run that,' Warlow said.

'Well, anyway, seeing you gulp that tea and your Adam's apple bobbing up and down like a ship in a storm reminded me that this woman I spoke to today had a prominent Adam's apple, too.'

'Is that relevant?' Warlow, tired and irritated, grunted out the question.

'To our case? Of course not. I'm employing distraction techniques to get your mind off the obvious. My point is that I had an argument once with a bloody-minded DI about Adam's apples. Don't ask me how or why, but he was adamant – see what I did there – that women didn't have one. Hence Adam's apple. Well, if that's true, this woman today must have had a gobstopper struck in her throat, that's all I can say.'

'Common misconception.' Warlow pursed his lips and tilted his head. 'Everyone has an Adam's apple. And I should know because my son is an ENT surgeon and I've had the lecture. It's called a laryngeal prominence and is a cartilage over your voice box. It's just that it's more prominent in men. An anatomical thing. But every single pronoun on the planet has one.'

'*Diawl*, where were you when I needed you? That bugger swore blind that only men had one and called me a rude name. Shame the *pwrs* is dead.'

'Shouldn't speak ill of the dead, Gil.'

'This is KFC we're talking about. Kelvin, Foxtrot, Caldwell.'

'Ah, then speak as ill as you like.'

They sat in silence while they finished their tea. KFC had been a thorn in both men's sides until his involvement in criminal activity had been exposed. He'd died at the hands of a psychopath before paying his dues. Rough justice, as Gil had said at the time.

'Think I'll give it another go.' Warlow creaked up off the kitchen stool, remembering not to groan as he did so. 'Let's hope Morpheus has his arms open.' He yawned. 'Maybe your distraction technique should be patented.'

'You think so?'

Warlow wiggled a hand as a maybe signifier. 'But the shot of whisky did no harm, either.'

Gil grinned. 'I note you drank it all with no complaint.'

'Damned right.'

'See you in the morning.'

Warlow raised a hand in response as he left the room. This time, when he put his head on the pillow in the bedroom, he fell asleep instantly.

———

AT THE SAME time as Warlow and Gil shared their whisky-laced tea in the early hours of the morning, a car slid unseen into Angle, a village on the titular peninsula jutting out into the haven at Milford. A village where people had lived for many centuries. A place with ancient Iron-Age roots.

In the nineteenth century, when the village's population had reached almost four hundred, Angle was a hub of industry, albeit of an unusual kind. Women painstakingly plaited straw for bonnets and mats, while the men ventured out to sea in pursuit of oysters during their elusive season. For centuries, Angle had thrived on the twin pillars of agriculture and fishing, a testament to its seafaring heritage. The lifeboat station, standing proudly as a sentinel, bore witness to the village's maritime history. But it was not only the waves that had shaped Angle; the wind had played its part, too. An ancient windmill, a thirteenth-century relic, had once graced the landscape, only to be repurposed as a pillbox during the tumultuous days of World War II.

Mediaeval buildings with their aged stones and secrets still stood tall, preserving the echoes of a bygone era. Angle's most perplexing anomaly was a fourteenth-century tower-house, a peculiar sight in these Welsh lands. Such structures were more at home in the distant corners of Ireland or northern Britain, yet here it stood, the absence of its precise origin adding to the mystery.

Nature, too, lent its enigmatic touch to Angle's landscape. In the daytime, the marshes echoed with the songs of elusive birds like dunlin, grey plover, and redshank, drawing bird-watchers into their hidden world. Kilpaison Marsh concealed secrets of its own, sheltering the elusive Cetti's warbler amidst the reeds and scrub.

The man now heading deep into this part of the Pembrokeshire coast knew all about these creatures from a different life. From a time before the all-consuming darkness that was his need for revenge had possessed him. Now, into this place of secrets, DS Catrin Richards's Mazda, moved.

Hunt's eyes raked the street. He needed somewhere to park, where it would be unobtrusive. He'd taken his time to get here, finding his way south and west along unobserved byways and tracks that meant he could park and pull in when other vehicles approached. It had taken him hours using this technique, aided by a judicious use of mud on licence plates front and back to begin with, until he'd purloined some others from an abandoned vehicle in a farm field.

He'd needed the car to get here, but now that he'd arrived, it could be left somewhere. He'd underestimated just how far away this corner of Pembrokeshire was from anywhere else. But he was here now. His map showed only the one road through and, at this hour, no lights burned in the neat houses, though the streetlights made him feel exposed. He read a sign for The Promontory House and turned off, hardly believing his luck when he drove through to an unlit parking area with the refinery lights glinting across the bay, and a stone wall on his left. This was open ground, but he tucked the car in up against the wall. His lights picked out reed beds and marsh leading to the water where boats sat high of the tide, and a bridge over the inlet leading up the coast.

An ideal spot.

Hunt turned off the car's lights and sat, waiting to see if his arrival had sparked any interest. Ten minutes later, he decided it had not. He had two hours in which to get to the cottage and set himself up to observe. He'd need to infiltrate the area without being seen. But he was a patient man. A man used to observing wildlife, camouflaged and equipped. He had no fear of travelling in darkness with an infrared headlamp.

He set off carrying the heavy bag he'd taken from the observation bunker. He could not risk it being found if the car raised suspicion. Best to take it and stash it somewhere safe. He had the tilt switches set apart from the pipe casing for now, with no risk of setting off the explosives. Separated from the trigger mechanism, they were harmless enough. But he'd read too many horror stories of inadvertent explosions not to be acutely aware of the need to be careful.

There were WWII pillboxes scattered over the peninsula, as well as an old RAF airfield. He'd looked it all up and marked them on his map. There would be plenty of places to hide his equipment.

At a little after 3am, Hunt set off, heading south and east until he could cut inland and head towards Angle Turn Farm and the cottage on its land. He crept along the line of the coast, keeping low and moving swiftly. The sound of the sea was soothing, but this was no time to stop and appreciate its beauty. He had to make it to the farm before dawn. If he was seen, he'd have to answer too many questions. Or even silence the questioner. But martyrdom, for himself or someone else, wasn't on his agenda just yet. He had extermination in his sights; a better term when it came to vermin.

His line inland took him across the B4320 and towards the old airfields. RAF squadrons had flown Supermarine Spitfires, Westland Whirlwinds, and Hawker Hurricanes on convoy protection duties from here. In 1943, the airfield became the home of the Coastal Command Development Unit which tested weapons against German U-boats. Hunt was not the only person interested in wartime history. Online, he'd found recent images of a bunker or generator room with GPS coordinates. A little after 4.20, he found the very room, out of sight behind a hedge. A red brick building with most of its structure below ground level. Hidden and unused. An ideal spot to stash his "equipment".

An ideal spot to hide in.

He ate a protein bar and drank some water. The cottage was half a mile from where he was now. He'd need to find a hide, or set one up, before the sun came up. He could see a faint light glow above the eastern horizon already.

Time to move.

CHAPTER SIXTEEN

THE TEAM WAS in by 8am. Gil and Warlow half an hour before that. The PolSA-organised search party were about to begin a march across the moor, targeting the area behind *Cân-y-barcud*. This was something that had to be done, yet Warlow was not hopeful. The absence of both Lane's and Catrin's vehicles argued strongly that they were not close by.

A search, however, was essential. Warlow left that to the experts.

At 8.10am, Rhys looked up from his screen.

'Email from Dr. Tiernon. His preliminary report on Denzil Williams.'

Though it would be easy to dismiss the Williams case and confine it to the back burner in light of Catrin's disappearance, they were all glad of the distraction.

'What does he say, Rhys?' Warlow asked.

Rhys did his thing, reading the screen and moving his lips in tandem with the words. Gil sent both Warlow and Jess a chin tucked look of strained patience.

'Early tox screen was negative, and there was a confirmed absence of defensive wounds. Cause of death, intracranial bleed.'

'So, hit on the head, then?' Gil added.

Rhys frowned. 'Hmm. What it says here is that, umm,

there is evidence of intraventricular haemorrhage. The cause of the bleed appears to be a ruptured intracranial aneurysm arising from the anterior communicating artery. Two intact aneurysms present in the same location, attesting to pre-existing disease. It is entirely possible that the ruptured aneurysm could have caused unconsciousness. As a result, the nature of the contusion on the head looks secondary. No suggestion of the use of a sharp or hard weapon is obvious.'

'He's blown a gasket,' Gil said.

'Ah,' Warlow muttered. 'That changes things a little.'

Rhys swivelled in his chair. 'We talked about this, sir. We wondered if a single blow might mean involuntary manslaughter. But if he blew a gasket—'

'I'd rather we didn't use that term, Rhys,' Jess said.

'Sorry, ma'am.'

From behind Jess, Gil shook his head at the DC.

'If he ruptured an aneurysm, then there is no charge to answer, is there?'

Jess answered immediately, 'There is something called Unlawful Act manslaughter.' She turned to her computer and called up a page she read a paragraph out from, nice and loud for Rhys's sake. 'An individual will be found guilty of committing involuntary manslaughter because of an unlawful or dangerous act should it be proven they intentionally committed the act and the act directly contributed to the death of another individual.'

'Wow, so would Denzil Williams blowing a ga... rupturing an aneurysm chasing a thief qualify?'

'That'll be for the CPS to decide.' Jess flattened her mouth.

Rhys turned back to his screen.

At a little after 9am, Alison Povey walked through the Incident Room door, an unusual sight devoid of snowsuit. But she looked exhausted this morning. This season's look, judging by the drawn faces that turned in her direction.

'Have I walked onto a set from Police, Action, the Walking Dead cut?'

'You have looked in the mirror, have you?' Gil said. 'How many hours' sleep did you get last night?'

An enigmatic shrug was her only answer. 'Let me put you all out of your misery.' Povey put both hands up, palms down for emphasis. 'I come with no fresh news. All the samples we've tested so far are from the same person. As yet unidentified on the database.'

'Not Catrin's, though,' Rhys said.

'No.'

'Can we assume they're all Lane's?'

'That's one reason I've called. It would be useful if we could get something of his to sample.'

'Like a toothbrush or a comb?' Rhys asked.

'Either would do.'

'Right. I'll get out to his house. We need to talk to the partner, and I'll get something from there.' Gil pushed away from the desk and stood up.

'Good idea,' Warlow said. 'He's not on the PNC. But we need to look at Lane's social media pages, too. See if anything stands out. And you could run that past the partner. Any relatives in the area, favourite spots he liked to visit, etcetera.'

'I'll get this to you by lunchtime,' Gil said to Povey.

'Good. We have another dozen samples to run.'

'I thought you had your QuikFix gismo?'

'It doesn't do multiple sampling. It'll take us a day or two to get everything sorted.'

Warlow glanced around at the tired, anxious faces. Everyone was worried. A word would not go amiss.

'I realise this is difficult. Sitting around doing nothing is the worst feeling. But we all know how this works. Bums on seats, phones to ears, fingers on keyboards. That's how we get intel. And that is what we need at the moment. Rhys, you need to concentrate on the Williams case. Jess and I will put Lane under the magnifier. We meet back here in three hours. That enough time for you, Gil?'

'More than enough.' Gil was already walking towards the door.

———

TWENTY MINUTES LATER, Gil drove through the market town of Whitland and pulled up at a terraced property on St Mary's street. An old town with centuries of history, Whitland's name reflected the ancient parliament sited here because of its strategic position on the county border between Carmarthenshire and Pembrokeshire. Of course, there was also the river Taf, with one f and pronounced as always in Wales as a "v". There was talk of the University Health Board building its new hospital somewhere on the outskirts. A new build to replace the old decrepit dinosaur that was Glangwili Hospital. A building that started life somewhere around the last World War. But, as with all large projects, the powers that be were taking their time over it. Gil had seen mountains move more quickly.

His knock was answered by a thin man in pyjama bottoms and a fleecy top. He was smooth shaven, both facially and on his skull.

'Dr. Shetty?'

'It is.'

Gil had his badge on a lanyard and held it up. 'Detective Sergeant Gil Jones. We spoke briefly yesterday.'

'About Geraint?' Shetty's eyes widened. 'Has something happened?'

'Could we talk inside, do you think?'

'Please, come in.' Shetty stood aside to allow Gil entry. The house's interior appeared tastefully furnished, reflecting an eclectic blend of modern and vintage decor.

'You renting?' Gil asked.

'For now, yes.'

Gil followed into a cosy living room, where they settled into armchairs overlooking a fireplace adorned with family photographs. Mostly, by the look of them, of Shetty's extended family. There was only one of Shetty and Lane on a beach somewhere not in the UK. The room was cool. The house's stone walls were thick enough to keep the sun, beaming in through the window, from turning it into an oven.

'Thank you for meeting with me, Doctor Shetty,' Gil began, his voice carrying a weight of empathy.

'It's Amol,' Shetty said.

'Geraint has not contacted you since we spoke?'

Amol's eyes got bigger. 'Should I be worried? You're here, so of course, I should be worried. What's going on?'

'Geraint met with one of our officers yesterday at a remote cottage up past Talley Abbey. Do you know it?'

'No. But I know he had a meeting. He's been interviewing one of your detectives for a piece of work.'

'We have not heard from the officer either since yesterday morning.'

'They're both missing?' Amol's expression betrayed genuine shock and surprise.

'You told us over the phone that Geraint is often away?'

'He follows stories up. I get a phone call or a text to say all is well, but it isn't unusual for him to be away.'

'And would you say he's been himself of late?'

Amol latched on to Gil's leading question hungrily. 'He hasn't been himself for weeks.' He paused, searching for the right words. 'Ever since the mugging and getting locked in the trunk of his own car.'

Gil recalled the incident. At the time, the team had noted it and the consensus from them was that it could not have happened to a nicer person. A consensus Gil was already beginning to regret.

'After that incident, he became more anxious. Something changed.'

Gil leaned forward, his voice softening with genuine interest. 'Can you elaborate on that?'

Amol sighed heavily and his gaze became distant, focused on some point beyond the room. 'Geraint has always been fearless, never afraid to chase a story. Some people see that as belligerence. I call it persistence. But after the mugging, he got a bit frightened, though he would never admit to that. Not even to me. But something changed in him. He even bought a bike to avoid using his car. It was as if he didn't want to be confined inside a vehicle again. I mean, don't get me wrong. He was unfit, and the exercise was only ever going to be a good thing.'

Gil noted down the details in his notebook.

Amol hesitated, then added, 'There was something else. He had a run in with some online vigilantes who were catfishing paedophiles. He'd wanted to do a story on them for ages, but they were aggressive and distrustful of him. They threatened him and made him feel unsafe. He dropped that story. So unlike him.'

'When was this?'

'Six months ago.'

Gil's pen paused mid-note as he processed this new information. 'Online vigilantes? What can you tell me about them?'

Amol leaned back in his chair, arms crossed defensively across his chest. 'Geraint never shared all the details with me, but they operated anonymously, communicating with alleged predators online. Pretending to be underage kids before confronting the people they entrapped publicly. It all sounded murky to me. Geraint thought it a fascinating story and wanted to approach it from both ends. Find a target that the vigilantes were chasing and show it from their viewpoint.'

Gil blinked once, slowly, unable to mask his surprise. His tone sharpened slightly as he sought clarification. 'A paedophile's viewpoint?'

'Geraint said that sometimes the vigilantes got it wrong. That could be just as bad. That was his angle. But when he tried to reach out to them and explain that angle, they shut him out completely.'

The detective furrowed his brow. 'So, Geraint's encounter with these vigilantes added to his anxiety?'

'Yes, it did,' Amol replied. 'He felt like he was being watched, and it made him paranoid. He became more guarded and secretive, so unlike him. Geraint convinced himself he was onto a big story, but he never shared the details with me.'

'The vigilante story?'

'No. Something else. That came after the mugging. Then he shifted his focus to the police and your detective, Richards. He's been like a dog with a bone ever since.'

Gil frowned. This case seemed to grow more complex by the minute. 'Doctor Shetty, do you have any idea what Mr Lane might have uncovered that made him so determined to pursue this story, despite the risks?'

Amol sighed, his gaze falling to the floor. 'I wish I knew, sergeant. Geraint is a passionate journalist, and he believed in exposing the truth. He must have stumbled on to something significant.'

Gil continued to ask questions and gather information, unable to shake the feeling that Lane's disappearance might be tied to a different story. One that now Catrin had become embroiled in. 'Had he spoken to you of any direct threats?'

'No. Not that I recall,' Amol said.

Gil nodded and kept probing, convinced now that what-ever had happened at CYB was a piece of a bigger puzzle.

As the afternoon sun cast a warm glow through the window, the two men sat in the dimly lit room, united by a common goal – to find Lane and uncover the truth behind his odd transformation from a fearless reporter into a bike-riding wimp.

CHAPTER SEVENTEEN

In the SIO room, Warlow faced a man he was accustomed to seeing in uniform. Craig Peters, as a traffic officer, spent a lot of his time charging up and down the A48 and the M4. But today, he'd dressed in a plain t-shirt and jeans, with trainers on his feet. Comfortable clothes. Chosen because they were one thing he needn't give much thought to.

Craig had gone up to *Cân-y-barcud* first thing. Warlow had sanctioned the visit as he had never been to the cottage, and he needed to understand its position and its remoteness because it informed the discussion and approach that Warlow and Buchannan were adopting. There was none of the "go home and let us do our job, Craig" nonsense. Catrin was his life partner, and he was one of them.

The PolSA had not wanted Craig to be a part of the search team, though. He'd drawn a line in the sand there in much the same way he hadn't wanted Warlow or any of his team along. Searches were a laborious, meticulous time-suck and better done by people who knew what they were doing.

Warlow and Craig sat and talked about what Catrin had been doing with Lane. Although it remained conversational, the DCI was subtly trying to find out if there was any context here.

'I mean, she doesn't like the bloke,' Craig admitted. 'She told me he always seems to have an agenda. When he asked her things, it was like he was waiting for her to slip up. Like he was looking for a different answer or knew something she didn't. Like I say, she didn't like him, or the situation. But she did it because she was told to.'

'She never felt threatened?'

'No. She'd have told me. She was just looking forward to getting it over with. I mean, he'd never tried anything, if that's what you're asking. If he had, he'd have been in cuffs.'

Warlow conceded the point. Catrin was not one to suffer fools, but these were questions that needed to be asked. 'This is unpleasant, I know.'

'Can't deny the touch of déjà vu, though.' Craig allowed himself a fleeting smile.

Warlow reciprocated. He'd called on Craig to help locate Catrin once before in a case where she and Rhys had been locked in a shed by a disgruntled farm worker they'd been investigating as a suspect in a murder case. Then, they'd utilised Craig's phone app to find Catrin's phone and, subsequently, the officer. But that would not happen here.

'Think she left her phone there at the cottage deliberately?'

Warlow remembered the phone sitting on the kitchen worktop in full view. There'd been no attempt to hide it, and that was how he formulated his answer. 'Not by her. I think she was made to leave it so that we could not track it.'

'And Lane? What is it he…' Craig let the sentence drift.

The DCI sensed that Craig did not want to use words like want or need here because any want or need in the situation they now found themselves in had all kinds of iniquitous connotations it was best not to contemplate. At least not contemplate from Craig's point of view.

'He's got no record, and he's gay. Gil is out seeing the partner…' Warlow was about to elaborate when movement caught his eye. Gil had returned from his visit to Lane's partner, his timing impeccable as ever. 'Why don't we ask him what he's found?' Warlow suggested, smoothly shifting gears.

They both walked out into the Incident Room. Gil immediately shook Craig's hand. 'Congratulations, I hear,' he said, adding the briefest of smiles.

'She told you, then?'

Rhys and Jess confirmed with nods.

'Ironic doesn't come near, does it?' Craig's mouth twisted in a parody of a smile as raw emotion gripped him momentarily.

Warlow turned to Gil to spare his younger colleague's blushes.

'What did you make of the partner?'

'He's as confused as we are. Okay, Lane, we all know, is a fully paid-up bloodsucker. Chases stories. Notice I didn't say ambulances. Therefore, is away a lot. But Shetty has received no communication, which he claims is unusual.'

'The mobile provider says Lane's phone is off,' Jess said.

'Shetty said Lane had been odd of late. Got cold-shouldered or maybe worse by a group of online vigilantes—'

'Vigilantes?' Warlow paused Gil to ask the question.

'Of the "we'll pretend to be thirteen and drag you out into the light" variety. Lying in wait for predators. Lane saw a story there, but it fizzled out somehow. Details were sketchy. But Shetty thought it might be tied up with Lane's mugging. That weird thing where he was found in the boot of his car in Kidwelly Quay.'

'I remember that,' Rhys said. 'In the middle of the Ronnie Probert investigation.'

'Anyway, Shetty wonders if it's all linked to what's happening now.' Gil held both hands out palms up at the sides as a demonstration of his bewilderment.

'What's any of that got to do with Catrin?' Craig asked. Though his tone remained calm and neutral, they all heard the crackle of frustration underlying it.

'That, we do not know, Craig.'

The traffic officer nodded and looked at Warlow. 'Is this

the point where you tell me to go away and read a book? My sergeant has already told me not to go to work. He said I'll be bloody useless. But I can't just—'

Warlow held a hand up. 'We can find you something to do. Lane has a significant online presence. Likes to blow his own trumpet. There are links to other journalists. They all need chasing up. Why don't you take his Instagram account? I'm doing his Twitter account –I'm buggered if I'm calling it X – and Jess has dug into his Facebook account, though she and Rhys are also working on another case.'

Craig nodded. His gratitude obvious.

'Cup of tea?' Rhys asked.

'Great. But I can do that, Rhys.'

'Not allowed,' Gil said. 'You do not wander into the Langham and ask Mr. Roux if he'll let you boil an egg.'

That brought a brief smile to the constable's lips.

'Is that a compliment, sarge?' Rhys asked.

'It might well be, Rhys. Treasure it as the rare and wonderful gift that it is.'

―――――

WITH TEA MADE and Craig settled at a desk, Rhys turned his attention back to the Williams case.

Jess had taken him aside and told him to adopt a strategic approach. Specifically, to take a step back and not get too bogged down in the specifics. 'A bit like looking at a photograph with slitted eyes.'

Being not yet thirty, Rhys used his phone for everything. But Catrin had told him not to underestimate the notebook as a tool. Phones could run out of battery, but the worst that could happen to a notebook was to run out of ink. And it was a damned sight easier to find a pen or a pencil than a charger, especially when you were out and about.

And so, Rhys had his notebook open as he jotted down his thoughts.

1/ Williams's aneurysm.

2/ Cans left. Technically, has the thief stolen anything?

3/ The descriptions.

He looked again at the last entry. He'd studied the CCTV footage a dozen times and not seen anything of use when it came to the thief's face. The hat and sunglasses made it difficult, and he'd kept his head down. It made the footage less than useful. But there were also witness statements.

Kaylee Francis said that the man standing next to her at the till had been about forty. But Mrs Lound's statement given to Gil and Libby's statement given to DI Allanby suggested they'd thought him to be much younger. Closer to thirty, perhaps. Had it been his voice, maybe?

He brought all this to Jess, who listened and then asked, 'Right, how would you go about reconciling the differences here?'

Rhys thought about it and recalled a piece of Gil's advice. One that felt apposite and not too off the wall.

'First impressions matter, but always dig deeper. There might be a Chippendale under the chalk paint.'

'But what does chalk paint have to do with male strippers?' Rhys had asked Catrin afterwards. Remembering her pithy reply brought a smile to his face. Her sharp wit and no-nonsense attitude were quintessentially Catrin, a trait he both admired and occasionally found intimidating. It was moments like these that made him grateful to have her as a mentor, even if her bluntness sometimes left him feeling like a schoolboy But at least he'd learned what the metaphor meant... as well as the name of a famous furniture manufacturer. He applied that same wisdom now in reply to Jess's question.

'Might be worth another chat with Libby, the shop worker, and Kaylee Francis. The girl who'd stood next to the thief at the till.'

'Good,' Jess said. 'Right, off you go.'

'But what about Catrin?'

'What *about* Catrin? There are four people sitting in this

office plus an army of fifty combing the countryside. We won't miss you for a couple of hours, Rhys.'

And so, just before lunch, Rhys set off in the job Audi back to Ffynnon Fach and the little store as his first stop.

CHAPTER EIGHTEEN

Hunt watched the VW Tiguan leave Angle Turn Cottage and wind its way along the drive.

John Napier sat in the driving seat. Next to him sat a woman, coiffured hair candy-floss stiff in the passenger seat. Behind, in the boot and separated by a wire guard, was a dog. A small dog, one of those amalgamations that people liked so much. A Cockapoo, or a Cockachon maybe, given its size. Hunt did not know the woman, but he guessed she was Napier's wife.

He could see them clearly through his Hawke binoculars, but they could not see him from his vantage point atop the pillbox at the edge of a field which offered a view of the Haven and the cottage. He lay flat on its concrete roof under a camo blanket and observed. The only car in the driveway was the VW. Napier drove an old Jaguar by preference. From Hunt's discussions with Lane, he was aware that the police used the Jag as a decoy vehicle whenever Napier deigned to go to work to avoid detection. Lane had followed it once, and it led him straight to police HQ in Llangunnor.

Hunt tracked the VW as it headed up and out onto the B road, turned and made for the village of Angle. He memorised the number plate. He'd track the car down later.

But once the cottage was empty, Hunt watched and

waited for any sign of activity. For fifteen patient minutes, he saw nothing and no one. It was now 11.45am. Almost lunchtime in the normal world.

Not so in Hunt's.

He eased off the pillbox, sliding out from under the blanket to slip down behind. He had his wares in a rucksack he shouldered carefully as he moved off towards the corner of the field, sticking close to the hedge on the left-hand side, heading towards a gate. His legs brushed against the knee-high barley, the air warm under a white, bright sun in a sky empty bar the occasional cloud and the contrails of passenger jets on their way across the Atlantic.

The breeze moved the barley to-and-fro in a slow-motion dance, like an ocean's tide. A crow cawed overhead, and the sound of a tug in the haven below drifted up to him. But his thoughts were only on his targets. If he crossed the next two fields, he could approach the cottage from the left-hand side.

Properties, even this far off the beaten track, had security systems these days. Most commonly, camera doorbells. There might even be a system at the rear of the property, too. If so, he'd know soon enough. But his plans did not involve breaking into the cottage itself. There were outbuildings, and he'd noted Napier entering and leaving one in particular twice during his period of observation. That was his target as he moved stealthily, camouflage jacket melding him with the greenery of his surroundings until he got within twenty yards of the rear of the cottage.

The field here ran down towards a feeding shed for the farm. A huge new building with steel-profiled walls that housed stock during the winter months. But nothing stirred there today. He'd need to expose his position to slip through a gate. He did so quickly, hearing no shout as he crossed the space to the cottage and its land.

He moved with purpose, concentrating on his task. He'd long ago given up on any kind of self-analysis. In effect, he'd obliterated his self-awareness and evolved a new reality. Psychologists would no doubt line up, salivating, to analyse his state of mind. They'd use words like idealised hate and revenge fantasy based on a need to emerge from the shame and vulnerability his demise had triggered. His retreat from the world, his cultivated ability to remain invisible, had denied his need to interact, other than with the despicable tool, Lane. And if he felt any jot of remorse or pity for the female sergeant, he brushed it away from his mind as he would an irritating horsefly. He was too far along the path to allow such thoughts to intrude.

Besides, some collateral damage was inevitable.

Close to the outbuilding, he crouched lower, moving like a cat towards the entrance. He put his ear to the door, listening intently. Nothing except the chirp of birds on a willow nearby in the garden. He tried the door, closed by a latch arrangement but no lock. It opened on oiled hinges, though Hunt half expected an alarm to sound and alert Napier to his presence.

Nothing happened.

Inside, the small windows covered by slatted blinds meant the room remained dark. With his heart pounding, he felt along the walls until he found the light switch. A cold fluorescent light flickered on, illuminating shelves laden with jars, and bottles, and boxes filled with tools. The back of the room, however, was different. There stood a new desk with a computer, accompanied by a well-worn office chair and an armchair. A wooden shelving unit, serving double duty as a bookcase, completed the setup. Hunt glanced at the titles. Some looked work-related, others, novels. Historical adventure fiction; mainly Cornwell and Patrick O'Brien. And on the top shelves, he made out painted models of Napoleonic artillery as well as unmade box-kits and paints.

Napier had hobbies, that was clear. Good. That meant he'd be back in this room soon. Hunt turned back to the door and studied it. It opened inwards, with enough travel for his murderous purposes. He slid off the rucksack and found the first of his pipes and the tilt fuse. This one had a ball bearing that would slide down to close the electrical circuit once a tilt rod was pushed or pulled. The rod had a hole for a trip wire he'd link up with the door handle after taping the pipe to an upright on a shelf behind some books. He'd set a five-second timer for safety during set up.

Once he completed the task, he'd head back to the village and pretend to be a tourist, stash the camouflage jacket, and feign interest in the church while he searched for the Tiguan. The car would be his second target.

He was sweating as he used silver duct tape to set up the bomb.

He was sweating twice as much as he ran the trip wire and wound it around the inside door handle before connecting the fuse with the door left a foot open and with enough slack in the wire for him to get out.

When he finished at the outbuilding, satisfied with his work, he retraced his steps and made for the village.

——————

WARLOW SAT in a room full of people wearing serious expressions, all of whom, like him, wishing they were somewhere else. He'd been summoned to the Assistant Chief Constable's office for a briefing on the Catrin Richards abduction, as it was already being labelled.

He sat between Povey and Buchannan around an oval table. Superintendent Drinkwater and Goodey were the show runners. Drinkwater like a balding pug, his bushy eyebrows in need of a trim, his round face shiny with a film of sweat. Pamela Goodey, known to everyone in the room and the building as Two-Shoes, sat primly. The nickname was a brilliantly ironic contradiction, given to her by someone who had quickly seen through her facade. Despite the prim appearance and doll-like features, lack of humour, ingratiation, and a willingness to throw anyone under the bus were true hallmarks of her character.

Both she and Drinkwater feigned impatience and haste, as if their rushed demeanour could somehow deflect the pointing fingers. After all, it was their actions that had left Catrin Richards vulnerable to kidnapping in the first place.

'The decision has been made to release details to the press,' Drinkwater said, his jowls quivering. 'It is not a decision we take lightly, as it were. Suffice to say that in view of the significant lack of evidence, an appeal to the public is entirely in order. Someone might have seen something. We have the usual hotline set up to accept calls, and now I will read to you the statement I have prepared. There are two reasons. Firstly, so that you are aware of it, as it were. Secondly, if anyone feels they would like to modify the statement, feel free. No one will be judged here.'

Two-Shoes, who had not yet looked up from her note taking, did so now to contemplate the audience, but ended up glaring at Warlow, her pen poised above the paper. Warlow felt a chill of warning run through him. This stare seemed to counter the sentiment that no one would be judged. Judging was Two-Shoes's MO.

Warlow returned her gaze, arms folded, his face set, and eyes locked.

'As of 9am today,' Drinkwater began, 'we have filed a missing person's report for two people. The first is a journalist by the name of Geraint Lane. The second is a Dyfed Powys officer, Detective Sergeant Catrin Richards. Sergeant Richards was driving a dark-blue Mazda 2. Lane a silver Renault Captur. We know that they visited a cottage near Talley in Carmarthenshire. An extensive search has yet to reveal their whereabouts. We would like to appeal to anyone who may have any knowledge of these two individuals or their vehicles to come forward immediately.'

Drinkwater paused to look up. He was met with silence until Buchannan posed the obvious, 'They're going to ask why they were both there.'

Drinkwater nodded. 'Mr. Lane was interviewing Sergeant Richards as part of the Force's transparency programme. The cottage was recently the scene of a brutal murder.'

'Is that enough detail?' Buchannan asked, his eyes darting between Drinkwater and Two-Shoes.

'It is for now,' Two-Shoes interjected, and there was a note of the definitive about the way she said it.

They ran through everything they knew. Povey's work up was still unfinished, but she was happy to inform the meeting that the blood found at the scene had now been confirmed as that belonging to Lane. Warlow gave them his assessment, what they knew about Lane and his previous run-ins with vigilantes, but was unwilling to commit to how relevant he felt this might be when asked. The PolSA had come in and explained how he was going to extend the search parameters. Roadside enquiries of the sparse commuter traffic had yielded no new intelligence. Half an hour after it was called, the meeting was over.

Buchannan and Warlow walked out together. 'Quick word before you get back to it, Evan. In my office,' the superintendent said.

Buchannan's office, a Spartan enclave in the heart of the police station, was a stark contrast to the bustling chaos outside. The office walls were painted a tombstone grey, adorned with a few fading plaques from the Buccaneer's earlier years on the Force. A single window offered a limited view of the fields outside, but it was mostly obscured by half-closed blinds that filtered the sunshine enough to keep the room tolerable. Air conditioning was an unnecessary extravagance still in the United Kingdom, though the way things were going thirty-degree heat was becoming a regular summer torture. A filing cabinet, a well-worn leather chair and an uncluttered desk excluding a coffee-stained mug were the only furniture in the room.

Once they were safely ensconced behind the closed door, the atmosphere grew tense. Warlow leaned against the desk, a deep furrow etched between his brows, while Buchannan settled into the creaking leather chair.

'How's Craig taking it?' the super enquired, his voice low and filled with concern.

'As you'd expect. Terrified but managing to hold it together. I've got him looking into Lane's social media. Better he feels involved, you know?'

Buchannan approved. 'Good idea. And you? How are you holding up?'

'I'm angry, and I'm worried,' Warlow admitted, his frustration evident. 'Gil doesn't like Lane, never has.'

Buchannan couldn't help but offer a wry smile. 'That's because he's a journalist and Gil is allergic.'

'Aren't we all,' Warlow conceded. 'But Gil feels, like me, that something isn't right here. I know none of it is right, but Lane as the predator? Seems too easy. And Catrin isn't the jam he butters his toast with. Plus, his partner says he hadn't been himself over the last few weeks.'

'Since the mugging?' Buchannan asked, a hint of scepticism in his voice.

Warlow shot him a pointed look. 'Exactly. What kind of mugger steals only your phone and then drives your car to an estuary car park with you locked in the trunk? It stank of BS at the time. Reeks of it now.'

Buchannan furrowed his brow, deep in thought. 'What do you think that was, then?'

'Not a clue,' Warlow said. 'But like two and two equalling five, it doesn't add up.'

Buchannan leaned back, momentarily shifting his attention away from the grim situation and towards his stiff limbs.

'How are the hips?' Warlow asked, injecting a momentary respite.

'Bloody nuisance,' Buchannan replied with a half-smile. 'They're ruining my breakdancing.'

Warlow let out a chuckle. 'I bet.'

As the tension in the room lingered, Buchannan shared a glimmer of good news. 'I got a call from a Chief Super at Greater Manchester Police. Apparently, there have been arrests in a big, organised crime operation. They're moving Jess's husband back into the city from his secondment further north. They feel the risk has diminished enough. The hyper vigilance business means Jess doesn't need to be on amber alert.'

'She'll be glad to know that.'

'You want to tell her?'

Warlow hesitated, conflicted about his role in this matter. 'No. It'll be better coming from you. I mean, it's not any of my business, really.'

'Okay. I'll do that. I just thought because you two worked so closely—'

Warlow interrupted firmly. 'This is her business, so—'

'Fine,' Buchannan conceded. 'I'll speak to her today.'

CHAPTER NINETEEN

THE STORE at Ffynnon Fach was open for business as usual. Mick Semple stood behind the post office counter as Rhys waved to him. He held up his hand with the fingers splayed to indicate five minutes. Rhys had another wander around until Semple finished with a customer and then joined him in one of the aisles.

'Sorry to disturb you,' Rhys said.

'No problem. I'm allowed to take a five-minute break. Any news?'

'About?'

'The thief?'

'Not yet.'

Semple looked disappointed. 'I spoke to Denzil's daughter. She says they think Denzil ruptured an aneurysm.' He added a tremor of incredulity to the word.

'Yes,' Rhys said. This was a small community. Word travelled quickly.

'So, that bastard hit him and made him bleed.'

Rhys did not agree or disagree. For now, he'd let Semple believe what he wanted to. 'I was wondering if you'd checked through your inventory properly. See if anything else might have been stolen?'

'To be honest, I haven't checked everything. We have a lot

of stuff here. Turnover isn't huge. We get a big delivery every Thursday and someone comes in to help with stocktaking. I thought I'd wait until then to go over everything. And with Denzil gone, we're short of personnel.'

'Totally understand,' Rhys said.

'But I know you asked, and it will be done.'

'Good.'

A silence, like a slow-motion clam shell, opened between the two men until Semple broke it. 'Are you getting anywhere with finding out who did this?'

'We are chasing some leads. The CCTV footage was not that useful. And that's partly why I'm here. Would it be okay if I spoke with Libby?'

Semple glanced over at the till where Libby was ringing up a customer's haul and then glanced over his shoulder at the post office desk. 'I've got no one waiting. So, now is as good a time as any.'

Rhys spoke with Libby outside the shop. He'd seen her before but had not spoken to her directly. Up close, she had her blonde hair in dip-dye pigtails and wore her false lashes dark and long. A single diamond stud glimmered in her left nostril and under the store bib, she wore a faded-black band t-shirt and a denim miniskirt. Her pale legs had seen little sun and the Doc Martens on her feet had seen no polish, ever. Libby stood a foot smaller than Rhys, but that was not unusual. She didn't ask permission when, with casual grace, she lit up a cigarette and leaned against the wall to talk to him.

'You knew Denzil well?'

'I knew him. I mean, he was older than my dad, so—' She slowly blinked, inferring their relationship was purely circum-stantial. 'He was a lovely man.'

'In your statement, you said that the man at the desk, the thief, only spoke a couple of words. He asked for a scratch card?'

'Yep. I mean, we didn't have a conversation. He only had two things in the basket. Besides, he kept his head down and he had shades on, and I prefer to see people's eyes when I speak to them.' She looked up into Rhys's.

'You've had a chance to think it over. Was there anything else about him you remember?'

'Like what?'

'His age. Other witnesses thought he might have been around forty—'

She laughed. 'No way. I'd say late twenties, max. And you know, maybe even a touch… they.'

'A touch what?'

'They.'

Rhys waited for a fuller explanation. 'They, as in the pronoun?'

'Yeah. I don't know, but the gloves were weird, and maybe I saw some dark nail varnish. Touch of the Van Dykes going on with facial hair, too.'

'Van Dyke?'

'Yeah. You know. A bit of a 'tache and stubble up the jawline. And dark, like, really dark.'

'Dyed, you mean?'

'Maybe. So were his eyebrows.'

'So dark nail varnish maybe, and dark eyebrows and facial hair?'

Libby sucked in some smoke and whistled it back out.

Rhys did the notebook trick and studied what he'd written. These days someone with a stubble and nail varnish meant sod all. A means of expression only, though his dad still had problems buying into people with beards and lurex dresses on TV. Unless they were in a Monty Python sketch or the League of Gentlemen.

'Thing is, I didn't really look too hard,' Libby explained. 'Not polite, right?'

'No, not polite.'

'You know who it is, then?'

'Not yet. But this is helpful?'

Libby twisted her mouth. 'Really?'

'Yes, it is.'

'Weird place to rob, though, right?' Libby bent one knee and put her foot flat on the wall she was leaning against.

'Why do you say that?'

She snorted. 'It's crazy. Like, who the fudge steals a six-pack of beer?'

Who indeed, thought Rhys. Not the first time he'd heard that sentiment expressed.

'You'd have to be really desperate is what I think.' Libby sucked in another lungful and exhaled blue smoke. 'So, what do you do when you're not chasing bad guys?'

'I play a bit of rugby and live with my girlfriend.'

'Ooh, very grown up. Is she sporty, too?'

'She's a police officer.'

'Nice. Bring your own handcuffs, eh? Match made in heaven, then.' Libby's smile was tinged with defeat. 'Of course, if she's ever too busy, I'm pretty good at football. You could come around and we could be Messi together.'

Rhys thanked her with a smile, made a mental note to remember that line to tell the boys in the club, and made his way back to the car park, retracing the steps taken by Warlow on his recce earlier. Rhys had the map of the village in his head. Straight ahead were fields. Left was a doubling back towards the village. He stared out over the open countryside, trying not to think about getting messy with Libby, searching for answers that were 'deffo' not to be found there.

———

CATRIN WAS HUNGRY. She wasn't cold exactly, but neither was she warm. Above her, in the real world, the thermometer was hovering around twenty-six degrees on a lovely summer afternoon. But in the shelter, or post, or whatever she was meant to call her prison, not that. She didn't know the actual measurements, but she remembered that the temperature was a constant ten feet underground. That's how heat exchangers worked. She'd talked to Craig about it once as an alternative for central heating. Part of their plan-making for their forever home, if and when.

Thoughts of Craig made her teary. Some of that, a lot of that, had to do with the little hormone factory churning away inside her. Catrin's hand strayed to her stomach. The pregnancy was still so new, a fragile hope she and Craig had been nurturing for months. She put it all to one side. Not to forget it, but park it. So that it did not overwhelm her. Which it had tried to do more than once.

Think about the temperature.

Right. The bunker's underground location meant it stayed at a steady, cool temperature. While it might be sweltering above ground, down here the earth's natural insulation kept things cooler

She'd turned off all but one light in an attempt at preserving power.

The effort of climbing up the ladder and hammering on the under surface of the hatch to make noise had got her circulation moving. Her watch read 3pm and hunger pangs were gnawing at her. She'd found a pair of scissors in a drawer and cut the zip ties that bound her wrists. It was a minor victory, a taste of freedom, but it brought her no closer to escaping.

Now she sat in her behind-the-door corner, her eyes fixed on the map pinned to the board with her position at its centre. Ironically, she knew exactly where she was, but no one else did. Her mind jittered with frustration, a little fear, and the growing hunger that had become her constant companion.

Hunt's effects were a reminder of the man who had brought her here. His clothes lay in a heap in the corner. She shivered, resisting the urge to pull one of his coats around her shoulders. The thought of wearing it sent a thrill of disgust down her spine. A faint but perceptible fusty aroma oozed out of the pile. But she knew she'd have to put that to one side if she needed warmth later.

For now, she'd keep busy.

The bunker itself was a proper relic. Old communication equipment lay scattered about. It was a time capsule from when the threat of war hung heavy in the air, and the Royal Observer Corps had been tasked with monitoring the apocalypse.

Hard to believe.

What had it been like to be stationed in one of these, she wondered. Hidden here on the premise that a missile carrying a nuclear warhead might land at any moment, even in this remote part of Wales. How reassuring it must have been for these officers to hear familiar voices on the radio every day.

She no longer had that luxury; this place had been forgotten by time and hidden from the world above.

The walls were dry, though some moisture had found its way down the access way, rendering the air a little stale with the hint of wood and wet sock in a mildewy concoction. The ends of her fingers tingled as she examined her surroundings. As regards to her possessions, all she had in the pocket of her jacket were some chewing gum, tissues, and a small spray bottle of perfume. Fat lot of use any of those things were now. Climbing up the ladder and pounding on the under surface of the hatch above remained her go-to plan. But there had been no response so far, no sign that anyone had heard her. The suffocating silence was maddening.

Twenty-four hours had passed since she'd arrived, and her watch mocked her with its meaningless readings. Time and hunger were her patient companions. She wished she'd doubled up on the fruit and yoghurt she'd had for breakfast… was it really the day before?

She'd found his food stash: A sparse collection in a cupboard next to the decrepit desk; canned goods – tuna, corn, carrots, mushrooms, one of each – enough to sustain her for a day or two, and two bottles of water, one already a quarter empty. He hadn't stocked up for an extended stay in this forgotten bunker, and she wondered if he had other places he hid out in with further supplies. She would not have been surprised. Hunt had planned for every contingency, but these had not included a long stay in the bunker, judging by the lack of food and water.

Catrin's stomach grumbled. There were crackers – a third of a packet – but no bread. Powdered milk since there was no fridge. She had the means to survive for a while, but the lack of variety was hardly enticing. She chewed on a cracker, letting her mind drift back, as it did every few minutes, to Hunt and his cold, calculating conversation.

She'd been stupid to discuss Napier with Lane, but the journalist had been persistent and sharp. Hunt had latched on to that knowledge. With a little luck, even if he made it to Angle, he would find nothing. Napier's cottage was difficult to find. Then again…

Minutes stretched into slow hours. Catrin battled exhaustion. The cold, hard floor offered no comfort, and what sleep she'd managed through the artificial night had been troubled and fleeting. Yet, she needed to stay alert during daylight hours, to be ready for any opportunity that might arise.

Plus, she now had some scissors.

She pored over her prison, painstakingly examining what she found: faded maps, dusty manuals, and photographs of long-forgotten officers who had once manned this post. Their eyes seemed to watch over her, their silent presence a haunting reminder of the bunker's history.

At least she wouldn't starve. Not immediately, anyway. She would not give in to fear or despair, either. While she waited for Hunt to return, she would do her job. Go through the bunker's contents to find out as much as she could about him, his motives, and likely targets.

Not that she could do anything about them.

But it was the professional thing to do.

CHAPTER TWENTY

THE ROLLING HILLS rose and fell around Constable Mark
Andrews, an endless sea of green and brown, dotted with the
occasional stone wall or gnarled tree. Lower down, the neatly
parcelled fields with their hedgerows looked lush. But where
he was, the isolated moorland was bathed in the golden glow
of the late afternoon sun and the only thing spoiling the tran-
quillity of the setting was the urgency of his mission.

He adjusted his police cap, tugging it lower against the
glare, and scanned the horizon.

Normally on his shift, he'd be patrolling the streets of
Aberystwyth, one eye on the early tourists. But not today.

Andrews had joined the search team scouring this remote
corner of Carmarthenshire for two missing individuals: a
journalist named Lane and Detective Sergeant Richards.
While he supported the cause fully, he was regretting his
participation today. The summer heat was relentless, and he'd
foolishly forgotten his water bottle in the car, leaving him
parched and uncomfortable as he trudged through the countryside.

PolSA had the officers fanned out, ten to twenty metres
apart, forming a ragged line that traversed the open
moorland.

The terrain was unforgiving, its rugged beauty hiding its secrets well. Quiet lanes wound through the hills, many with grass growing merrily down their centres, attesting to the paucity of traffic this area encountered. Here and there were abandoned stone buildings that had seen better days.

Andrews, boots snagging on the tufted grass, approached an old feed shed with a crumbling tin roof and a weather-ravaged rickety door hanging off its hinges. He could hear the distant shouts of his fellow officers, calling out the names of the missing pair where access to clumps of trees on dangerous slopes was difficult.

The isolation of the place weighed on him. The Iron Age circles of stones dotted randomly on the landscape spoke of ancient cultures and practices. There was no escaping the sense that this land had seen its share of struggle and death. That and his thirst had his senses on edge as he neared the stone hut swathed in a temple of brambles and heard, or thought he heard, something that made his heart hiccup into his mouth.

Was that a moan?

No. Impossible.

But the series of muffled thumps that followed were real enough.

Andrews gripped the handle of his baton and carefully pushed the rickety door open. It creaked ominously in protest, revealing the dimly lit interior and the prize within. There, parked haphazardly inside, was a silver car. A Renault Captur with its windows fogged up. Andrews couldn't see inside the car, but the source of the moans and thumps became clear as he approached the rear of the vehicle.

He called out, 'Hello? Anyone here?'

The moans returned. Urgent and desperate.

Andrews stepped out and called to a colleague, waving his arms to attract attention. On the hill twenty yards above, Jason Roblin, another uniformed constable, returned the shout and ran down.

'I've found the car and there's someone inside,' Andrews yelled.

Roblin immediately called it in on his radio. But the hammering from inside the boot got louder. Andrews slid on nitrile gloves and fumbled for a catch before swinging the boot lid up. A man, bound and gagged, lay crumpled, knees bent up on the floor. Blood had congealed on his face, and his clothes were torn and dirty.

'Lane?'

The man nodded feebly.

'Control, this is Jason Roblin.'

Andrews heard his colleague behind him stammering into his radio. 'We've, uh, we've found Lane. Repeat, we've found Lane. He's in bad shape. We need an ambulance here.'

Andrews carefully removed the tape from Lane's face. One eye was swollen shut, his breathing shallow. When the tape came off, the journalist moaned in pain.

'Where is Sergeant Richards?' Andrews demanded.

Lane shrugged, mouth open, his jaw working to relieve the stiffness from the tape.

Roblin joined them. 'I've called it in. Christ, what happened?'

Lane's cracked voice croaked out a reply. 'He was waiting for us. In the cottage.'

'Who was?'

Lane half collapsed against the car. But Andrews needed answers.

'Who? Who was waiting?'

The sound of sirens in the distance meant help, primed and waiting, was on the way. Roblin untied Lane's hands and gave him a drink of water. The journalist grabbed the bottle and swallowed thirstily.

'What happened?' Andrews persisted, his voice low and soothing. 'Where's Sergeant Richards?'

Lane's eyes flickered open, and he coughed weakly. Blood smeared his lips as the words finally emerged. 'Hunt... Hunt took her. I don't know where.'

The cryptic message sent a shiver down Andrews's spine. For a moment, the word perplexed him. Who or what was Hunt? But one glance at his colleague, Roblin, and the look of horror on his face as he stared at Lane told him he was the only one confused by what he'd heard.

'Hunt? You mean Roger Hunt?' Roblin demanded.

Lane let out a whimper.

All Roblin could do in reply was whisper, 'Shit.'

———

WHILE ANDREWS and Roblin waited with Lane for medical assistance miles away, in his office, DCI Warlow was unaware that the investigation was about to be turned upside down. He'd been back from his meeting with Buchannan for no more than half an hour when Povey knocked on the door of the SIO room. Jess had been summoned by the super for him to break the news about Greater Manchester Police arrests, and Rhys had gone out to interview the witnesses regarding the Denzil Williams case. Warlow felt the odd pang of guilt about that, but he trusted Jess's judgement. Rhys was the most junior of the team, but he was developing into a good and thorough investigator. It would do no harm to give him his head and let him show some initiative. Warlow had Denzil Williams's daughter in his mind as these thoughts pin-balled around in his head.

Once Rhys was back, they'd have a briefing.

The last person he expected to knock on his door at that point was the CSI lead.

'People will start talking,' Warlow said, looking up.

But Povey was in no mood for banter. She didn't even bother closing the door.

'I've just had the results back from a sample we took from the stairs at *Cân-y-barcud*. Not much, just a smudgy grease mark one of my lot spotted. The profile has a match on the database.'

'What? I thought Lane's DNA wasn't on—'

'It's not Lane's,' Povey said. 'If I was being pedantic, we don't actually know whose it is, but we've made a pre-emptive assessment because the sample matches samples we took from a site during the investigation into the Moyles's murder.'

She had all Warlow's attention now.

'What site?'

'A site up near Gwynfe. An unfinished Airbnb project that someone had rented out.'

Warlow thought frantically. The Moyles investigation had been complex, and perhaps it was no surprise that it was coming back to bite him on the leg. After all, Lane and Catrin had gone missing from the very place Moyles had been murdered.

'Wait a minute,' Warlow said, still searching his mental database. 'Are we talking about the place that Hunt—'

He got no further. Povey's nod stopped his flow of words and sent his mind into a tailspin. '*Ty Coed*,' he muttered. Woodsman's cottage–a half-renovated hut with an incomplete roof. Inside, one wall had served as Hunt's macabre gallery, divided into three sections. Each section featured a different man. Royston Moyles dominated one, captured unaware outside *Cân-y-barcud* and in various locations around the town of Llandeilo. The depth and quality of the photos at the rental property hinted at prolonged surveillance.

The second section showed Daniel Hughes, Hunt's second victim, while the third displayed John Napier - the man Warlow and Jess had saved from being roasted alive, and whom Catrin still protected.

Images and snippets zipped through Warlow's mind. Povey was right. They had biological samples from that spot where hHunt had holed up and planned his assassinations.

'Evan,' Povey said his name, but she got no further.

Gil appeared behind her, his face flushed, his demeanour serious and unusually grave. 'Sorry to interrupt. I've just taken a call from the PolSA. They've found Lane.'

'Where?' Warlow was on his feet in seconds.

'Locked in the boot of his Renault four miles from *Cân-y-barcud*.'

'Alive?'

'Yes. Battered and bruised, but alive. They've taken him to Glangwili.'

'What about Catrin?'

Gil shook his head.

Warlow moved from around his desk but stopped when Gil didn't move.

'There's something else. Lane said someone was waiting for him and Catrin at the cottage—'

'Hunt,' Warlow said and speaking the man's name felt like a physical blow.

Gil's expression would have been amusing in any other situation. Shock and surprise sent his eyebrows skywards.

'How the hell did you know that?' he asked.

Povey answered, 'We've just analysed a sample from *Cân-y-barcud*. It wasn't Lane's. We think it's Hunt's.'

'It *is* Hunt's,' Warlow said, clenching his fists, fighting to maintain his professional composure even as a mixture of dread and determination coursed through him.

'Do you think he has Catrin?' Povey asked.

'Christ, I don't know what to think. But we need to speak with Lane.' Warlow motioned the other two out of the office and followed. 'Gil, you and I are going to the hospital. Alison, can you wait here for Jess and fill her in? Tell her I'll contact her as soon as we know something.'

As they exited the room, Warlow's mind did a whole series of floor exercises worthy of at least a silver at the gymnastic world championships. What the hell was Hunt up to? And where the hell did Catrin fit into all of this?

Outside, as he and Gil walked to the Jeep, neither man spoke. The afternoon's heat came at them from all directions, from the sun, in the wind, and in hot smoky waves from the tar beneath their feet. Both men were sweating when they got to the car. They found no respite there; the vehicle had become a furnace.

But it barely registered.

Warlow cranked up the air-con and drove out, trying not to let his hands shake too much as he headed towards the town and the hospital at its eastern fringe.

CHAPTER TWENTY-ONE

WARLOW DIDN'T LINGER in the A&E department's reception for long. The urgency of the situation was evident to everyone, prompting the duty consultant to approach him as soon as he announced his presence. For once, he and Gil were let in immediately.

The medics had triaged Lane. He'd broken nothing and denied losing consciousness. In all probability, they would not keep him in. Warlow considered the possibility of interviewing him outside the hospital, but that would consume valuable time, a commodity the DCI couldn't afford to squander.

The main acute care area buzzed with activity. A dozen people in scrubs and a few in civilian clothes swirled about like electrons around a nucleus. Amid this organised frenzy, healthcare workers multitasked, engrossed in conversations on phones or diligently documenting their actions, zipping in and out of rooms behind drawn curtains. God alone knew what was going on there.

But a quiet environment it was not.

Most of the activity seemed to come from one cubicle in particular, the epicentre of an ongoing medical emergency. Whatever was taking place there, it seemed urgent.

Mercifully, a nurse directed Warlow and Gil to an area on

the other side of the room. One with the drapes only half drawn.

Lane's face looked like an oil painting after a white spirit attack by a climate change activist. His left eye was half shut, his lip bloodied and thick, and some butterfly sutures held closed three cuts on his forehead, one of which had oozed a scarlet rivulet that gravity had rolled towards his eyebrow.

Warlow showed his badge knowing full well that Lane was aware of who he was, but there'd be no room for error here. 'Mr Lane, you've been in the wars.'

'Full marks for observation,' Lane replied, his mouth distorted by a swollen lip.

Gil joined Warlow in the room. 'We meet again,' he said, addressing the man in the bed.

'We do, sergeant. I won't pretend that it's a pleasure.'

'Some might call it fate,' Gil said.

Lane did not reply.

'Up to talking?' Warlow dived in.

'Fine,' Lane said, clearly not.

'What happened at the cottage?'

'Is she okay? DS Richards?' Lane asked, his good eye darting between Warlow and Gil.

'Why don't you tell us.' Warlow stepped closer to the bed, his expression hardening.

Lane gingerly touched his swollen eyelid, wincing at the contact. 'I have no idea. He told us nothing.'"

'You mean Hunt?' Gil asked.

Lane's bloodied hand trembled. 'He was in the cottage. The door was open as arranged by your lot. He must have got in before I got there. Hiding upstairs, listening to us. Sergeant Richards and I went outside for a short while to discuss how the killer might have got to the cottage when Moyles was murdered. Bloody ironic.' Lane's laugh ended up in a phlegmy cough. He cleared his throat and continued, 'Hunt showed himself when we went back in. Armed with a hand-gun. Like some bloody Kafkaesque nightmare.'

'Armed?'

'He fired the thing into the ceiling to make sure we knew it was real.'

Gil and Warlow exchanged a rapid questioning glance. The sergeant left to make a quick call.

'What happened to DS Richards?' Warlow asked.

'Like I say, Hunt had a gun. He made me use zip ties to restrain her hands, and then I was bound to the stairs with zip ties, too. He took the sergeant to her car and came back in. That's when he attacked me. They drove off. I was out of it. He disappeared for a while, when he came back, he bundled me into my own car, drove to the deserted shed, and left me there.'

'Did he say anything?' Warlow asked.

'Called me some names I won't repeat here. He blamed the press for dragging his name through the mud after what happened to Moyles. Bloody ironic for a murderer, but that's what he said. I didn't think he'd stop when he was attacking me. Firing that bloody gun again into the garden. I wasn't going to argue.' Lane sipped at some water from a plastic glass that wavered alarmingly on its way to his lips.

'Did he give any inkling of where he might take her?'

Lane shook his head.

Gil came back in, his expression suspicious. 'No evidence of any bullet hitting the ceiling, according to Povey.'

'What? But he fired a gun,' Lane protested.

'Maybe they were blanks,' Warlow said.

Lane's head fell forward, and the part of his lip that could move shifted into a sardonic grin. 'Shit.'

'You couldn't have known that,' Gil remarked. 'A gun remains a gun until it either lights a cigarette or a tiny flag pops out with the word "Bang" on it.'

'Not funny,' Lane protested, swallowing thickly.

'Who's laughing?' Gil said. 'You're here, Sergeant Richards is not. I do not find that the slightest bit amusing. In fact, I find it… bewildering.'

Warlow steered the conversation away from the gun. 'How did Hunt get to the cottage?'

'He had a bike. I saw him carry it to the sergeant's car while I was tied to the stairs.'

'So, he cycled to the cottage?' Gil asked.

'I'd say so. He had no car of his own.'

'How did he know you were there?' Warlow asked.

'No idea. But he wanted information. The man is unhinged. He wanted information on Napier.'

'John Napier? The solicitor?' Gil asked.

'Yes. The man Hunt has already tried to kill,' Lane answered. 'He thinks Catrin… DS Richards, had that knowledge, and we all know she does.'

Warlow had a hundred questions, but he let Lane finish.

'That's why Hunt took her. He wants to find Napier.' Lane let out a choked laugh. 'The really bloody weird thing is I'd asked Catrin about him, too.'

'Why?' Warlow demanded.

'Because he's tied to the Moyles murder. Why do you think we were at the cottage? To get a sense of the case. I knew Napier was still under police protection. I was trying to be clever.' He shook his head, and his eyes drifted away. 'I mentioned he had a second property down in Pembrokeshire. In Angle.'

'How do you know he has a place in Angle?' Gil demanded.

'I'm a journalist. It's easy to find that stuff out. Catrin didn't answer, but what I'm saying is that Hunt must've heard that. He'd been hiding in the loft.'

Warlow turned to Gil. 'Find out if Napier is in Angle.'

'I'll need to make some calls.' Gil grunted. Once more the sergeant disappeared through the curtain like a scruffy Wizard of Oz. Warlow turned back to Lane. 'It doesn't look like they're keeping you in.'

'No.'

'We'll need to speak again. A more formal interview. Tomorrow. I'll be in touch, but if anything comes to mind, ring me or Gil Jones.' Warlow handed him his card.

'I will.'

One last question struck the DCI. 'How would you describe Hunt's state of mind?'

Lane didn't hesitate. 'Single-minded. Obsessed. Full of bitterness and a need for vengeance.'

'Is Catrin in danger?'

'She most definitely is.'

Warlow clenched his jaw, nodded at the journalist, and left.

———

'So, ANGLE, THEN,' Gil said as Warlow drove out of the hospital on the way back to HQ.

'You ever been?'

'No, never. Hardly get past Folly Farm these days with the little ones.'

'Not exactly a place you'd stumble across. Very much an end of the line spot.'

'Looks like it on the map. I checked with a mate in Pembroke Dock. Apparently, there is a DC based there who monitors things as well as Catrin. But guess who the supervisor for Napier's protection is?'

'No idea.' Warlow was in no mood for games.

'None other than your favourite superintendent and mine. Goodey Two-Shoes.'

'What?' Warlow looked startled. 'I thought they'd sidelined her after everything she's done. All very well overseeing some administrative issues relating to press relations, but this… Christ, they should rename her King Merde-ass. Everything she bloody touches turns to shite.'

'Merde-ass for Midas.' Gil nodded his approval. 'That's one for the Christmas letter. Apparently, she's been tasked with budgeting cuts, so she's been overseeing a reduction in the protection offered because there's been no sign of Hunt for months on end.'

'That means I need to speak to her.' Warlow's lids went to half-mast. 'She'll have all the details, no doubt. But you get going. I'll contact you in the car once I get an address. Come to think of it, someone ought to ring Napier.'

'I'll get the Pembroke DC to do that,' Gil said. 'Best he hears a familiar voice telling him the bogeyman is about. What about Lane?'

'What about him?'

'Do you believe all of that?'

'Don't you?'

Gil made a derisive noise that was half snort and half tut. 'If that bugger told me the sea was blue, I'd want photographic evidence. Why was Hunt already there? How did he know they'd be there?'

'There is that,' Warlow admitted.

'It's not as if he could've followed Lane on his bike, is it?'

Warlow thought about that before answering. 'You say that, but these days, on an e-bike maybe it's not impossible. But what's the alternative? Who else knew they'd be going up there?'

Gil had his eyes on the traffic but found no answers there. Eventually, he said, 'I hate to say it, but only those involved in the press nonsense.'

'Drinkwater? Goodey?'

Gil sighed. '*Argwlydd,* I don't know what to think. Lane's injuries are real enough. Though it's possible, he hasn't had a feed of blood for a while and that's the way vampires look when the tank is empty. I had a curry last night. See the way he flinched when I got too close? That was probably the garlic.'

'I'll leave that observation out of my report, if you don't mind,' Warlow muttered and put his foot down.

———

Lane's partner, Amol, picked him up from A&E at 5pm. Full of concern, he'd half carried the journalist to his car.

'Oh, you poor thing,' Amol said, and not for the first time.

'I'm okay, honestly. Could've been a lot worse.'

'Do not say that.' Tears sprang to Amol's eyes. 'Don't ever say that. Are you hungry?'

'Not very.'

'You must eat something. There's some of that lentil bake left. I'll make a salad—'

Amol's veggie cooking was brilliant. Though sometimes, Lane simply felt like murdering a sausage. 'I'm too knackered,' Lane cut him off. 'And I still feel a bit sick. Being in the car isn't helping.' They were approaching the lights at the bottom of Jail Hill, at the western edge of Carmarthen.

'Take some deep breaths,' Amol suggested.

'I am.' Lane leant forward in the passenger seat and dropped his head down low. Without looking up, he mumbled, 'Can you stop at that car park at the roundabout under the bridge?'

Panic raised Amol's voice an octave. 'Are you going to throw up?'

'I might,' Lane grunted.

'Hang on. The lights are just changing.'

'I need some fresh air.'

Amol sped up through the lights as they turned orange. The car park was two hundred yards away. He pulled in, and Lane opened his door and half tumbled out. He hurried to the railings at the riverbank where he leaned forward, his head hanging down.

Amol joined him and put his hand on Lane's back, rubbing it gently. 'Can I get you anything?' He asked, his voice laced with concern.

Lane kept his head down, avoiding eye contact. 'Is there any water in the car?'

'No, but I can run across the road. It'll take me two minutes to pop up to Blue Street.'

'Would you?' Lane twisted his neck and attempting a lopsided smile, suppressing a wince as the movement pulled at his bruises

'Of course,' Amol said, his dark eyes angled in concern.

Lane waited while his partner crossed the road at the

lights just off the roundabout. When he was sure Amol was out of sight, he reached into his pocket for the phone that Hunt had returned to him as part of their bargain. The phone Hunt had taken from him at the supposed mugging.

Fake gunpoint, according to the cops.

He stifled a dry laugh. The chubby sergeant was right. There was no way he could have known it was a fake. You didn't question that kind of thing in a known killer.

He glanced left and right.

No one looking. Lane pressed buttons. He hadn't backed this phone up to the cloud. He'd long considered that way too dangerous. He had local backups but those he had long ago discarded after the run in with the paedo-hunters.

Hunt had turned off the Find my Phone function already, too. But Lane double-checked, then he signed out of his account, opened settings, general, reset phone. He kept glancing over his shoulder, but Amol was out of sight. The screen blanked out and rebooted. A factory reset. Then he turned the phone off and threw it out into the river flowing slick and brown beneath him as the tide drove the estuary waters inland. No one would find it there. Even if they did and made the thing function, he'd wiped it now.

Belt and braces. Too bloody right.

Lane exhaled with relief and stood up straight.

Hunt, the bastard, had hurt him. Taken pleasure in the beating. Going way over the top to make it seem genuine. More than once Lane had begged him to stop.

But when he stopped, eventually, he had kept his word and given Lane his phone back.

Intact. With all the damning evidence it contained.

If Hunt was caught and he broke the Faustian pact he and Lane had made, it would be a question of one man's word against the other about the contents of the phone. Respected journalist working with the police versus a known murderer. Lane would ride out that storm if it came. But for now, despite the bruises and the mother of all headaches and his aching limbs, Lane felt freer than he had for months.

The police would want to grill him about the missing sergeant. But he'd tell them the truth. He knew sod all. He had no idea where she was. The only person who could answer that was Hunt.

With a bit of luck, the twat would do what he needed to do and sod off to Mexico or some eastern European backwater, where Lane would never see or speak to him again.

That might mean the loss of the detective sergeant. But what was one less bloody copper in the world?

Lane smiled.

His lip hurt when he did that, but he embraced the pain, smiled a little more broadly, and heard the healing tissue rip open again just before he tasted blood.

It felt good to be alive.

CHAPTER TWENTY-TWO

RHYS PARKED the job Audi in front of the row of tightly packed, three-storey terraced houses. He checked the address on his notepad, then climbed out, sliding on a jacket despite the warmth of the afternoon as he approached the nondescript building that housed Kaylee and her three children.

He rang the bell, eventually to be buzzed in by a woman in her fifties with short hair, ragged features, and an extensive set of keys hanging from the belt of her unfashionable jeans. Despite the heat, she wore a flannel shirt. Through the partially open inner door, secured with a six-inch chain, that was the extent of what he could discern.

Rhys introduced himself, flashed his lanyard, and smiled.

The woman did not reciprocate. She took a photo of his ID, said, 'One minute,' and shut the door.

Rhys stood and studied the various notes stuck up in the little vestibule. Most were instructions about entry and warnings about behaviour that would not be tolerated. Halfway through reading a warning about noise after 9pm, the inner door swung open, unveiling the woman in the flannel shirt.

This time, she identified herself. 'Miriam Noakes. I'm the supervisor here. Sorry about the wait, but we always check before admitting. Routine. Kaylee is on the second floor, room ten. Is she expecting you?'

Rhys took the stairs. Noting the thin nylon carpet and scuffed white gloss on the balustrades.

Number ten was the last room on the left on the second floor, its door some kind of pale wood with metal handles and metal kick plate running across the bottom eight inches. He knocked, and Kaylee opened the door. Inside, the accommodation was modest but clean. The furnishings were worn, and the small TV sat atop a battered wooden stand. The scent of Cheerios lingered in the air from some bowls on a small table, while cartoons played on the TV. Two sets of bunk beds lay against one wall, a sofa against the other. A tiny kitchenette sat at the back. There were no toilet facilities.

Birthday cards adorned the small table.

Kaylee's freckled face didn't smile. She wore jean shorts and a sleeveless t-shirt.

'Didn't expect to see you again so soon.'

Rhys, though, was still coming to terms with the room. 'Is this it? Is this where you live?'

Three children, two girls and a slightly older boy, did not look up from the TV.

'We had a bigger place, but I got evicted for not paying the rent.' Kaylee's shoulders slumped.

Rhys's eye caught the birthday cards. 'Someone's birthday?'

'Danny's. Four today, right, Dan?'

A boy with long hair turned and nodded.

'Happy birthday,' Rhys said.

Danny had his mother's smile. 'I got presents.'

'Good for you.'

'Glass of water?' Kaylee gestured towards the kitchenette.

'That would be great.'

'No ice. Sorry. Fridge is downstairs.'

'That's not a problem,' Rhys said. 'Look, I won't keep you long. I'm here about Mr. Williams, the man from the store.'

'What's happened?'

'There's been a postmortem. The pathologist thinks there may have been an underlying medical condition. Running after the thief might have triggered it off. He bled from an aneurysm.'

'Shit,' Kaylee said.

'I'm here just to go over some things you said.'

'Let's sit. Sorry about the telly.' Kaylee gestured to the narrow, wobbly chair opposite her small flyaway table.

Rhys took a seat, his discomfort evident but masked with politeness. 'It's fine,' he replied, taking in the cheap wallpaper and the scattered toys. 'It's none of my business, but you don't have a partner?'

Kaylee sighed, a mix of resignation and bitterness in her voice. 'Did. He's the father of the three of them. Dreams of being an MMA fighter. Only, he likes a drink and tends to forget I'm not a sparring partner.'

Rhys offered a sympathetic nod. 'Sorry about that.'

Kaylee's eyes narrowed, studying Rhys for a moment. 'You are, too, aren't you?'

'It can't be easy,' Rhys said.

'I'd rather be here than waiting for him to come home from the pub,' Kaylee replied, her voice firm.

'Do you have any other family?' Rhys inquired.

'A brother. I don't talk to my mother and father. But my brother comes around. He helps.'

She poured some water from a jug into an enamel cup, handing it to Rhys. He sipped at it, the tepid water hardly refreshing.

'So, about yesterday,' Rhys began, getting back to the matter at hand. 'You said you thought the thief was what, fortyish?'

'Definitely older than me. Us. What are you, twenty-five?'

'A bit older than that.'

'This guy was older than you.'

'And he wore gloves?' Rhys continued.

'Yep,' Kaylee confirmed. She leaned forward, her gaze hardening. 'I'm telling you; I saw what I saw.'

'But he spoke?'

'He said, "scratch card".'

'Okay. I wanted to check. To make sure I hadn't misheard.'

'Fine,' Kaylee tone was clipped, her patience clearly wearing thin.

A knock on the door drew Rhys's attention. They both heard a voice from outside. 'Kaylee, it's me, Abby.'

'Hang on.' Kaylee got up, but before she got to the door, it opened, and a woman stood there. Tall, thin, long in the face, short dark hair.

'Oh,' she said on seeing Rhys. 'Didn't know you had visitors.'

'This is the detective constable I told you about.'

Abby's eyes stayed large. 'You were right about him being a big one.'

'Abby,' Kaylee chided the woman.

Danny turned from where he was sitting on the floor. 'Abby, is my mote in your room? I think Luke's got it.'

'Probably. Why don't you go and look?'

Danny got up in one movement and ran out of the door and through another door opposite.

'Abby's my neighbour. She has two of her own.'

Rhys stood and held out his hand. 'Nice to meet you, Abby.'

'A polite copper. Wonders never cease,' Abby said. She did not shake Rhys's hand.

He turned to Kaylee. 'Thanks for the chat. I may be in touch again.'

'You know where I am. Living my best life,' Kaylee said, arms folded, leaning against the door frame.

Rhys wrote that down when he got back to the car.

———

Hunt followed Napier, wife, and dog to the beach at West Angle Bay. He knew the car and spotted the VW easily enough. They parked in the beach car park a few yards from the busy café. Trouble was, this was a very public place.

People and cars were coming and going at a steady rate. Many of them were dog walkers. This beach was one of the few that allowed dogs access during the summer. Though anyone with a dog who did not pick up after it was likely to be named and shamed on social media given the number of people on the beach with and without dogs. Hunt was sure the place would be heaving come the school holidays. The presence of a nearby caravan park was also a contributory factor to the number of people milling about.

He'd come with everything he needed in his backpack. But the harsh fact was that there were too many bodies and eyes around. He'd quickly realised that fact as he'd walked through the village, stopping at the odd sight to feign his tourist credentials to anyone watching, and on to the bay, turning north where the coastal path climbed up and around the headland. He'd gone only fifty yards before jumping across a gate into a field which rose on his right until he found some suitable cover to observe his prey.

The day sizzled with warmth, yet the coastal breeze lent a refreshing coolness. An hour post-cottage departure, Napier, his wife, and dog hopped into the car and headed back toward the village. Meanwhile, Hunt, hurrying ahead on the road, observed them taking the exact turn on the street where he had turned during the wee hours the night before.

Reaching his concealed car parked behind a wall, he glimpsed Napier's vehicle navigating a curve along the track, delineating the boundary of the small estuary. But that road led to only one place. The Promontory House pub: a hostelry that served drinks and food. Pubs had gardens. But pubs also had parking areas and once parked, cars were left alone until a pint, or a meal, had been consumed.

An ideal situation for someone wanting not to be seen whilst they attended to their business around a parked car.

Adjusting the heavy backpack so that it sat more centrally, Hunt set off at a brisk walk in pursuit of his target.

CHAPTER TWENTY-THREE

LATE AFTERNOON, Warlow found himself once again seated at the oval table with Buchannan, Drinkwater, and Two-Shoes. It had been just a few hours since their last meeting, but the stakes had risen considerably. Lane's ominous revelation had cast a long shadow over their already tense situation, and Warlow couldn't shake the feeling that they were treading on increasingly dangerous ground.

He wasted no time in recounting Lane's disclosure. The room grew heavy with an unspoken understanding that the investigation had taken a sinister turn. There were now two pressing priorities: finding Hunt and locating Catrin. Warlow leaned forward, his voice low and intense. 'They may not be mutually exclusive.'

Drinkwater cut straight to the chase. 'But are you sure Hunt has gone to Pembrokeshire?'

Warlow hesitated for a moment, his gaze locking onto Drinkwater's. 'We can't be certain of anything,' he admitted. 'But it is the only lead we have at the moment—'

Buchannan interjected with a hint of urgency. 'Sergeant Jones is on his way to Angle as we speak.'

'We need eyes on Napier,' Warlow explained.

Two-Shoes, always the shrewd one, attempted to steer the conversation away from their missing colleague. 'Is it possible that Sergeant Richards told someone she was meeting Lane at *Cân-y-barcud*?'

Warlow saw through the thinly veiled deflection. 'She told us,' he said firmly. 'Told her partner, too. But then whoever arranged all of this with Lane could have let it slip as well, don't you think?'

Two-Shoes sat up straighter, her demeanour shifting from evasion to confrontation. 'I spoke with Lane,' she said, her admission hanging heavily as a challenge in the air.

Warlow allowed the silence to linger, letting the weight of Two-Shoes's statement settle among them. Drinkwater cleared his throat, breaking the impasse. 'The real question is, should we go public with Hunt? Warn people to be on the lookout and to stay away.'

Buchannan chimed in, his voice filled with a sense of inevitability. 'I don't see we have any choice in the matter.'

'Pamela?' Drinkwater redirected the conversation, seeking her input.

Two-Shoes responded, her eyes locked onto Warlow's with defiance. He met her challenging stare, leaning back but refusing to look away.

After a moment, she turned to Drinkwater. 'I'll prepare a report,' she said coolly.

Drinkwater placed both hands firmly on the table. 'This case keeps taking darker turns, but we must not shy away from our responsibilities.'

Warlow added a sombre reminder, 'Or forget that we have one of our own still missing.'

Drinkwater's expression darkened. 'Any news on DS Richards?'

'Not yet. But I would suggest we do not dilute that effort in order to search for Hunt.'

Two-Shoes exchanged a tense look with Drinkwater. 'We're already committing significant resources,' she argued.

'Why does that make me think of Custer's last stand?' Warlow said.

Two-Shoes bristled. 'Much as you'd like it to be otherwise, DCI Warlow, I cannot magic up personnel.'

The deputy ACC, however, sided with Warlow. 'Then we call for help from South Wales police if needed. I'll speak to the commissioner.'

Two-Shoes moved her head up and down once with a glance at the senior officer, gracious in defeat. Or at least able to control her burning need to hiss like a snake at him. 'Of course, sir.'

Warlow showed no emotion. This wasn't about scoring points. This was about his people. He didn't give a monkey's about the power play here. The time for checks and balances was long gone, and to let the idea of budget and spend enter the discussion was beyond him. But that was why they had the Two-Shoes of this world. That was how she'd got to where she was. The calm voice of stultifying reason. She looked at the numbers where others only saw the need. But if you went too far down that road, you started stratifying. Picking cases that were and were not worthy of the spend. And that was a slippery slope. Not the same as the slippery slope the CPS negotiated, but a mudslide, nonetheless.

The room went silent. Everyone understood that the darkness surrounding the investigation was closing in. Decisions made now could mean the difference between resolution and disaster. And Warlow, for one, couldn't care less if someone's ego got bruised along the way.

———

Rhys returned to HQ to find a sombre Incident Room. Jess was the only other team member there, her face etched with concern as she hunched over a desk, poring over documents.

'What did I miss?' Rhys asked as he approached the DI.

She didn't waste a moment and filled him in on the latest developments concerning Lane and Hunt. Rhys listened intently, his expression hardening with every detail of this harrowing information.

'Hunt? That doesn't sound good.'

'Gil's headed down to Angle,' Jess continued, her gaze locking on the young DC's troubled face. 'I sent Craig home, though he didn't want to go. DCI Warlow is meeting with the bigwigs. He'll be back any minute. How did your interviews go?'

Rhys let out a sigh and leaned against a nearby desk. 'Okay-ish, ma'am. There's still some discrepancy between what the shop assistant believes she saw and Kaylee Francis, the shopper who was next to the thief, says she saw. Both provide a similar description of the clothing, but Kaylee is certain the suspect was older. Meanwhile, Libby, the store employee, puts him at roughly my age.'

Jess scrutinised Rhys with a thoughtful expression. 'Do you think that's significant?'

Rhys hesitated, his mind working to make some sense of the conflicting accounts he still had not worked out. 'I need to review that CCTV footage again. Maybe I can get a better look, but something just doesn't sit right. I can't quite put my finger on it yet.'

'I'll take another look, too, if you'd like.'

Rhys nodded, appreciating the support. 'Thing is, they're both absolutely certain, which is the odd part.'

Jess leaned back in her chair. 'Well, witnesses can be tricky, Rhys. Ask Molly. She's been studying this stuff for her Psychology A-level, and since I'm her main sounding board, I've had a bit of a refresher.'

Rhys couldn't help but grin at the thought of Jess assisting her daughter with her studies. 'My mother used to help me with English, too, ma'am. Handy that it was her specialist subject.'

Jess smiled briefly, but got back to business an instant later. 'Eyewitness testimony is often considered compelling in court, but we know it's highly unreliable and has led to wrongful convictions. I can't recall the exact stats, but something like seventy-five percent of DNA exoneration cases have been attributed to mistaken eyewitness accounts.'

Rhys's eyes widened in shock. 'That's a big number.'

'It is. That's why we need to treat it carefully. Memory can be easily manipulated, especially when exposed to post-event information. It's called the misinformation effect. Molly had me quizzing her on this topic. Vital details of a perpetrator's appearance or even non-existent objects, like cars or buildings that weren't there, can all corrupt a memory, like a damaged file in a computer.'

'I can't work it out. I've seen the CCTV, and he was standing next to Kaylee and in front of the shop assistant, Libby. It's weird.'

Jess nodded. 'It's good that you're being thorough, though. It's appreciated. Keep running with it. Something will surface, I'm sure.'

'Thanks, ma'am.'

'And if you want a change, take a dive into Hunt's past. There's a lot to go through. He's had an interesting life. Even before he became a TV wildlife expert.'

'Anything in particular you want me to look at?'

'No. Take your pick. There's sod all on the PNC, so it's public domain stuff we're after. Just so long as it's done quickly.'

Rhys turned away, logged onto his computer, and pulled up a search engine before typing in Hunt's name once again.

———

At 5.10pm, John Napier, accompanied by his wife Olwen and Tonks the dog, settled onto a weathered bench in the pub garden. It was the perfect hour to arrive; the midday hikers had long since departed, leaving the garden relatively quiet. The temptation of dining alfresco coupled with the pub's dog-friendly policy made being outside a no-brainer. They chose a quiet spot in the narrow garden, knowing that by six o'clock, it would be standing room only.

This old watering hole, with its storied history dating back to the 1800s, was rumoured to have once been a haven for pirates. In modern times, it had carved out a niche as a renowned seafood spot. The sea breeze carried with it the invigorating scent of saltwater, mingling with the subtle aroma of freshly prepared dishes sourced from the bountiful waters surrounding this corner of Wales. Gulls swooped and yodelled overhead, their cries punctuating the otherwise peaceful seaside scene. Beyond the pub and its garden lay a meandering path leading back to the village, and steps down to a pebble beach where the placid inlet lapped hypnotically against the shore.

One notable disadvantage marred Napier's otherwise idyllic evening. The pub was just far enough to make walking impractical, which meant limiting the amount of alcohol they could enjoy. Not that either of them was likely to be breathalysed here. Still, nine times out of ten, Olwen would be the designated driver.

Still, few things could rival the pleasure of enjoying dinner at a seaside pub on a British summer's evening. Napier relished this moment, finding it far preferable to being stuck in his stuffy Llandeilo office, grappling with difficult clients. He had nearly forgotten the reason for their prolonged stay at their second home. The name Hunt, which once dominated his thoughts, hadn't crossed his mind in months. While time hadn't completely healed all wounds, it had certainly eased the pain.

As far as he was concerned, Angle and their cosy cottage made for a perfect hideaway.

Napier didn't ask Olwen what she wanted to drink; he knew their routine. Two gin and tonics always kicked off their evenings, and tonight would follow suit. He planned to enjoy some wine later at home, but for now, a G&T would quench the thirst they'd worked up while walking their dog, Tonks.

He didn't bother stepping all the way into the bar. He slipped through the entrance with a discreet nod to Nina, the friendly barmaid who knew their routine. She held up two fingers with a smile, and inquired, 'Two large G&Ts, John? You're in the garden, yes?'

Napier responded with a thumbs-up and retraced his steps.

During winter, food service ceased at four, but in the summer months, the pub extended its hours to six – an insider's secret that kept the Napiers from going hungry, but which would see people being turned away disappointed in an hour's time.

He made his way back to where Olwen and Tonks sat, smiling at strangers on the benches, their faces bathed in the warm glow of the late afternoon sun. Tonks caught sight of him and bounded toward him with enthusiasm. The diversion momentarily preoccupied him, preventing him from noticing the lean, bearded man in sunglasses with a rucksack slung over his shoulder strolling along the lane toward the car park.

Even if Napier had glanced in the man's direction, he wouldn't have recognised him. His memory of Roger Hunt had faded. Now, sporting a beard and dark glasses, Hunt had altered his appearance significantly, to where even his own family might struggle.

However, the lack of recognition was one way. Hunt was well acquainted with Napier, and that familiarity was enough to prompt a fleeting, cautious glance toward the man leaning over to pet the dog. The hesitation lasted only a moment before he swiftly continued his path.

Oblivious to the near encounter, Napier joined his wife and reached for some titbits for the dog and turned his attention to the menu.

Crab or lobster roll this evening, he wondered.

CHAPTER TWENTY-FOUR

HUNT STOOD on the periphery of the pub's car park. His eyes, hidden behind dark sunglasses, scanned the scene before him. Amid the laughter and clinking glasses, he'd found his quarry – Napier. He didn't think of him as a man. He didn't even think of him as an animal because they, no matter how savage or cunning, had survival as their driving life force. Napier and monsters like him were driven by something else. Something far less pure. A darkness that fed on misery. Hunt had fallen victim to Napier and Moyles' schemes. In turn, Hunt's actions had left one man dead and another in a coma.

But the wheel turned.

He had with him an instrument of revenge. Brutal but effective. He'd seen IEDs used and their effectiveness. He was no terrorist, but he'd been to some of the world's worst places, war zones where he'd been tasked with monitoring the effect on wildlife. Most often after conflict had ended, but not every time. The result was always brutal.

More than once he'd been in difficult situations, appalled by how cruel men could be to other men, and even more so to animals. A couple of times, in Afghanistan, his path had crossed with a British Counter IED task force. These were paratroopers, training local forces as well as defusing bombs.

He'd learned a lot from 2 Para. And not the kind of thing

you'd pick up in a library, or from the internet unless you wanted someone from the intelligence services knocking on your door.

Today, he put that education to good use. His plan was to attach the second pipe bomb to Napier's car. Duct tape it underneath with a pull switch that would go off once the car pulled away. There might be collateral damage. He'd regret that. But the switch was rigged for a thirty-second delay. Enough for the car to pull out. As he approached the parking area, he took his glasses off to wipe the sweat from his eyes. He was hot and nervous as the weight of his murderous intent bore down on him.

Hunt spotted the VW and hurried over, crouching down beside it. Suddenly, he heard footsteps. A young girl in a Promontory House pub t-shirt had emerged from a nearby car, likely killing time in air-conditioned comfort before her shift.

Her sharp eyes fixed on Hunt as she approached. 'Are you okay?'

'Dropped my keys under the car,' Hunt lied, forcing a smile. 'Clumsy of me.'

'I can help you look,' she offered, her gaze uncomfortably keen.

'No need, I see them now. Thanks anyway.'

The girl nodded and turned towards the pub's back entrance. As she walked away, Hunt caught her glancing back, her expression now tinged with suspicion. He held his breath, waiting for her to disappear from view before resuming his covert task.

'Shit,' he muttered. The encounter had unnerved him. His senses, already on high alert, brought his heart rate up to a gallop. He'd only removed the duct tape from his pack and stuffed it back in now and got to his feet just as a man, dressed in an identical t-shirt to the girl, came through the gap. Hunt ducked low again and moved around the cars, keeping out of sight.

The man – Hunt assumed he was the landlord – walked

forward, brow furrowed with suspicion. Hunt moved towards the line of cars furthest away, searching for an exit, but saw only a fence. Panicked, he hurried towards a camper van and crawled underneath. He heard the crunch of the landlord's feet as he walked the length of the park before they stopped and he heard a voice.

For a second, Hunt thought the landlord was addressing him, but then realised he was speaking to someone else in a jovial tone.

'John, you're leaving early?'

'Yeah. Bit of a domestic problem and we need to get home.'

Hunt recognised Napier's voice.

'All okay?'

'Yes and no. I'll have to pass on the lobster roll this evening. What are you doing out here?'

'Kirsty said she saw someone acting suspiciously. Said he'd lost his keys under his car. I can't see anyone.'

'Oh,' Napier said. One vowel, but laden with disquiet.

'What's up, John?'

'Nothing, but don't be surprised if the police call.'

'Why? What's this all about?'

'Maybe nothing. But I need to get home. I'd keep an eye open, though, if I were you.'

'Are you going to tell me what's going on?'

'I can't. It's a police matter. They might be in touch… that's all I can say. Look, we'd better go. I'll see you tomorrow night. I'd call it in. The fact that someone's been snooping around, I mean.'

'Okay, but—'

Car doors slammed shut, and Hunt's ears pricked up at the growl of the VW engine purring to life, followed by the crackle and pop of tyres on the car park stones. A moment later, the engine noise faded into the distance to be replaced by voices of revellers in the garden. He bided his time until the landlord's footsteps retreated, then stealthily uncoiled from his concealment, and slipped away up the narrow lane toward the headland trail. Hunt had to take a roundabout route, following a long, winding path to maintain his distance. He needed to find another spot to observe Napier's cottage without being seen. Despite the sense of urgency, he prioritised staying hidden, keen to disappear from view as quickly as possible. He'd now lost the advantage of surprise. But that didn't matter. For now, all he needed to do was avoid detection.

———

GIL CRUISED down the road towards the peninsula, gliding past an iconic white building with its two-storey turret overlooking the haven. Startling in both its appearance and isolation, Rocket Cart House, built in the nineteenth century to house a cliff-rescue team that used rockets and breeches buoys, it served now as a holiday home. But it remained a listed building and a monument to the coastguard service. All around it, the flat, serene landscape painted a pastoral picture, but Gil kept his foot down, conscious that beneath this tranquil façade, trouble brewed like an impending storm. As he navigated the winding roads, he couldn't shake the sense of dread that gripped him. A few yards past the house, his phone rang. The call came through the car's speaker.

'Hello?' Gil answered.

'Sergeant Jones? This is Zoe, one of the dispatchers. We have a flag up on the system to contact you if we get anything in relation to Angle, in Pembrokeshire.'

Gil's eyes darted to the rear-view mirror. The B4320 stretched clear ahead and behind him. He slammed on the brakes and pulled into a lane entrance, affording himself a clear view of the sloping fields that led to Milford Haven. In the distance, the Valero Refinery's towers reached towards the heavens. He leaned in, engrossed in Zoe's voice.

'The landlord of the Promontory House pub just called in to report someone behaving suspiciously in the car park,' Zoe explained. 'Apparently, one of his customers recommended he called it in.'

'Which customer?' Gil inquired, his pulse quickening.

'A John Napier.'

'*Argwlydd mawr*,' Gil muttered, a sinking feeling gnawing at him. His grip on the steering wheel tightened. 'It's bloody happening.'

'Sorry?' Zoe asked.

'When was this?' Gil demanded.

'Seven minutes ago.'

'Good. Thank you. Well done. Keep me informed immediately.' Gil ended the call, but his mind raced. Instead of driving on, he reached for his phone and dialled a number provided to him by the detective sergeant in Pembroke Dock. The voice that came over the line was young. Not as young as Rhys, but a lot younger than Gil.

'DC Tobin? This is Gil Jones, DS out of Carmarthen.'

'Oh, hi, sarge,' Tobin responded. 'They told me you'd ring. I was expecting a call—'

'Have you spoken to Napier?' Gil cut Tobin off, his voice sharp.

'Yes, sarge. Ten minutes ago,' Tobin replied, his reply this time laced with concern.

'And what did you tell him?'

'I told him to stay home and be vigilant. I told him that Hunt had been spotted. Funny thing, he was in the pub with his wife when I called.'

An icy hand closed around Gil's heart. 'Where is he now?'

'On his way home, if not already there. I mean, Angle isn't exactly a big pla—'

'*Mam fach*,' Gil interrupted.

And though Tobin was not a Welsh speaker, he could sense the desperation in Gil's voice. 'Is something wrong, sarge?'

Gil fired up the engine. 'Get some bodies down to Angle. I'm five minutes away from Napier's cottage, according to

Miss Go-ogle. I'm near, but I think we're going to need the cavalry.'

'Why—'

'Just bloody well do it, detective constable. That's an order.' Gil hung up and floored the accelerator, barely able to believe that his fishing expedition had turned, in an instant, into what might be a life-and-death pursuit.

CHAPTER TWENTY-FIVE

WARLOW STRODE into the quiet Incident Room, where Rhys and Jess were intently focused on their screens. What had begun as a straightforward investigation into Denzil Williams's possible unlawful death had spiralled into a convoluted mess, complicated by Catrin's disappearance and Hunt's emerging involvement. Warlow felt like he'd been thrust into a relentless merry-go-round with the speed dial cranked up to a dizzying maximum.

The clock had long ticked past 5:30, yet no one in the room showed signs of leaving any time soon.

Rhys, his eyes briefly leaving the screen, offered, 'Cup of tea, sir?'

Warlow exhaled, fatigue etched across his face. 'I could murder one.'

A faint grin curved Rhys's lip. 'The old ones are the good ones, sir.' With that, he stood and left, with only the two senior officers and a pair of data-entering indexers remaining in the Incident Room. Warlow made his way to Jess's desk and spoke in hushed tones.

'Buchannan let it slip about Ricky,' he began, deciding to grab the bull by the horns.

'You mean, it's a relief to know no one is going to turn up

at the door with a shotgun?' Jess asked, her gaze locked on her screen.

Warlow's expression remained serious. 'I wouldn't quite put it that bluntly, but yes.'

'Agreed. It's a huge relief.'

'And Ricky is going back to Manchester, I hear.'

'All the more reason for me not to, then.'

Warlow winced inwardly at Jess's words but chose not to comment.

'And,' Jess added, 'no reason for us to impose on you any longer.'

'We've had this conversation already, haven't we?' Warlow replied. Exhaustion tugged at the corner of his eyes.

'We have. I'm only laying it out, that's all.'

He let that one slide.

'It's hard to think about anything but the job at the moment, though,' Jess said, a pen poised in hand.

Her screen revealed an image of Roger Hunt from a TV programme he'd been featured in. 'Anything from Gil?' she asked.

'Not yet. He should almost be there by now. I think we'll get Napier moved somewhere else and then decide on the best strategy. Two-Shoes, predictably, accepts no blame for what happened to Catrin. She prefers to suggest that the leak of information, because there must have been, must have occurred lower down the food chain.'

Jess snorted. 'I can hear the sweaty slap of closing ranks from here. Any news on that? Catrin, I mean?'

Warlow grimaced. 'Our best bet is finding Hunt. He's the one with all the answers.'

Rhys reappeared, balancing three mugs with tea bags still steeping. 'Old school for speed, I'm afraid,' he explained, nodding at the brew.

'Hot and wet, that's all that matters,' Jess said, catching the look Rhys shot her over the rim of his cup. 'Don't you dare,' she added, but with no venom attached.

'Ma'am,' Rhys spluttered, his cheeks turning crimson. 'I wouldn't… I didn't…' He trailed off, flustered.

Warlow chuckled. 'We'll let you off the hook, Rhys. Sergeant Jones's innuendo shadow stretches a very long way, does it not?'

———

NAPIER PARKED the VW in the driveway, silently urging Olwen and their faithful Tonks into the cottage. He didn't want to betray the anxiety that coursed through him since the ominous phone call. With a soft click, the door locked behind them, cocooning them from the uncertain world outside.

Olwen sensed something was amiss, but she assumed it was work-related and didn't share her husband's unease. She ventured into the quaint kitchen and opened the fridge. 'Plan B, then. What shall we have for supper? I think we still have some frozen lasagne from last week.'

Napier, his thoughts still tangled in the unsettling telephone conversation at the pub, had lost his appetite but knew he couldn't say this without betraying his disquiet. 'Fine,' he said, biting back irritation. 'How long will it take?'

'Ten minutes to defrost and reheat,' Olwen replied, sticking her head around the kitchen door, seemingly ignorant of her husband's mood. Or perhaps quite used to them.

Napier nodded absently, his gaze distant. 'Then I'll nip out to the office and bring back some Pinot Noir. Does that suit? Or maybe the Bordeaux that you like?'

Olwen nodded, but her eyes betrayed a flicker of concern. 'Either. I could do with a drink after rushing away like that. Is everything alright, John?'

'Fine,' Napier replied tersely. The walls of the cottage seemed to close in on him, and he yearned for the solace of his makeshift office. 'I have a couple of emails to respond to anyhow.'

Tonks trotted after Napier as he made his way to the back

door. He glanced down at the eager dog. 'No, girl, you stay here with Mum. How about a chew?'

Tonks's tail wagged excitedly as Napier fetched a treat and handed it over. The dog promptly retreated to her beloved mat to enjoy her prize.

Napier unlatched the back door and stepped out into the late afternoon air. The yard stretched before him, leading to the small outbuilding that doubled as his office down here in Angle. As he approached the door, a crow flew overhead, its raucous cawing shattering the quiet of the yard. Napier's gaze drifted up to the trees, their branches swaying gently. It was a near-perfect summer day, marred only by the unsettling call he had received.

The young constable, Tobin, had been anything but subtle. Napier had preferred the female sergeant, but it was Tobin who had informed him that Hunt, after all this time, was on the loose. He'd kept this alarming revelation from Olwen so far, but he knew he would have to share it soon. Over a glass of red, perhaps, to fortify her for what lay ahead?

Trouble was, he had no idea what might.

Napier understood he had to tread carefully, to keep his emotions in check. Tobin had mentioned that the police were on their way, and Napier couldn't help but feel a glimmer of hope. Presumably, they had a plan. More relocation, he presumed. He sighed.

If Hunt had resurfaced, then perhaps the police had a chance of capturing the elusive man once and for all. Drawing strength from that thought, Napier extended his hand, gripped the office door handle, and pushed it open.

———

GIL JONES GUIDED his car onto the narrow drive leading to Angle Turn Cottage. The stone building remained concealed from view at the turnoff, a hidden spot tucked away from prying eyes. Fifty yards in, the road turned a forty-five-degree angle to reveal the little house, all stone and slate with a steel and glass sunroom at the side and a clutch of little outbuildings across a small yard. The whole place looked like a child's drawing. All that was missing were chickens and the odd goat. He was straightening up with another fifty yards to go when, without warning, the world before him tore apart.

An earth-shattering explosion rent the air, and a blinding fireball consumed the outbuildings. The sheer force of the blast sent a shockwave rippling through the surrounding landscape. In a fraction of a second, the Arcadian scene had morphed into chaos. The world seemed to split asunder, debris hurtling into the sky.

Gil's heart hammered in his chest as he slammed on the brakes, his car skidding to a screeching halt. The windshield before him displayed a tableau of devastation. The roof of the stone outbuilding had been obliterated, stones from the wall still tumbled yards over the manicured lawns. Smoke and dust swirled in a frenzied dance in the blue sky.

Moments later, the door to Angle Turn Cottage creaked open, revealing a woman and a trembling dog. The woman, Napier's wife, Gil assumed, clung to the doorframe, her wide eyes reflecting the confusion and the horrors she was witnessing.

Gil leaped from his vehicle, his heart pounding as adrenaline coursed through his veins. 'Mrs. Napier!' he called out, his voice raw with concern.

The woman turned to him. She tried to speak, but the words caught in her throat. She gestured frantically to the mangled ruins of the outbuilding. 'John… he's in there!'

Without hesitation, Gil dashed toward the wreckage, his mind racing with dread. The acrid smell of burning wood and singed earth stung his nostrils. He clambered over chunks of debris, his eyes scanning for any sign of life amid the devastation.

In the smouldering rubble, he spotted a twisted beam, and beneath it, a form, bloodied and unmoving. Whoever this was, their body had been battered and broken by the explosion. One look told Gil there was no hope.

With trembling hands, he reached out to the blood-spattered neck to check for a pulse, but it was futile. Half the face was missing, as was one arm.

John Napier was gone.

Olwen Napier, her face streaked with tears, approached slowly in a stuttering walk. The dog, Tonks, whined softly, its tail between its legs.

Gil turned with both hands in front of him, clambering back over the stones and wood.

'No, you don't need to see this. He's gone. I'm so sorry, but he's gone.'

She tried to push past him, but Gil held her back. The dog inched forward and then raised its snout and whined once more.

'I'm so sorry,' he whispered, his own voice choked with shock.

Olwen turned to him, her eyes filled with anguish. 'What happened? How did it happen?'

Gil struggled to find the right words, his mind still reeling from the explosion. 'A bomb. That was a bomb.'

A noise, half cry, half wail, oozed out of her mouth, and Gil realised she was pointing. He followed her gaze and saw the remains of an arm, still clothed in the sleeve of a shirt, lying on what was left of the off-its-hinges door. He pulled her away then, back towards the house. But they didn't go in. One bomb had been triggered. There could be more. There might be more booby traps. Instead, he held her, shuddering and keening against him. But he turned her away from where the body lay and stared over her head to peruse the damage.

The piercing wail of approaching police sirens shattered the eerie silence. At ground zero, the devastation was stark: a building reduced to rubble, a woman collapsed in grief for her lost husband, and a loyal dog whimpering for a master who would never return.

Questions would be asked. The wisdom of sending the Napiers back to the cottage with Hunt at large would be at the top of that list. That had been naïve. But then, who would have suspected the killer would have been monstrous enough to attack the home? This was obviously a man who paid no heed to who else could be killed or injured.

That harrowing thought led back to Catrin, and Gil muttered out an oath, which might just as easily have been a prayer.

CHAPTER TWENTY-SIX

DAYLIGHT HUNG ON AT 9PM.

The unease in the room was palpable. It was a room with a past, one that had seen its fair share of gatherings and events, now repurposed as a makeshift command centre. Metal chairs upholstered in rose-red material occupied the space, some neatly stacked against the walls, others drawn around collapsible tables. The cream walls, adorned with framed photographs and posted-up information, looked recently decorated. The polished wooden floor, like the rest of the building, bore the tell-tale signs of recent refurbishment.

Rhys was studying the images of lifeboats on the far wall.

Warlow's restlessness was palpable. He did not want to be in the hall. He needed to be at the cottage, where Napier's lifeless body lay tangled in the rubble. Yet, they were trapped here, awaiting clearance from the bomb squad.

Hunt had been reputedly spotted by numerous supposed witnesses before and after his altercation in the pub's car park. As dusk crept closer, Warlow couldn't shake the sense that the more they procrastinated, the more opportunity it afforded for their prime suspect to go to ground. And since he had successfully stayed off the radar for months, Warlow suspected that was something Hunt was an expert at.

This room, more accurately a hall, bore the name "Angle

Village Hall" on its entrance. Its imposing exterior was a testament to the community's history, featuring a stone-built façade with large wooden doors under a porch. Memorial plaques honouring the village war heroes hung on the walls on either side. It quickly became the nerve centre for the police operation, the ideal location to coordinate their efforts in capturing an elusive killer.

Despite its functionality, the waiting was wearing thin on Warlow. They'd all dropped everything upon receiving the call from Gil, and now they were stuck here, their hands tied. Even as the Explosive Ordnance Disposal unit and their support team set up shop, Warlow felt time slipping away.

Gil returned from the crime scene, and the ordeal had left him visibly shaken. Jess sensed the tension in the room and suggested, 'Why don't we head to the pub? Gil looks like he could use a drink, and we need to talk to the landlord.'

Warlow nodded in agreement. 'Great idea. I wouldn't mind getting a better sense of the lay of the land.'

Outside, the evening was gently transitioning into night, a warm breeze still lingering in the air. The village hall stood proudly opposite St. Mary's Church, a structure that dominated Angle since the fourteenth century. At the rear, a Seaman's Chapel existed as a sentinel next to the salt marsh, bearing witness to centuries of history. Angle had that in spades. For all the wrong reasons, it was now poised on the threshold of a new chapter, too.

The group departed into the fading light, their footsteps echoing the tension that hung in the air. The picturesque surroundings provided a stark contrast to their grim reason for being there. As they reached the gravelled lane leading to the bridge spanning the tidal creek, Rhys paused, taking in the scenic view. In the distance, the refinery's lights blinked, and small boats rested high on the marsh, safely above the tide's reach. Behind them loomed a fortified tower with arrow slits, a living relic from the fourteenth century.

'Wow,' Rhys said, clearly awestruck, while his companions pressed on.

Warlow had walked ten yards along the road when he realised the DC was still standing at the bridge. 'Come on, Rhys. You can take photographs later.'

'Sir, it's not that,' Rhys replied, his voice animated. 'There's a blue Mazda 2 parked against the wall there. I can't see the licence plate from here but hang on.' Rhys trotted back a few yards to a position slightly behind the car and then turned back, a frown evident in his expression. 'Sir, wrong licence plate but… it's Catrin's car. I recognise the sticker on the back window and she has that renewable air freshener thing hanging from her rear-view mirror.'

Warlow hurried to join the young officer, the others closing in behind him. Jess peered at the vehicle. 'Are you sure?'

'He's right,' Gil said. 'I've been in this car with her enough times. Hunt could have switched plates.'

Jess, now gloved up, moved forward.

'No.' Gil put a hand on his arm. 'I've seen first-hand what Hunt's explosive skills are like. We can't risk it.'

'Shit,' Warlow growled and took a step forward. 'Catrin? Are you in there? If you are, make some noise.'

Nothing but silence came back as a response.

'Rhys, run back to the Hall and get that bomb squad lot here,' Gil ordered.

The DC didn't need telling twice, and he sprinted off back along the lane.

'Think she's in there?' Jess asked.

'*Arglwydd mawr*, I hope not.'

Rhys came back at a trot five minutes later with two men in military uniform who took over and told Warlow that they couldn't stay where they were. Once the team had gone over the car, he'd let him know.

'It needs to be done quickly. We have a missing officer.'

The man nodded.

'Looks like we're going to the pub after all,' Gil said grimly.

THE EVENING AIR had grown cool as Warlow and Jess stood in the Inn's car park. The landlord offered to guide them through the events that had prompted his concerns. Kirsty, the young barmaid who encountered Hunt, joined them, her eyes now reflecting the fear she felt on realising how much of a lucky escape she'd had. The landlord's name was Peter. He went by Pete.

'Christ, and to think he was planting a bomb,' he muttered.

Warlow, however, remained cautious in his assessment. 'We don't know that for sure, but it seems likely.'

Kirsty pointed out exactly where the Napiers' VW had been parked and where she had seen Hunt on his knees. She'd attempted a description, but what with the glasses and the beard, the rest of his face had left little to describe.

Warlow stepped away from the group, heading towards the car park entrance. He pondered the possibility of Hunt escaping unnoticed. 'And no one saw him head back down towards the village?'

Pete shook his head. 'Nope. He'd have had to walk past the people in the garden. They saw him walk up alright, but not back.'

At the gate, Warlow turned his gaze uphill. 'So, this way, you think?'

Pete answered, 'That leads back up towards the lifeboat station and the coastal path.'

Warlow probed further. 'Anything else?'

Kirsty chimed in, 'Loads. Old farm buildings, Chapel Bay house, and the Chapel Bay Museum. But then it's open fields until you see the fort.'

'Fort?' Warlow asked.

'Thorn Island,' Pete explained. 'A Victorian fort in the Haven. Only accessible by boat. They built it to stop the French invading back in 1850. Hard to believe now, right?'

Kirsty expanded on this. 'It's always on telly. A kind of

off-grid place to go. I'm pretty sure someone lives there full-time now, too.'

Warlow fought a sinking sensation. Roadblocks and stationed officers along the established paths leading off the peninsula were already set up, but the more he learned, the more he suspected Hunt hadn't ventured far. Not with buildings and even an island to hide in. There were countless hiding spots within throwing distance. It made their task more daunting than ever.

Warlow thanked both Peter and Kirsty for their cooperation before re-entering the pub, where Gil and Rhys were seated, nursing glasses of orange juice and lemonade with plenty of ice. But no laughter. Every voice that spoke did so in subdued sentences, mirroring the anxiety that had taken hold of the entire village.

'Anything?' Gil inquired as the senior officers joined him and Rhys.

Warlow sighed, his frustration simmering beneath the surface. 'Not yet. But it's clear we can't let our guard down. We need to cover every escape route.'

Warlow's phone buzzed, and he swiftly answered the call. The voice on the other end was terse and urgent. 'Bomb squad,' he muttered, hand over the mouthpiece.

He listened some more and then thanked the caller before putting the others out of their misery. 'They've finished their sweep of the car. No explosives found, and the boot is empty.'

The tension in the room eased. The possibility of a hidden bomb had weighed heavily on their minds, but what had weighed even more heavily was the prospect of finding Catrin trussed up and dead.

Gil leaned forward, brow furrowing. 'Right, what's our next move?'

Warlow contemplated their options. 'We'll have to contact whoever is on that island. Make sure they're okay and get a search team over there tonight. We can't leave that to chance.'

Jess added, 'The chopper is going up.'

'It has heat-sensing infrared, right?' Rhys asked. 'If he's hiding outside, they'll find him.'

'I doubt he's that stupid,' Warlow said. 'But there's no point in us being here. The bomb squad people said they'd be another couple of hours at least at the cottage.'

He'd reluctantly made a decision that weighed heavily on him. 'I want everyone to go home and rest. We'll regroup in the morning. And not here. In Carmarthen. This won't be over until we have Hunt in custody, but this place is going to be like a zoo. We'll be better off out of it.'

'What if Catrin is here somewhere, sir?' Rhys asked with the candidness of youth.

But Warlow had considered that. 'I doubt she is. Having her along would make no sense. Lane said that Hunt had gone with Catrin in her car for a while before coming back. He had no reason to lie to us about that. If so, then Hunt would have taken her somewhere first.'

'Let's keep the car under obs for now. He might come back.' Warlow doubted it, but they had enough bodies on the ground to stake it out.

The team exchanged weary glances, the realisation sinking in that their pursuit of Hunt was far from over. They left the pub, the burden of an unsolved crime heavy in their thoughts. Night had fallen, casting a shroud of darkness over the unlit road, skirting the marsh and leading back to the Hall.

At the village, they dispersed, each to their own vehicle. Warlow followed Jess back to Ffau'r Blaidd. There, they sat in the kitchen, both exhausted by the day's events.

'Have you told Molly about her dad yet?'

'Not yet. She has enough on her mind. I will but let her get her exams done first.'

'Sounds like a good idea.'

Cadi, her favourite stuffed bear, Arthur, in her mouth, moved from Warlow to Jess and back like a fondle-seeking, slow-motion missile.

'You don't think Hunt has done anything to Catrin, do you?'

Warlow squeezed his eyes shut. 'I'd be lying if I said I hadn't thought about that. Bombs are bloody crude. Obviously, he knew that if he put one in the car park, other people might get hurt. But so far, he hasn't lashed out randomly in that way. I'd like to think that applied to Catrin.'

'Oh, God, I hope so,' Jess said. She glanced at the wall clock. 'It's only eleven, but it feels like two in the morning.'

Warlow leaned over and took the dog's head in his hands. 'It'll be light at half four. Perhaps you and me should go for an early morning stroll, eh?' He avoided the use of the 'w' word. Any mention of walk would send the dog into a tailspin.

'I'd offer to come with you, but I… c.b.a.'

Warlow grinned. The acronym for Can't Be Arsed was one of Molly's favourites, as her mother knew only too well.

'Let's see what tomorrow brings,' Warlow said as Jess left the room.

CHAPTER TWENTY-SEVEN

GINA MELLINGS, Rhys Harries's partner and a fellow officer in the Dyfed Powys Police Force, was already pyjama-clad when Rhys returned home, just before the stroke of midnight. She immediately threw her arms around his neck and turned her face up, eager for a brief kiss.

'You didn't have to wait up,' Rhys said, weary but appreciative. 'But I'm glad you did. Hugs were on my list of things to do before bed.'

Gina grinned. 'What else?'

'Shower and food.'

'Okay. You shower, I'll heat the food.'

'Sorry I'm so late,' Rhys muttered as he headed toward the bathroom. 'It's been manic.'

'So I heard. So everyone heard.'

Ten minutes later, Rhys sat at the table, suitably showered and smelling significantly better than when he'd first arrived home. He wore bedtime shorts and a t-shirt, while Gina sat cross-legged on a chair opposite him, sipping a glass of water.

'How bad? In Angle?' Gina inquired, her expression grave.

'Bad enough, so Gil said,' Rhys confirmed. 'But I didn't see any of it because the bomb squad was still there.'

Gina's head shook in disbelief. 'Oh, my God. A bomb in Pembrokeshire.'

'Hunt spent some time with bomb disposal groups from the army,' Rhys explained. 'He was in Afghanistan doing research into the effect of conflict on wildlife. But he saw these guys in action, and I think they adopted him. He obviously knows about IEDs. Gil said there wasn't much left of the building or Napier.'

'Gil saw it, then?'

'He was fifty yards from the place when it blew up.'

Gina looked appalled. 'Is there no sign of Catrin?'

'We found her car. Hunt must have used it. But Warlow thinks he took her somewhere before he came back for Lane.'

'Oh God, Rhys. This case is horrible.'

Rhys idly moved his food around his plate.

'Are you not eating that?' Gina's eyes widened.

'Weird. I'm suddenly not that hungry.'

Gina raised an eyebrow. 'Did I just hear you say you weren't hungry? Did you eat something on the way home?'

Rhys shook his head.

Gina let her mouth fall open. 'Then things must be really bad.'

Rhys sighed. 'To be honest, it's what happened this morning that got to me.' He recounted the heart-breaking visit to Kaylee and her three kids, crammed into a one-room temporary accommodation. 'Four of them in that one room. It isn't right.'

Gina's expression softened as she walked around the table to put her arms around Rhys's shoulders from behind and rest her chin on his head. 'There are lots of things that aren't right in the world, Rhys.'

'I know,' Rhys admitted. 'I shouldn't let these things get to me. Gil says I need to become tougher. Develop a hard outer shell.'

Gina gently squeezed him. 'No. I like your skin just the way it is, Rhys Harries.'

Rhys turned to face her and grinned. 'I quite like your skin, too.'

Gina quirked a smile. 'Good, it's so hot, skin is probably all I'll be wearing to bed tonight.'

'That's not fair.'

Gina's smile was enchanting. 'Who said anything about being fair? Come on, I'll clear all this up in the morning.'

———

IN THE UNDERGROUND GENERATOR SHED, Hunt once again found shelter. The summer air hung heavy with the scent of damp earth and old machinery. He'd sought vengeance relentlessly. Months spent plotting and planning, culminating in the explosion that had, he hoped, finally obliterated Napier. From his hiding place atop the pillbox, he'd watched the emergency services descend. He'd smiled on seeing the ambulance leave with only a zipped-up body bag.

Vindication.

Now, as he lay in the shadowy recess of the underground chamber, his mind swirled with a mixture of triumph and emptiness. The bomb had done its job, but it also left him adrift in the aftermath. Two foil blankets, taped to the underside of the ceiling, served as his camouflage, shielding him from the prying eyes of the police helicopter's heat sensors as it droned overhead. The rhythmic thumping of rotor blades reverberated through the ground, a relentless reminder of his precarious hideout.

Hunt remained attuned to the sounds of the world outside his makeshift sanctuary. He detected the distant hum of approaching vehicles, but they never stopped near him. Fear, once pushed aside by his unrelenting need for vengeance, now crept back like a dark and shapeless presence in the night. The kidnapped detective sergeant impinged onto his thoughts, securely locked away in a hidden bunker where she remained unharmed, a mere pawn in his calculated game. He could leave her there. Perhaps no one would find her for a hundred years, by which time she, and the foetus she carried, would be nothing but dried skin and bones.

But she'd played no part in Moyles' and Napier's sick games. She and her child were innocent. An inconvenient fact that gnawed at his conscience. He sensed the irony in that. He'd killed two people and rendered the third a vegetable. To the outside world, he would seem a callous murderer.

But the detective sergeant deserved better. She had not given up her secrets, and he admired her for that. Lane had forced her into falling into his journalistic trap by suggesting an address for Napier. And even then, it had been more a lack of denial than a confirmation. A slip he'd been able to act upon. So, now he needed to find a way back to the bunker near Tregaron where she was hidden. There, he'd let her out after he'd made his escape. Because that was where his focus now shifted.

The peninsula's treacherous waters and sheer distance rendered swimming far too risky an option, but the rugged coastline promised a way out. Hunt's mind raced as he lay in the stifling darkness. The helicopter's blades whooshed over-head, a constant reminder of the narrowing window of escape. He had to vanish into the rocky terrain, and soon.

A sudden change in the helicopter's sound jolted him awake. Had they spotted something? His heart pounded as he held his breath, listening intently. After a moment, the rhythmic thumping resumed its pattern. He exhaled slowly, the adrenaline leaving him drained.

In that moment of terror, a realisation struck him: for the first time in months, he wanted to live. The madness that had driven him to this point had dissipated with Napier's death. Now, he yearned for solace, somewhere far from this land and its ghosts.

But first, he had to survive the night. The coastline's rocky cliffs and hidden coves beckoned, promising escape if he could just reach them. Hunt tensed, ready to move at the first sign of the helicopter's departure. His family, his old life, was past. The other victim in all of this, the teacher he'd fallen in love with and whose image had also been exposed to the world by Moyles and Napier in their sick Peeping Tom set up, might be the only other being who would understand why he did what he'd done.

But there could be no future for her in his fugitive life. He'd burned that bridge when he murdered Moyles.

He would leave once the helicopter stopped sweeping. Plus, he needed some light for what he had planned. The outside world beckoned, a world of danger and uncertainty, but Hunt was ready. He liked to think he'd calculated every step, every contingency, though it had been a near thing in the pub car park. Still, he was determined to slip through the fingers of those who were casting a net around him.

But for now, he lay still. The distant wail of yet another siren serving as a grim reminder that time was of the essence. The coast called to him. But he'd hold on a while longer. Until the helicopter's fuel ran out.

Then he would move.

———

GIL GRIPPED the steering wheel of his unmarked police car, knuckles white as he navigated the winding roads back from the scene of devastation at Angle. Burdened with the weight of what he'd just witnessed, the explosion that claimed the life of John Napier, partner to Royston Moyles, and the victim the murderer had targeted. The acrid smell of burning debris still lingered in his nostrils. As he drove, he couldn't shake the image of the charred remains of Napier's office and the severed arm in the debris.

All haunting reminders of the chaos and death that had unfolded.

Gil had seen his fair share of gruesome crime scenes, but this one got to him. Largely because of what else they'd found. The discovery of Catrin Richards's abandoned car shocked him. On the surface, of course, they'd known that

Hunt had been involved in her abduction; Lane witnessed that first-hand. But seeing her car at the scene brought it keenly home.

Worse was knowing he had to share that painful knowledge. Gil wanted to make the call and had told Warlow as much. He pulled over to the side of the road, his heart heavy as he dialled the number. After a few rings and despite the late hour, Craig Peters answered.

'Craig, it's Gil,' he began, his voice steady despite the turmoil within. 'I won't pussyfoot… we found Catrin's car down in Angle—'

'Angle?' Craig's voice cracked with disbelief. 'Where the explosion was? It's all over the bloody news—'

'The car wasn't near where the bomb went off. But there's no sign of her. We don't think she is anywhere near.'

'How do you know?' Craig demanded.

Gil could almost picture Craig pacing. 'We don't. Not for sure, but it makes no sense that she was down there. That's what we concluded.'

'Then where the fuck is she?'

'That, I don't know.'

The silence on the other end of the line stretched for several seconds until it was broken by a choked sob. Craig, normally stoic, was crumbling under the weight of uncertainty.

'Catrin…' Craig's voice broke as he uttered her name, a whispered plea for her safety.

Gil felt a pang of empathy, a shared sense of helplessness. But that was not what Craig needed. 'We won't stop until we find her, Craig. And we will. You know that. We never leave one of our own unfound.'

Strangled inhalations came over the line and then words. 'Sorry, sarge, I know you're doing everything. Can I come in tomorrow? Sitting here, it's doing my head in.'

'DCI Warlow says you're welcome.'

'Thanks.'

The connection ended, leaving Gil numbed. The priority

now was to capture Hunt, interrogate him, and to bring Catrin back safely. His fingers tightened on the steering wheel as anger surged within him. He didn't want to think what he might do if Hunt had done anything to her.

He let his head fall to the steering wheel, breathing deeply. He quelled these thoughts, replaced them with a different anger. Napier's death meant that they'd lost their chance to question him about the enigmatic little boy, Sillitoe, whose photograph they'd discovered on tapes recorded by Moyles.

'*Na beth y'w blydi mess*,' he muttered to himself. That was one he would not need to translate for DI Allanby. She'd muttered, 'What a bloody mess,' herself as they were leaving to get to their cars.

With a sigh, Gil resumed his journey. The horror of the day's events churning in his mind and his gut, threatening to crush his resolve. He had seen things that no one should ever have to witness, and he was keenly aware that the trauma of it all was taking its toll. There were demons in his head, vile thoughts about what might be. He turned to the entertainment system to deflect his thoughts.

His daughter's friend was a psychologist, and they'd chatted about cognitive behavioural therapy. He'd listened to it all, aware of how he might appear cynical, to his daughter anyway, but her friend had been interested to hear how he dealt with the job. Coping skills weren't taught when he'd been a young Uniform, but he'd worked out some of it for himself. In his previous vehicles via tape decks, then CDs. Now it was all linked up to his phone. He found what he was looking for in a file entitled "most played".

Gil was made of stern stuff, a seasoned detective who had weathered many storms in his time. He wouldn't let his emotions get the better of him now. There was work to be done, a dangerous criminal to catch, and a colleague to find.

Yet, as he drove, he allowed himself a moment of vulnerability, acknowledging the horror and anger that coursed through his veins. Now he had to channel that rage, to use it as fuel to propel him forward. Catrin's life hung in the balance, and he wouldn't rest until she was safe.

With grim determination, he pressed on into the night. And somewhere in his soul, as Tom Waits offered his *Invitation to the Blues*, he found some consolation knowing every member of the team felt the same way as he did.

CHAPTER TWENTY-EIGHT

A DAY and a half had passed by at the speed of a racing snail since Catrin had arrived at *Cân-y-barcud*. She'd put the lights out overnight and spent hours in complete darkness, sleeping on and off, occasionally lighting up the space with a flashlight she'd found. Her key problem was boredom. She was in no immediate danger, and she'd eaten some crackers and cheese. Twice. Once for lunch and once for supper the night before. There was an electric hotplate, but given the lack of obvious ventilation, she had not wanted to use it. Maybe she would for lunch. A single tin of baked beans sounded delicious.

Craig liked his with cheese grated on top with a little Lea & Perrins sauce. She preferred hers with toast and nothing else. And she was hungry most of the time these days.

'Eating for two,' Craig had joked. 'Wish I could get pregnant.'

She'd given him a mouthful for that.

During the night, Catrin had slept in her clothes under a spare sleeping bag, and it had not been that uncomfortable. So far, she'd avoided meddling with Hunt's belongings – apart from the food – not wanting to antagonise the man.

But, as the long hours wore on, and after having set herself an exercise regimen of two hundred steps up and down the bunker every fifteen minutes, gradually, she turned her attention to its contents. More specifically, what Hunt had brought with him and left with her. In her own methodical way, she'd made lists in her notebook. And being the officer that she was, she kept it formal.

Reporting Officer: DS Richards

Summary of Incident:

During my time held captive, I have used the opportunity to review items and materials and possessions of Roger Hunt.

Itemised Food and Water:

Perishable goods – one small square of cheese. Canned and non-perishable food items –1x mushrooms, 1x corn. 1x Tuna, 1x baked beans (1x carrots, already eaten)

Dried fruits and nuts – one packet.

Bottled water – approximately 1.3 litres.

Three cans of Hazy Jane beer.

Small portable stove with fuel canisters.

Fishing equipment – rod/flies/lures

Clothing:

Weather-appropriate clothing for all seasons. Some of it camouflage attire.

Hiking boots and trainers.

Gloves, hats, scarves, some adapted for cycling.

Rain gear and waterproof clothing.

Survival equipment:

First aid kit and Swiss Army knife. Fire-starting equipment (lighters, waterproof matches, fire starter).

1. Shelter supplies (tent, sleeping bag).
2. Compass and maps.
3. Headlamp or flashlight with extra batteries.
4. Binoculars and navigation tools.
5. Camouflage netting.
6. Emergency blankets.
7. Maps.

———

PERSONAL ITEMS:

Some paperback books – military thrillers mainly – and some non-fiction books on wildlife, several of which had been authored by Hunt, as well as playing cards and a solar charger for electronic devices. Some handwritten journals.

Technical equipment:

A variety of packages scattered at the base of a cardboard box appear to have contained nuts, bolts, and nails. All are empty. Also noted; trimmed wire ends and insulation, together with fine screwdrivers and pliers, rolls of wiring and batteries, and a section of metal piping as per an old drainpipe.

Conclusion:

Hunt appears to have been living in the old Observer Corps Outpost bunker for an extended period, possibly months. Though the lack of food suggests this might not be his only bolt hole. It is my intention to further examine the written material. There does not appear to be any residual combustible or explosive material. Though black powder, consistent with fireworks judging by its smell, is residual in the box.

The likelihood that he has been engaged in the construction of an IED is high.

In a plastic folder, she found a schematic of the bunker that went a long way to explain what she could not work out. The structure looked very basic. A cutaway diagram showed the shafts – access ways and ventilation. Behind that was a document that gave her an insight into where she was and what it had once been all about. She guessed it might have been printed from an official site somewhere.

In the 1980s, the Royal Observer Corps (ROC) played a unique role in UK civil defence. Though civilian volunteers, members wore RAF-like uniforms and operated under RAF command. Their history of collaboration dated back to pre-WWII, when they served as aircraft spotters. ROC posts were stocked for two-week emergencies. Not permanently manned, members were rostered for duty until bombings began, after which on-duty personnel stayed in bunkers, aware that exposure meant certain death.

Participants were often young singles or older childless couples. Uncertainty loomed over who would respond in real emergencies and how civilians might react.

the ROC's utility was primarily envisioned for limited nuclear strikes, aiming to prompt diplomatic solutions before total devastation. Most people were unaware of wartime plans, which included strict control over communications and movement, with potential martial law.

Each monitoring post had essential equipment for nuclear detection and survival. Exercises simulated attacks, with members conducting assessments while recognising the drills' artificial nature.

As ROC facilities were decommissioned, former members faced disillusionment. Despite their service, they were denied membership in RAF associations and later excluded from Cold War medal distributions due to their civilian status.

CATRIN READ ALL THIS TWICE. But mainly, her interest revolved around the structure, particularly the ventilation system. It meant it would be okay to light the Primus stove and make some tea or coffee with powdered milk. That was what she did now. It would mean another visit to the latrine bucket and the swirling blue liquid in the bowl. But needs must.

There were photographs in the folder, too, and she found several of an older man in uniform in and around a bunker. On one, she found the name Walter Hunt scrawled in handwriting.

Roger Hunt's father?

She'd never heard of nuclear war observation units dotted all over the country. It sounded dystopian, to say the least.

A soft, self-aware chuckle escaped her dry throat. She'd

read Day of the Triffids in school, and while she later watched both the film and TV adaptations, both had been disappointing. And why being here, in this underground prison, brought a science fiction novel about an invading plant species to mind, she wasn't sure. Perhaps it was the vibe. After all, John Wyndham's book was written in the 1950s and had a post war feel to it. And here she was, in a building built around that time, cut off from the world.

She lit the stove, boiled water, made tea and began to wade through the rest of the literature to see what she could find.

CHAPTER TWENTY-NINE

EMMA AND JAMES HUCKSTABLE, known among friends as "outdoorsy," balanced their nine-to-five managerial jobs with a frugal, eco-friendly lifestyle. Childless by choice, they dreamed of owning a second-hand camper van. The trouble was, refurbished ones cost an arm and a leg, and they were some way away from paying off the mortgage on the house in Walsall. For now, their weekends were filled with impromptu cycling and camping adventures. They'd pack their bikes and tents, finding campsites or secluded spots wherever they ended up. To stretch their holidays, they took strategic breaks, often turning five days into nine-day getaways.

While foreign travel was out of reach, they explored new domestic destinations, with Emma favouring coastal areas and James enjoying local history. Their carbon-neutral approach extended to their eating habits, typically cooking their own meals and rarely indulging in eating out. Or rare occasions, they'd seek a local pub and share the cheapest main course on the menu. On special occasions they might indulge in a shared dessert.

This June break, their first of the summer, they caught the train from Birmingham to Cardiff and then hopped across to Carmarthen and all points west with their bikes. James had the idea of spending the night somewhere near the coastal path in Pembrokeshire. Airbnb's were out of the question. Too expensive and an unnecessary luxury when they had everything they needed strapped to their panniers and on their backs.

And with the weather on their side; hot and dry and positively balmy, the less time they spent indoors, the better.

But James knew that this path was a national park. And you could not cycle on it – at least not on the majority. Not only disallowed, but also impractical because of the rocky and uneven terrain. Still, a jot of rebelliousness now and again did no one any harm. He'd studied his maps and saw that the Angle Peninsula had a bit of military history.

He'd spied what looked like semi-circular bunkers on the map and a little digging told him that these were Bofors gun emplacements. An East Blockhouse had been turned into holiday accommodation, but it looked like you could still walk to the gun emplacements and there was a small building just on the other side of the coastal path. The unobstructed views from there would be staggering.

With a hazy plan in mind, as Hunt stalked Napier, they had cycled to Angle Bay, enjoyed a cup of tea at a café, and then ventured down a private road to the Blockhouse and the gun emplacements.

Oddly, no one had questioned their presence, despite the road's private status. Remarkable what one could achieve on a bike.

They had reached the Bofors guns when the explosion caught their attention that afternoon. James ascribed the noise to the nearby military firing ranges and paid it little heed. After securely locking their bikes next to a farm gate, well out of sight, they embarked on a stroll along the southern and western path to Freshwater West, a location famous for Dobby's demise in the Harry Potter film franchise – an attraction that had piqued Emma's curiosity.

But, instead of riding back to the main roads, at dusk, they returned to the farm gate and wheeled their bikes down from the Bofors emplacements to the path, and across it to the building James had spotted. From their vantage point, they gazed out at the Haven, with Thorn Island in the center and St Anne's Head lighthouse visible to the west, waiting to see if anyone would ask them to leave. No one did.

The unlit path remained deserted as dusk fell. A patch of land just to the side of the little hut looked dry and flat. Big enough for a tent.

'Do you think we should, Jim?' Emma asked, her voice tinged with excitement and a touch of anxiety.

'If someone comes and tells us off, we'll plead ignorance. I mean, look at this view.'

It was, indeed, splendid and unique.

'We'll get up early and go before anyone uses the path. Come on, Em, it'll be fun.'

And so, with practised efficiency, James set up their Summit tent, and they sat on the far side of the hut, hidden from the path, whispering and drinking tea from the thermos they'd filled at the café hours earlier. Hand in hand, they gazed out at the tranquil waters of Milford Haven on this rare, warm summer evening as the daylight faded.

'No wonder they chose this area to film in,' Emma began, referring again to the Potter franchise. 'It's—'

'If you say magical, I will scream,' James interrupted.

Emma punched him playfully on the arm.

They heard the distant helicopter and sirens but were mostly shielded from the sounds by the onshore breeze. Whatever the reason for it circling, it was someone else's concern.

True to his word, James got up early, awakened by the seagulls. They packed up quickly, retrieved their bikes and set off on the B4320, unaware of the heightened police activity and transport lockdown. They had no inkling that a dangerous criminal was on the loose.

When, a few moments into the trek, Emma called to James, he slowed his bike, waiting for her to catch up, assuming she needed a break.

'Did you see that?' Emma called out.

'What, Em?' James stood astride his bike, twisting back to talk to her.

'Across the field. Somebody doing something in a hedge.'

'What you mean, relieving themselves?'

'No,' Emma said. 'Something else. I couldn't see properly.'

'Where?'

'Back there. As we passed a gate.'

'You sure he, or she, wasn't just having a pee?'

'A he, most definitely. And yes, I am sure about that. I think I saw some smoke.'

'Oh wow, it is dry. Don't tell me he was setting a fire?'

'I don't know.'

James turned his bike around in the deserted lane, heading back the thirty yards with Emma following.

'This gate?' he asked.

'Yep.'

James pulled up just in time to witness a man crouching low, running back toward a dip in the terrain, to disappear on the other side. Emma was right; smoke curled up from the hedge, and flames flickered.

'What the hell is going on? That's malicious. And look, on the other side of the gate here, see?'

'Is that a bottle of lighter fluid?'

James got off his bike.

'What are you going to do, Jim?' Emma's question sounded wary.

'This is arson, Em. I'm going to take a photo of that lighter fluid container. I might even pick it up since it's evidence. I'll use something. Don't want to contaminate it for fingerprints and such.'

'Hark at Sherlock.'

James dismounted and, in a very stagey English accent, said, 'Do you know where lemons come from, Watson?'

'What?' Emma asked.

'A lemon tree, my dear Watson.'

Emma laughed.

She was still chuckling when James put his hand on the kissing gate and pushed.

————

So far, everything had gone off without a hitch, just as Hunt had meticulously planned. The day remained silent. Eerily so. The only sound he had produced was the dull thud of the lighter fluid bottle as he indiscreetly discarded it on this side of the weathered kissing gate. He'd retraced his steps to the dense hedge and ignited the fire. Now, adrenaline flowing, he stood in the cramped generator room, everything stacked and piled at the door, ready for a quick exit.

The tilt fuse he'd fashioned himself was rigged and connected to the trip wire. Hunt had decided against adding a timer element this time; precision was paramount. He'd secured the end of the wire to the bottom of a small plastic bottle with a half-inch of mercury nestling within. When the wire tightened, the bottle would tilt. Hunt had run the trip over a piece of exposed rebar poking out of the wall, ensuring that the bottle would flip, spilling the mercury into the narrow-sealed neck, closing the circuit with the two live wires exposed there.

Now, those live wires were connected to the battery, poised for action. Nothing to do except leave. Still, he stood there, checking his work, wanting to ensure he'd done everything correctly, his own steady breathing the only sound in the room. Outside, nature held its breath too – no wind, no morning gulls, just a dead silence that was almost oppressive.

Then, amidst the stillness, a woman's laughter. Hunt's blood ran cold. Someone was out there, someone on the road nearby. Panic surged through him. Had someone spotted the rising smoke from the fire already? He needed to check; Christ, it was too bloody soon.

Hunt reached forward to disconnect the wire from the battery, heart pounding. Just as his fingers touched the mechanism, the trip wire tightened, and the plastic bottle flipped, mercury coursing to seal the circuit.

Only the Huckstables had seen the smoke. But everyone on the island heard the second pipe bomb explode.

The exception, of course, was Hunt himself. In a cataclysmic instant, Hunt's world fell apart. The shearing, tearing shards of the pipe bomb severed his auditory apparatus from the rest of his nervous system, instantly destroying his ability to perceive sound.

In those final, fleeting moments before darkness engulfed him, Roger Hunt's ears registered one last sound. It wasn't the explosion he'd meticulously planned, nor the chaos he'd intended to unleash. Instead, in a cruel twist of fate, the last thing he ever heard was Emma Huckstable's carefree laughter, echoing from beyond the gate—an innocent response to a silly joke about a lemon tree.

CHAPTER THIRTY

TEN MINUTES after the Huckstables tripped the wire that set off the second pipe bomb, several things happened at once in the Incident Room at Dyfed Powys police HQ.

Dispatch took half a dozen calls from the public about a loud noise, "like a bomb going off." The press, already encamped at the edge of the police cordon and roadblocks, miraculously set up before any of the hyenas had sneaked through, saw the smoke and heard a noise too. They wasted little or no time in posting this as a headline – second explosion rocks a peaceful beauty spot.

The BBC were quick to get it up on their news app. An urgent fanfare trumpeted a notification on Jess's phone. She ignored it while she continued searching on a web page for things Hunt-related. But a second notification, almost demanding a response, coincided with Warlow's phone ringing. He recognised Povey's number and responded.

'Alison,' he said. 'What news?'

She replied in a breathless, high-pitched staccato. It made the expectant grin on Warlow's face evaporate within seconds.

'You've heard?' Povey asked.

'Heard what?'

Across from him, Jess glanced at the news app and immediately raised her troubled eyes from the phone screen.

Warlow's frown deepened as he noted how full of horror they were. But he was still engaged with Povey on the phone.

'Another bomb,' she said. 'The EOD group is there now. An old generator shed on the ex-RAF site. One confirmed fatality so far, two shocked but unharmed cyclists within the bomb radius.'

'Shit,' Warlow hissed out the elongated oath.

Jess was holding up her phone with the screen towards Warlow, mouth open, as if she wanted to interrupt. Warlow covered the mouthpiece of his phone with his hand and turned to Jess.

'Povey,' he said. 'Second bomb.'

Jess let her phone drop to her side at the worst fear of confirmation.

Warlow shifted his hand from his phone's mouthpiece. 'Do you know who is dead?'

Povey was obviously in transit. Judging by the bumping noises, Warlow guessed she was jogging, and the repetitive muted thumping was that of equipment bouncing against her clothing.

'Only what the robot sent back. Not brilliant images and thank God for that. But it's male, bearded. That's about all they can say. The shed was a confined space. It's a charnel house.'

'If it's Hunt, we need confirmation.' Warlow was stating the obvious, he realised. But his brain was trying to compute all the ramifications and, as a result, his filters were off.

'You know how this works,' Povey said between breaths. 'They'll need to be happy there are no more booby traps before I get near. But when I do, I'll prioritise samples.'

'Should I come down there?' Warlow asked.

'I wouldn't. Wait until I get the nod. It might take a few hours. I'd say we assume it's Hunt until proven otherwise. The EOD guys told me that these IEDs are notorious. A lot of potential users end up being victims of their own aspirational excess.'

Warlow noted the pun but didn't respond. Instead, he

thanked her and rang off. Povey was a hundred percent right. He hated making assumptions, but they needed to plan for the worst. If Hunt had blown himself to smithereens either by accident or design, he couldn't think of any way it could be worse. Not only would it mean they'd lost their murderer, but they'd also lost their only link to Catrin.

He realised, when he eventually looked up, that Jess, Rhys, and Gil were standing in a little circle around where he sat to take Povey's call. Ironically, the same desk usually occupied by Catrin herself.

Gut churning, he repeated the words he'd spoken to Jess and added Povey's harrowing details. 'A second bomb. One fatality.'

Gil used his perspicacious hammer to hit the nail on the head for the others. 'The sod has blown himself up, hasn't he?'

'Unconfirmed, but we have to assume it's him. Povey says it's a bearded male.'

'But shouldn't we wait until we're certain, sir?' Rhys asked.

Jess answered with a shake of her head. 'We can't afford to. For Catrin's sake.'

They were stark words. Words Warlow had not wanted to hear, but which needed to be said. 'Jess is right. We keep working, but now it'll be twice as hard. I want to know everything there is to know about Hunt and his links to this part of the world.'

'Are we going down to Angle?' Gil asked.

Warlow sighed. 'The bomb squad needs to give us the all clear. No point hanging about down there for that.' He looked around. 'Where is Craig?'

'Went out to his car to fetch something,' Rhys said.

Warlow got to his feet. 'Best he hear this from me rather than some bulletin on the radio. A cup of tea ready for when I get back will not go amiss.'

'On it, sir,' Rhys said.

Warlow stood in the doorway of the Incident Room, half

turned and addressed the three of them. 'I'm going to tell you what I'm going to tell Craig. If Hunt is dead, then that will be a setback. But it also makes me twice as determined to find Catrin. I will not let this be another Branson.' With that, he left.

———

PRIOR TO POVEY'S phone call, Rhys had been busy studying the CCTV feed from the shop where Denzil Williams had worked. Specifically, at the pile of unpaid for groceries that Kaylee Francis had left at the till when the thief had run off. He glanced at Warlow's departing back and then sought clarification from Jess.

'Does that mean we should put the Denzil Williams case on the back burner, ma'am?'

'For now, yes. Instead, help me go through Catrin's notebooks. I've made a start, but another pair of eyes would do no harm. Anything Hunt-related.'

'I'll get a brew on first.' He levered himself out of the chair, but, just as Warlow had done a moment before, he hesitated on the threshold of the room, turned, and looked at Gil.

'Sarge. Who or what is Branson?'

For once, Gil did not respond with anything remotely pithy. Indeed, he swivelled his chair around and regarded his younger colleague with an unusual seriousness.

'Seven years ago, you were still in school then, right?'

'I was, sarge.'

'Then I'll forgive you your ignorance. It didn't happen on our patch, but Swansea isn't a million miles away, even if it does sometimes feel like home to one or two aliens. Damian Branson certainly deserved to be sent back to another planet, preferably one that is devoid of oxygen.'

Rhys stepped back into the room, the tea forgotten, as Gil summarised the case that made headlines for a short while. But which, like all things consigned to history, had faded into old news.

Damien Branson was unemployed at the time he was convicted. To feed his drug and alcohol habit, he burgled and stole. But he'd done none of these things when he worked as a forklift driver at a packing factory in Swansea. Then he'd been in a partnership with Lorna Risman. Even been in line for a promotion when their child, Lola Risman was born. And at the beginning, he'd been a good father. A doting parent. Showing off a child that had been bubbly and loving. Damian, like a lot of young men, enjoyed the company of other young men. Lorna, too, kept a posse of girlfriends, preserving a friendship circle as a wholly necessary perpetuation of youthful exuberance.

Nights out apart from one another were an acceptable and unspoken arrangement between the two. Having Lorna's mother living nearby as a willing babysitter when necessary, helped. But motherhood curbed Lorna's enthusiasm for late nights much more than fatherhood tempered Damian's. And with money from the job came opportunities for him to indulge in more recreational experimentation. He was well versed and tolerant of alcohol, but soon dabbled with a little cocaine, chased by a little crack. A little gravel did no one any harm.

Except, of course, it did.

More often than not.

Damien's habit spiralled. He lost his job. And, eventually, Lorna and Lola. What he had not bargained for was the bitterness of that loss. A bitterness that fed on Lorna's misery and her desire to move on and find a new partner. This she did by way of a fit, sporty Josh Makepeace.

Damian was no match physically for Josh. But his jealousy, fuelled by alcohol and magnified by crack, led to restraining orders and more than one arrest for aggravation. His justification for this behaviour, based on the warped paranoia that his daughter was being turned against him by Lorna and Josh, was a misguided belief he had a parental right of access.

The courts disagreed. Their only concern was for the

well-being of Lola. And allowing her time alone, or even supervised, with a crackhead like Damian found no toehold, even in the most liberal magistrate's heart. And despite Damian's tenuous argument being delivered via the voice of an expensive barrister paid for by Legal Aid, he got nowhere.

Thwarted, Damian resorted to revenge. He waited until Josh was away on a football tour with his local club and broke into Lorna's home. High on a cocktail of whatever he got hold of, he killed his ex with a hammer. The coroner's court reported seventy-eight blows in all: arms, legs, torso, and head. When Josh returned home to find his partner pulverised and Lola missing, the police swung into action. The car chase that led to Damian's capture got three million views on YouTube. But then seeing a woman fall into a fountain whilst texting gets four million views.

Damian refused to tell the police what he had done with Lola. The courts sentenced him to life for murdering Lorna, but all attempts of getting him to reveal where his daughter was fell on smug, sick, and very deaf ears. He even sniggered at Josh when they led him away to be incarcerated.

And then, last year, demolition began in an abandoned factory in Llansamlet. Stuffed into a black plastic bag under a small mountain of broken pallets, workmen found the remains of Lola Risman.

It was no consolation to anyone involved with the case to know that Damian was now held in solitary confinement for his own safety. Not because he was at risk of self-harm, but because the other inmates would show no mercy to a child killer. It had been reported that when he was told of the finding of Lola's body and asked to comment, he said, 'She was mine. If I couldn't have her, fucked if anyone else would.'

Rhys's lips formed a thin slash across his face as he listened to Gil's harrowing explanation. 'I wish you hadn't told me that, Sarge. That's bloody horrible.'

'Horrible is what we deal with, isn't it?' Gil gave no quarter.

'Get that kettle boiled before DCI Warlow gets back,' Jess suggested.

Grateful for the release, Rhys turned and left, but not before hearing Jess and Gil's last exchange.

'You could have softened that story a bit, sergeant.'

'True. But then Rhys might have hated that bastard Damian Branson a little less. We can't be having that, ma'am.'

CHAPTER THIRTY-ONE

WHILE THEY WAITED FOR HUNT, or whoever the bomb victim was, to be scooped up into jars, and for the bomb squad to wave and give them access, Warlow endured yet another bigwig meeting. They met once more in the room with the oval desk. Drinkwater, Goodey, Buchannan, Warlow, and Jess. What he read on the faces of the two most senior officers was a kind of distorted relief. They wanted desperately to believe that Hunt had become a victim of divine intervention and got his just rewards via half a kilo of nuts and bolts shredding his flesh at close quarters.

Goodey, her short hair impossibly dark to the roots, as if not one grey thread had the temerity to appear, betrayed a kind of barely restrained excitement at the news. It struck Warlow as not particularly decorous.

'Of course, we cannot use the term karma, but it is what springs to mind,' she said, looking from one officer to the other for approval. But the only nod she received came from Drinkwater. 'Karma indeed. He who lives by the sword, as it were.'

'How soon will we know for definite that it is him?' Two-Shoes fixed her glinting eyes on Warlow.

'I'd say by the end of the day. Povey is on it.'

'I hardly need to tell you, Evan, how much that will mean

if it turns out to be the case. I suggest we stand down the search effort until we know one way or the other.'

She meant the effort of looking for Hunt, of course.

'We could move that effort into looking for Catrin Richards,' Warlow said, his voice gruff.

'You're sure she was not with him in the generator shed?' Drinkwater asked.

Warlow winced at the crass clumsiness of the question. The idea of Catrin being trapped in the generator shed during the explosion was too horrific to contemplate. Besides, it made no sense for a stealth-conscious Hunt to have taken Catrin with him to Angle. But the question threw him. 'Povey says they're certain that there is only one fatality in relation to the second bomb,' he explained. 'And they are certain that it is male.'

'That's some consolation,' Drinkwater added.

'Not much of one. Hunt was the only person who knows where Catrin might be. Now that Hunt is dead, I would like to hand the nuts and bolts – no pun intended – of all that over to Pembs CID. This is well in their Operational Command Unit area. That would free us to concentrate on finding Catrin.'

Two-Shoes tilted her head. 'What's your strategy?'

'We're narrowing our focus down to determining Hunt's links to the area. As you know, he was a wildlife expert. He knew the quiet places on the patch. The hidden places.'

'Big patch,' Drinkwater said.

'All the more reason we're freed up to get on with it, then, sir,' Warlow said.

The glint remained in Two-Shoes eyes. 'Don't you think you're a little close to this, Evan? Are you sure you'll be able to apply objectivity to the situation?'

'With all due respect, ma'am, objectivity doesn't come into it. What we need here is terrier-like thoroughness and energy. There's a clock ticking. Catrin has already been missing for days. She's pregnant. I'm likely to be about as objective as a Storm Shadow missile.'

'No one is doubting your tenacity, Evan,' Two-Shoes said.

An unusual compliment from an officer who rarely praised attainment or skill in others because, as Warlow understood it, they were currencies she hoarded like a Zurich gnome. Or Smaug's gold, depending on your literary bent. Come to think of it, she might pass for a stern bureaucrat from a Dickensian novel, all sharp angles and cold efficiency.

'That's fair enough,' Drinkwater said, and Warlow could have kissed him. An act that would have gone viral on the Force intranet, no doubt.

'Okay. Once it's confirmed that it's Hunt's remains in that building, though.' Two-Shoes had to have the last word.

'That's fine,' Warlow said, glancing at his watch. 'I'll get down to Angle. If that is Hunt, I'll want to see what Povey's team finds. If he's dead, all we'll have left are his effects. I want a look at them. I'll brief CID once I'm there.'

On the way out of the room, Jess spoke. 'Want me to come with you to Angle?'

'I'd rather you stayed here and dug into Hunt.'

'I can do that.'

'Thanks.'

———

CATRIN HAD ADOPTED a submariner's approach to her captivity. She treated the steps up to the sealed and locked hatch as a ladder up the conning tower. Once every half an hour, at least during what she perceived to be daylight by her watch, she'd clamber up and thump the underside of the metal hatchway with a rusted wrench she'd found in a toolbox. Hunt had made no attempt to blindfold her on the journey up, and it had been in daylight. She knew it was in Cardiganshire somewhere because she'd seen signs for Tregaron. But the last few miles had been across a vast emptiness. She reasoned that anyone walking in that area would not be doing it at night. So, after dark, she would conserve her energy.

And conserve her food.

So far, she had not felt too stuffy. Indeed, the air vent leading up to the ventilator shaft could become quite cold at night. So much so that she'd contemplated blocking it off. But she'd abandoned that idea almost immediately. She would not suffocate in here. That was one thing not to have to worry about. On the cutaway drawing, she could see that the vent led straight up to sit a couple of feet above the ground. It did not look as if anything with air filtration was included, which made the whole construction, from a radiation perspective, not exactly lead-lined. Admittedly, a blast would hardly trouble anyone this far down, but the air would become toxic pretty damned quick. She suspected that gas masks would have been deployed in the case of a nuclear strike, at the very least. Maybe even Hazmat suits. Though she was doubtful that every volunteer for the corps would have been issued with one.

Water had become Catrin's primary concern. In her pregnant state, albeit early, proper hydration was crucial. She'd read that about a litre of water daily might be the minimum requirement, accounting for loss through sweat and urine. Fortunately, she wasn't urinating much or sweating at all. She had consumed a litre since her arrival, not having considered conservation initially. The realisation that Hunt's return was uncertain made her reassess her supplies. While she had enough food for several days if rationed, water was a different matter. With only a chemical toilet available, recycling wasn't an option.

To distract herself, she turned again to Hunt's notes. She'd found little in the way of reflection in them, but some entries detailing activities over the last couple of months had intrigued her immensely. In particular, the entries for certain days where a symbol had featured. She suspected these were GPS coordinates judging by the miniature circles and marks both single and double. Degrees, minutes, and seconds?

These were always entered carefully with the dates. But

the accompanying scribble was always added as a scrawl. Like an afterthought. Almost disdainfully.

And before the scribble was used in tandem with the coordinates, it appeared on certain written-in dates going back as far as January.

Catrin sipped the cupful of water she'd allowed herself for the next two hours and jotted down her impressions as she read on.

———

WARLOW RAN the security gauntlet on the way over to Angle.

He hadn't waited for Povey's call but got it anyway as he approached Pembroke. He got to within a hundred yards of the second bomb site and had to walk the rest of the way. Another calm, warm day. He glimpsed views over the green fields to the water of the Haven. The irony of the word wasn't lost on him. There'd been nothing peaceful about this day. He passed lines of response vehicles and EOD squadron vehicles. He noted a man in army uniform attending to a yellow Remote-Controlled Vehicle-tracked propulsion unit which, he presumed, had already done its job.

A couple of white tents had been erected near the corner of a field. The vague shape of an old and unused track, indicated only by the way the grass appeared to grow a little differently, led off towards open ground. Warlow presumed this was an old RAF road.

Povey, suited up but with her hood down, stood next to the tents.

'Any point me going into the generator shed?'

'It's a biohazard. We've recovered two limbs but left the remains of the corpse where it is.'

'Distinguishing features?'

'Not so far. HOP has been, though.'

'Not Tiernon?'

'No. There is always a silver lining. I've sent half a dozen samples back to HQ. We should get some comparison within a couple of hours. But in the meantime, we've recovered some things that were not destroyed, including a phone. We'll get it looked at.'

'If you find the number, let me have it. I'll get Rhys on to the service provider. Let's see who he's been contacting, if anyone.'

'Might take a bit of time. It's not switching on. But the tech bods might do something.'

Warlow looked towards the bottom of the building where a dark red pool of blood had spread out from the interior. 'What's the story here?'

Povey pointed to a coiled piece of wire that had been severed, the last four feet of which had curved into a coiled snake. 'Warrant Officer Class Two Meechum thinks that whoever was inside had rigged the wire to a kissing gate over yonder.' She pointed further down the field. 'The Huck-stables—'

'The cyclists?'

'They'd camped out on the path.'

Warlow frowned. 'Not supposed to do that.'

'They're regretting it now. Some of whoever was in that generator shed was blown through the open door and into the field where the gate was. They knew nothing about the Napier bombing. Assumed the noise was ordnance from the tank firing range further along. They saw someone setting a fire and investigated.'

'How do you read that?'

'Meechum suggests that the fire was to draw attention. He suspects that the wire was rigged such that whoever investigated the fire would set off the bomb, which would pull everyone here, allowing the booby trapper an opportunity to slip away – possibly towards the coast?'

'So, the bomb was rigged not to cause harm?'

'Looks that way.'

'Where are the cyclists now?'

'Down in the community hall, your remote outpost.'

'I'd better have a word,' Warlow said.

'I'll send you that number of the phone we found in the shed as soon as. Not much point you looking at it. At least not until we clean it up. It wasn't a pretty sight as it was on the body.'

'I'll take your word for it.'

Warlow returned to the Jeep and continued driving towards the village to talk to two cyclists who could be linked to the killer the police had been after for months. But he'd go easy on them. As Povey suggested, witnessing a severed hand waving at you as it flew through the air would be enough of a reminder of their foolish derring-do for a long time.

CHAPTER THIRTY-TWO

WARLOW GOT BACK to Ffau'r Blaidd a little after eight-thirty. Jess's black Golf and Molly's startlingly yellow VW Up were parked to allow him room to get the Jeep in. The Allanbys were mindful.

Jess had changed out of her work clothes into jeans and sweats and was sitting in the living room with the TV on. She turned down the volume as he entered. Cadi, her stuffed bear Arthur in her mouth and her rear end in hyper-wiggle mode, made a play run over to greet him. Warlow dropped to his knees to fondle the dog.

'How was it?' Jess asked, her chin on the backrest of the sofa.

'I took the call from Povey on the way back,' Warlow said, two hands buried in the dog's soft neck fur. 'Her quick answer DNA machine has come up with a match for Hunt.'

'Accident or design?'

'The way it was rigged, the explosives' boys think it was an accident triggered by a rogue cyclist who should have been nowhere near.'

'That'll please Drinkwater and Goodey, then.'

Warlow frowned at that. 'Do you think they're right? Should we step away from looking for Catrin and let someone else run it?'

Jess moved to sit on the sofa's armrest. Her t-shirt revealed arms toned from an increased frequency of gym visits. She went with Molly for whom physical exercise had become exam-stress release therapy.

'Two things spring to mind. Would you be happy to do that?'

'Not happy, no.'

'If it was you he'd kidnapped, do you think Catrin, or any of us, would have sat back?'

'Christ, no.'

'Then why are you even asking?'

Warlow turned back to the dog, who had pressed her head, snout down, to nuzzle into his chest. An almost human gesture which melted most of everyone who met the dog's heart. 'What if we don't find her?'

'We *will* find her. *You* will find her. You always do.'

Warlow squeezed his eyes shut, banishing the image that flared. 'Perhaps I don't want to find her. Not face down in a ditch with her underwear around her neck.'

Jess got up and knelt next to him, her hand on the dog's back. Cadi's tail thumped, delighted by the doubling of attention. Jess was two feet away from Warlow, and he suddenly wished he'd taken that last bit of chewing gum from the little coin well under the gear stick of the Jeep. She smelled wonderful; her grey eyes boring into his.

'This is Catrin Richards we're talking about. Wherever she is, I know she is going to feel a lot better knowing that it's you who is looking for her. I would.'

The slap of flip-flopped feet entering the room made both detectives look up.

'Why are you both inspecting Cadi?' Molly asked. 'Is she ill?'

Jess stood up, grinning. 'No. She just deserved an extra hug.'

'Yeah. She does. All the time.'

Molly looked a little pale from too much time indoors.

She wore a troubled expression. 'The second bomb is all over social media. Was it him?'

Warlow nodded.

'Oh, my God. Did you, like, have to look at it?'

'They wouldn't let me. But I saw enough.'

Molly turned down her mouth. 'I don't suppose you're hungry, but there is some risotto left.'

'Made by you?'

Molly narrowed her eyes. 'Yes.'

'Then I am definitely hungry.'

'It's mushroom.' Molly delivered this as an apology.

'I bloody love mushrooms,' Warlow said. 'As a kid, I used to have mushrooms sautéed with milk and a bit of mustard on toast.'

'Never tried that,' Molly admitted.

'Right. Then next time, I'll make that for you.'

'She's carb-loading before her last exams,' Jess said.

'Is that tomorrow?' Warlow asked, standing up and making for the kitchen.

'Biology A 2. Genetics and variation. And then I'll be free.'

'To do what?' Warlow asked.

'Might get a job. I need money for my week of sun, sea, and… socialising. And I might go up and see my dad.'

'That sounds good,' Warlow said and meant it. Relations between Molly and Tricky-Ricky had been fractious since he and Jess had separated, to say the least.

Molly shrugged. 'But mainly, it will mean I get to spend even more time with my bestie.'

'I'm sorry, but I'm going to be busy over the next few days, Molly.' Warlow kept a straight face.

She reciprocated with a toothless grin and walked over to Cadi. 'Your daddy thinks he's hilarious, doesn't he, Cadi? But we both know who my bestie really is, don't we, girl?'

The dog responded with a soft-eyed lick of the girl's cheek.

'But you also promised you'll help with finding us some-where to rent,' Jess said.

'Yeah, yeah. I know.' Molly did not return her mother's gaze.

'I'm not saying anything,' Warlow said. 'I've made my thoughts clear on the matter.'

'You have,' Jess agreed. 'I'll get your risotto in the microwave. I think there's some Parmigiano shavings left, though Molly was hoovering them up like nobody's business.'

'Mum, I do not hoover.'

'From the look of your room, I can attest to that.'

'My God, you two should sort a double act with me as the stooge.' Molly adopted her best affronted look as the popty-ping began heating the meal. As they ate, Warlow felt the day's tension slowly ebbing away. The simple act of sharing a meal with Jess and Molly provided a brief respite from the case weighing on his mind. But he knew he needed more than just food to clear his head

———

LATER, after stripping off his clammy shirt and changing into a t-shirt and shorts, Warlow took Cadi out for a walk along the lanes. The cottage was well out of the village, on higher ground than the little clutch of houses and even the castle, but remained within easy reach of them both. Its position allowed that glimpse of the river and the estuary he treasured so much. This evening, though, Warlow walked the fields. Many had been recently cut with black plastic-coated bales arranged like sleeping beetles awaiting collection. He'd brought a ball and a thrower, and Cadi fetched and retrieved as they walked the stubbly grass, the ground dry and hard underfoot. The air itself was heady with the tobacco musk of cut grass and the sun still oozed heat at 9:30pm, even as it slid inexorably towards the horizon.

Warlow's senses registered all of this at some level below

his consciousness. His mind, that part of it he could not ignore, fished other, more turbulent waters.

His earlier conversation with Jess still resonated. Wherever Catrin was, and if she remained capable of cognition, she might well be hoping, and expecting Warlow, her boss, the leader of her team, to be trying to find her. And yet, he could not help but feel that Hunt and all his murderous machinations were now nothing but a distraction.

He recognised this as absurd, since Hunt was the root cause of everything. But the afternoon and evening spent at Angle had revealed nothing of immediate or practical use in the search for the detective.

His mind swung around and around like the sweeping arm of a sonar screen, searching for any signal that might indicate a clue they could follow. Instead, his words of earlier came back to him now like a hollow echo.

Branson.

Christ, that had been cringe-worthy. Hardly an inspirational reference, even though his intention had been to use the case as an example of what he did not want this one to be like. But even mentioning it meant that his own brain had contemplated the possibilities.

Of Catrin being held somewhere.

Of Catrin already dead.

Of her corpse degrading in some sordid, god forsaken hole.

Warlow halted, taking a deep breath as Cadi trotted up, ball in mouth, her eyes bright with anticipation. She'd learned to deposit the saliva-soaked missile into his waiting hand. He loaded it into the thrower and sent it soaring into the field where it bounced high off the hard-packed soil. She took it in her mouth at full stretch the third time it hit the ground and recoiled into the air. She was well coordinated, never missed the ball, and it always gave him pleasure just to watch her. Much as you might gain pleasure from a footballer showing his skill of controlling a high ball.

But it was a mere distraction. He'd mentioned Branson as

a warning to himself and others. By doing so, he'd made an unspoken promise not to allow that ever to happen again.

'Believe it, then, Evan,' he muttered.

Cadi heard his voice and tilted her head. Warlow realised that she'd brought the ball back again, and he held it, moist and sticky in his hand. Warlow tossed the ball once more, watching the dog chase after it at full speed. He realised that same intensity was needed in the search for Catrin. But he could not do that if he was too tired to think. Deciding to call it a day, he turned towards the gate leading home, completing the last quarter of his walk around the field.

As he squinted into the setting sun, its final blazing arc dipping into the western sky, Warlow's thoughts drifted to his family in Australia. He imagined the same sun, slightly cooler in their winter, now rising to greet his son, daughter-in-law, and grandchildren on the other side of the world. A bitter-sweet smile touched his lips as he contemplated the vast distance between them.

Here, in Wales, on the western edge of Europe, it was almost mid-summer and the air and the earth were warm. A miracle after a soggy, bitter winter.

Catrin needed to be able to enjoy this, too. Let the sun bring its promise of light and warmth to her and her unborn child.

He'd make that happen, even if it killed him.

CHAPTER THIRTY-THREE

On Thursday morning, Warlow sat in Starbucks' car park reading the newspaper he'd just bought from the Tenby Road service station at Gil's request. He'd taken the call not ten minutes before.

'Lane is in the newspapers,' Gil had said. 'You need to see it.'

It was in a red top and the headline was bad enough.

———

Hunt for missing police detective intensifies after a second explosion rocks a quiet Welsh seaside retreat.

Brave Journalist Survives Horror Ambush by Notorious Killer – A Desperate Search for Detective Sergeant Catrin Richards Begins.

Under this, a white on blue quarter section had a teaser.

Do not miss this today's exclusive interview with the journalist at the heart of the Angle bomber horror.

Lane's bruised face next to a stock image of *Cân-y-barcud* cottage appeared on page 4.

**HORROR IN HIDDEN COTTAGE: KILLER HUNTS
COP AND REPORTER!**

In a terrifying turn of events, a routine interview with Detective Sergeant Catrin Richards in a secluded Carmarthenshire cottage became a nightmare when notorious killer Roger Hunt ambushed the meeting.

'It was like something out of a horror film,' recalled shaken journalist Geraint Lane. 'One minute we were chatting, the next this wild-eyed maniac burst in brandishing a gun!'

The peaceful setting erupted into chaos as the bearded lunatic took control.

'His eyes were crazed,' Lane reported. 'I've never seen such pure evil up close.'

DS Richards, displaying remarkable bravery, attempted to shield the journalist from Hunt's onslaught. However, the killer bound the reporter's hands and held both at gunpoint, subjecting them to a terrifying ordeal.

'I thought we were goners,' Lane admitted. 'But DS Richards was incredible - she never lost her cool.'

The horror intensified when Hunt forced Lane into the trunk of a car.

'I was sure that was it - my final resting place,' the journalist revealed. 'The darkness was suffocating.'

In a stroke of luck, police discovered the vehicle just in time, rescuing Lane from becoming another victim of Hunt's twisted game.

DS Richards remains missing, believed to be in the clutches of this cold-blooded killer. The situation has grown even more dire with reports of a second explosion and unconfirmed news that Hunt himself might be a victim, placing DS Richards in even greater peril.

'I can't stop thinking about her,' Lane confessed. 'She saved my life, and now she's out there with that monster.'

This harrowing incident shines a spotlight on the challenges faced by women in law enforcement. DS Richards' dedication to her job is particularly noteworthy given the ongoing struggles within the police, which has been plagued by allegations of bigotry, racism, corruption, and sexism.

Recent investigations into abusive behaviour, discrimination, and harassment among officers have led to public admissions of failure from high-ranking officials. A government team is currently reviewing complaints against nearly 1,100 officers, highlighting the urgent need for cultural transformation within the force.

As the hunt for DS Richards continues, this incident serves as a stark reminder of the dangers faced by those who serve and protect, as well as the pressing need for reform within law enforcement agencies. 'DS Richards is a hero,' Lane insisted. 'She deserves better than this - all women in the force do.'

Warlow read it all twice. The second time more slowly and with growing distaste and anger as the words sank in. When he'd spoken to Lane, he'd actually felt sympathy for the man. But this polemic, full of his usual police bashing rhetoric set Warlow's teeth on edge.

Of course, he had no sympathy for the criminal element within the Force. Who in their right minds could, or would? And every case, even in this quiet corner of the country, corruption and wrongdoing hiding under the umbrella of law enforcement, grated like ground glass in a milkshake. You could almost forgive Lane for pointing all that out. But to brandish the hackneyed racism and misogyny cards in a situation that had no relationship to either was simply showboating in the worst possible way. Lane's tilt to the activist fringe now wormed its way under Warlow's skin. He took pride in knowing his officers. And here he was, doubting himself.

Jess had delayed leaving for work to make sure that Molly was up and ready for her exam. They both knew that this was an unnecessary worry as Molly was as "on it" as anyone Warlow knew. Still, today was an important day in the Allanbys' lives. The key to a new life rested on Molly delivering the goods, which she would, Warlow had no doubt. But he was not Molly's parent. That came with an extra dollop of worry.

He rang Jess's number.

'She gone yet?'

'Almost. She's made an effort, though. Showered and even wearing a bit of perfume. I know because Cadi was doing her nose in the air thing as she came down the stairs.'

It was one of Cadi's little quirks. Whenever one of the Allanby women wore perfume, she'd signal an acknowledgement with a nose-up tail wag.

'A word?'

Molly came on the line. 'Hi, Evan.'

'All set?'

'Pencils sharpened. Favourite goofy rubber stuck on the end. Butterflies flapping in my guts. Anything else you'd like to know?'

'You'll smash it.'

'I'm waiting for you to say sock it to them. Or something equally last century.'

'Sock it to them, Molly.'

Her voice softened. 'Thanks for ringing, Evan. Now I have to brush my teeth with my lucky toothbrush. Byeee.'

Jess came back on. 'All okay?'

'No. Lane has written an article for one of the tabloids. It's drivel, but he claims Catrin was about to reveal to him how she's struggled with sexism and workplace bullying.'

Jess didn't answer.

'Christ, Jess. Am I that naïve?'

'You aren't naïve. And yes, there is all that stuff. Of course, there is. If you aren't strong, banter can come across as something hateful. I got some of that in Manchester. But not here.'

'Catrin said nothing to you?'

'No. Never. Of course, there are individuals you might not want to sit next to at a bar for more than ten seconds. And after KFC, I thought we'd lost her.'

Warlow wrinkled his nose. 'KFC,' he murmured. 'My skin

crawls even at the mention.' Kelvin Fucking Caldwell had been one of those worthy of Lane's criticism. He'd also tried to usurp Warlow and coerce Catrin into acting against him. Christ, when you thought about it in those terms, it sounded like something from Game of Thrones.

'You and me both,' Jess added. 'But she got over KFC. Catrin is a smart cookie, and she loves the job. I think she loves you a little bit, too.'

'Steady on.'

'A much-maligned leadership quality, Evan, making people believe in you. You don't know the half of it.'

For a moment, he was at a loss, but then he glanced down at the paper again. 'If you get a chance, grab a copy of this BS and have a look. Gil has always detested Lane as a self-serving bloodsucker. I took all that with a pinch of salt, but I am coming around to that way of thinking at a rate of knots. This is him on a bandwagon, playing the trumpet and banging a drum all at the same time. I'm surprised you can't hear the sodding thing from Nevern.'

'Anything we can do about it?'

'No. He's not breaking any rules. Other than common decency. Reading this stuff helps no one. I watch the news and see the spate of frankly ridiculous shoplifting and burglaries that go unpunished. It makes me sick. Be good to have a bit of support now and again. It would help with recruitment, too.'

'Agreed.'

Warlow smiled. 'Vent over.'

'Is that an order?'

He chortled. 'Save that one for Gil. But well done, I am cheered up.'

'Good. Right, I hear trainers on the stairs. One last pep talk, and I'll be on my way.'

CHAPTER THIRTY-FOUR

CATRIN WOKE up on Thursday morning to a raucous chorus of a murder of crows, their cries echoing above her. The sound filtered in through the narrow ventilator shaft, a stark reminder of the world beyond her confinement. The sound waxed and waned and she imagined the birds flocking from one tree to another. They would draw near, filling the air with their mournful cries, only to vanish into the distance, leaving behind an empty silence.

The bunker, once designed for practicality and function, had become her purgatory; its harsh fluorescent lighting illuminating every stain on the dingy walls and the Ordnance Survey maps. Maps she'd studied dozens of times as the only distraction during long hours in this bleak dungeon. She made her way to the makeshift restroom, breath held because the chemical stench mingling with her own body's ammoniacal contribution was even more unbearable than before. Her urine emerged a deep amber hue but thankfully not yet ochre; sparse but undeniable evidence of her dehydration. Thirst was her constant companion now, taunting her with sly glances at the paltry amount of potable fluid she had left.

Catrin wanted Hunt to return. Surely, he would return.

She huffed in a deep breath and let it out slowly.

Hunt.

She'd rationalised it in these terms.

He would get to Angle, realise how impossible it would be to remain inconspicuous, assess the surroundings, and inevitably come back for her.

At least, that is what she firmly believed in the beginning but, with each passing hour, shadowy doubt like a stalking beast crept ever closer.

People would search for her. It had been four agonising days since she first saw Hunt at the secluded cottage. There'd be a manhunt and a sergeant hunt in full swing. Yet, fear and despair gnawed at her, and she could not help but glance again at the dwindling supplies she had left. There, on a cabinet shelf, sat less than a third of a large bottle of fizzy water and two cans of Hazy Jane beer. She had consumed one of the IPAs yesterday, and its effects had hit her like a freight train.

Dehydration had made her body more susceptible to the alcohol. At least that was how she'd explained it away, and her dwindling collection of fluids brought the realisation home with a bang. Drinking was the key to enduring her captivity. And today it looked as though she would have to drink more beer. Yet, how could she stay alert, keep her wits about her, hang on to the sliver of hope that someone would come for her, when the alcohol made her woozy?

She shook her head to clear it of this pointless debate. What choice did she have?

Staying strong had always been her mantra. She turned her mind to Craig and the baby.

She'd try, for their sakes.

————

GRAVE but not yet desperate was the best way to describe the Incident Room. These were accepted police descriptive terms for misper situations. But Warlow was having none of it. For him, the adjective of choice would have been frustration. His morning had dissolved into a series of meetings with his colleagues in CID: Buchannan, the media officer, and a host of other people far less essential and who subsequently got less and less out of the DCI whose mind was fixed on the search for his colleague. But he'd spent the last hour with Craig and Catrin's parents. And they got one-hundred-percent Warlow. He'd made promises to them. That he would find her.

He should not have, but he had.

Thankfully, none of them had asked if he could promise she'd be alive.

As the meetings dragged on, Warlow's leg bounced rhythmically under the table, a silent metronome counting down precious minutes. What he needed to be doing was collating information and brainstorming the problem.

It was well after three when he finally freed himself from the clutches of administration and bureaucracy and joined the team.

There were no smiles. No high fives.

Wordlessly, Rhys fetched him a mug of tea as Gil wrote something on the Job Centre. There was no sign of the Human Tissue For Transplant box. No biscuits had been consumed during Warlow's absence. Whether that was a mark of respect or a mark of lack of appetite brought on by solemnity, he was yet to find out. He didn't need to ask. Once the mug was in his hand, Jess took the lead.

'We've taken a narrow approach, concentrating our efforts on Hunt and Catrin's car.'

Intrigued, Warlow sat at the desk Catrin would normally have occupied to listen.

'Rhys had the bright idea of looking again at the places that Hunt had visited here. We've sent Uniforms to the house he'd rented previously, including the half-finished Airbnb up at Gwynfe. We've also contacted that owner and other owners in the area to see if Hunt had ever been in touch when he was not on the run. Try to establish more haunts. It's taking some time, as you can imagine.'

'He came off social media, obviously, so there's not much there from him,' Rhys explained. 'I've trawled through the

Wildscene programme's website, though. They have not removed all content by him because it's intermingled with all kinds of other stuff. I'm trying to find any links with the area.'

'Get on to them. Ask them to send us anything they have and to not delete anything until we tell them to.'

'Already have, sir,' Rhys said.

'Of course, you have. What about the car?'

Gil replied to that question, 'It's back in forensics. It's her own car, and through luck she had two new tyres on the weekend. The place that did the change measured her mileage.'

Warlow listened, sipping his tea.

'I'm waiting for someone to come back to me with the current mileage,' Gil went on, 'If we subtract the two, and knowing what the mileage is from here to her house and from here to *Cân-y-barcud*, plus a rough estimation of the mileage between here and Angle, it might give us some indication of how far he drove it with Catrin before returning to deal with Lane. It might concentrate the search area.'

Gil had their attention.

'Brilliant, sarge,' Rhys said.

'That's assuming Sergeant Richards didn't do a sly recce up to John Lewis in Cardiff on the way to meet Lane, in which case the mileage theory is kaka.'

The ludicrousness of this statement, both in terms of the logistics, and in terms of suggesting anything other than total professionalism from their missing colleague, brought much-needed smiles.

'Anything else from Povey?' Warlow asked.

Jess wrinkled her nose. 'Not yet. Hunt's phone is still with the nerds.'

'Right. Sounds like we have enough to do. But we don't sit on anything. If anyone comes up with an idea or something useful, you shout.'

Nods all around.

'Worth discussing Lane?' Gil asked.

'Don't,' Jess warned.

Warlow sighed. 'On the one hand, we should have expected nothing less from him. He's exploiting the situation for his own ends.'

'I know what I'd like to do with his ends,' Gil muttered darkly.

'I spoke to Craig,' Warlow said. 'He says the only time Catrin ever said anything to him about feeling exploited was in Uniform and that was when a letch of a sergeant – we all know which one – commented on her appearance on a night out.'

Gil nodded. 'That would be McCormick. Aka Mick the Prick or Caveman Mick. He's long gone. Early retirement of the bugger-off-we-don't-want-your-sort-anymore variety.'

'The way Lane wrote it made it sound like we're wolf whistling at every turn,' Warlow murmured.

'Multi-tasking, that is,' Gil said. 'Rules Rhys out from the get-go.'

'Lucky I've got a thick skin,' Rhys said.

'Did I ever tell you I don't trust Lane?' Gil asked.

'Last count, I'd say a hundred times,' Rhys said.

'His article can't have come as any surprise,' Jess commented.

Warlow rubbed a finger over the little patch of stubble on his chin he always somehow missed on his morning shave. 'No surprise at all. But I'm not talking about his journalistic leanings which are so far left he's practically falling over sideways, waving his anti-police banner. Good luck with that, I say. It's a free country. But what I meant is that something smells off about the whole thing.'

'Still, we can't stop him from expressing an opinion,' Jess said. 'And I'm certain that suggesting he runs anything he prints past us will be met with wholehearted disdain.'

'Did I tell you that his partner mentioned he'd had a run in with paedophile vigilantes?' Warlow remarked.

'Remind me.' Gil frowned.

'Apparently, they did not take too kindly to him wanting to do a piece on them. There were threats.'

'Do we think it was they who "mugged" him and stole his phone previously?' Rhys asked.

'Mugged him and locked him in the trunk of his own car in Kidwelly Quay, as I recall,' Gil said.

'That is a weird coincidence.' Warlow sipped more of his tea. 'I mean, getting locked in the boot of your car happens to everyone at least once, correct?'

'Does it, sir?' Rhys blinked in surprise.

'No, it does not, Detective Constable Harries.'

'What the DCI is trying to suggest, Rhys, is that it is not at all common,' Jess said.

'But it's happened twice to Lane now…' Rhys followed his logic, only to run out of steam.

'C word,' Gil said.

'Bit of a coincidence, yes, sarge,' Rhys agreed. 'And we don't like coincidences.'

'No, we do not, Rhys.' Warlow stretched his legs out and held the mug in both hands, contemplating what had been written on the board. 'Write Lane's name in big letters. I, for one, cannot wait to see what further vitriol emerges from his poison pen.'

Rhys got up and wrote on the board. 'Are you being ironic, sir?' he asked, turning back to the DCI.

'Well spotted, Rhys,' Gil said and then turned to the DCI himself. 'We could get the *pwdryn* in,' he suggested. 'We haven't formally interviewed him.'

'Oh, we will,' Warlow said. 'But let's give him a little more rope before we haul it in.' The tea had made the DCI feel better. As had the chat. There were leads to follow up, and all was not yet lost. He sat up. 'Any other business? Rhys, Denzil Williams.'

'I probably need to go out to chat with the store owner one last time, sir. No urgency. But I'd rather stay here for now. Feel like I could be of more help looking for Catrin.'

'So do I,' Jess said.

'But you think you're making progress with that, too?' Warlow asked, narrowing his eyes at the DC.

'I do, sir. Just want to be absolutely sure about a couple of things.'

'*Diawl*, now you've got us all on the hook,' Gil said.

'Including more stuff to look at on the *Wildscene* website, sarge,' Rhys explained.

'As mentioned, if we find anything significant, we share it.' Warlow got up and made for the SIO room. He felt a little better for the meeting. Hard to use optimistic, but probably okay to suggest not completely defeated.

He clung to the positives.

He was still clinging four hours later when they'd come up with nothing at all.

CHAPTER THIRTY-FIVE

No one yelled Eureka that afternoon. Or evening.

It was well past six when Jess left.

'Go home,' Warlow ordered. 'Molly will be full of beans. Go and celebrate with her.'

'She'd prefer it if you were there, too?'

'I appreciate that, but—'

'Celebrating not on your agenda. I get it.'

'But that's not fair on Molly.' Warlow had spent years taking his work home, learning several unpalatable lessons from that habit. Now, he drummed the need for work-life balance into his team, repeating it like a stuck record.

'Maintain a clear boundary between work and life.'

He could have added some other platitude to inject a pithier, on-trend zing into it. But he didn't do that. Since he was allergic to any on-trend zing and any sentence containing a variation of those words. And yes, he was a fine one to bloody talk. But living alone meant he'd had no one to please but himself and a dog who thought the sun shone out of his every orifice.

But he wasn't living alone now. At least temporarily. And so, different rules applied.

'Molly's bought a nice Chablis to celebrate,' Jess said. 'Not my idea, but she's already taken Cadi on a beach walk. She texted to say how wonderful it is to be free from the tyranny of examinations.'

'Yes, well, she'll learn that the tyranny of examinations is a Disney family ride compared with the Gulag of a post A-level world that hurls crap at you from its shit-covered fingers at every turn.'

Jess had one eyebrow raised as she listened to this. 'I know it seems like it's weeks since Catrin left, but it's only a few days, Evan. We need to let people do their jobs.'

'You're right. I promise when I get back, I'll have my game face on.'

He didn't leave headquarters until almost eight but worked on his mood for the whole forty-minute drive home to Ffau'r Blaidd. By the time he got there, he'd managed to tuck most of his gut-twisting doom and gloom away.

Molly was full of it. Though she looked pale and tired, she was also emotionally intelligent enough to see that the case continued to weigh heavily on both adults.

'Why aren't you in the pub with other teenage hooligans?' Warlow asked.

'I would be, but some of the others still have exams. Besides, I'm saving for Spain.'

'When are you going?' Warlow had been told, but his filing system hadn't placed it under important.

'Couple of weeks. Just to chill. It's not too rowdy where we're going,' Molly explained.

'Won't you be clubbing it in some outdoor amphitheatre full of foam?'

'Nah,' Molly said. She'd had a glass and a half of wine by now. Her pallor had gone, and her colour was high, as was her mood. 'Not straight off the plane, anyway. I mean, we will end up in a bar or two, sure. But it's an all-girl group. And this weekend I'm off to Manchester to visit Ricky.'

She had, ever since he'd known her, often referred to her father as Ricky.

'You're staying with him?'

'No, I'm staying with an old friend. But I am seeing him on Saturday and Sunday for lunch. Aren't I a good girl?'

'I'm sure he'll be delighted.'

'Of course, he will. Besides, I need to get out. It's hardly a fun fest with you two.'

'Moll…' Jess began.

'No. It's okay. I'm just teasing. Truth is, I don't feel much like celebrating myself with Catrin still missing.'

'You're better off in the Hacienda.' Warlow dragged up this mention of a notorious nightclub from somewhere deep in his memory banks.

He got scathing looks from both females.

'Good to know you're still in touch with your acid house past,' Jess said. 'You know the Hacienda shut in the 90s.'

He topped up Jess and Molly's glasses before adding a quarter of an inch to his own. Molly watched him do it with barely veiled disappointment.

'It would be so good if you found Catrin before I came back,' she said, suddenly serious.

If he had been less generous, Warlow might have interpreted this plea as an entitled teen's bleating narcissism. But Jess told him that Molly had texted her to ask about Catrin four times over the last two days. And so, he took it at face value. A genuine plea from the heart.

'It *would* be good,' Warlow agreed. 'We'll do our best to make sure it happens.'

'That's what I like, DCI Warlow,' Molly said. 'Cocky determination.'

'I tried un-cocky, and it didn't work.'

'This isn't half bad,' Jess said, holding up her glass to inspect the wine.

'Well over a tenner at Tesco,' Molly explained.

'Ah, the sweet spot. More than ten and less than fifteen.'

'Are you taking the Michael, Evan?' Molly asked.

'Not at all. It is a general rule of thumb I apply myself. And this little beauty has notes of chalky soil on its front end. I get a hint of the fossilised sea creatures embedded in the limestone where the vines' roots have penetrated. The terroir must have a touch of salt in its core to produce such a clean edge to the mineral side of the palate.'

Molly turned to her mother. 'Are you going to throw something at him, or shall I?'

'Tell you what, I'll get some peanuts. We can toss them in his mouth every time he opens it.'

Warlow raised his glass. And though the thoughts of Catrin and wherever she was threatened to crowd out all else, he found it within him to offer up a toast. 'To the end of exams and the promise of summer. Let's see what tomorrow brings.'

The Allanbys raised their glasses in reply and clinked.

———

GIL HAD TAKEN his work home with him, and there was no pretence otherwise.

The Lady Anwen knew when to leave her husband alone when he was ears deep in a case. It did not happen that often these days, but when it did, she made him tea and gave him food. She'd never been jealous of his commitment. She wore his preoccupation as a badge of pride. After all, he was a man who loved his daughters and indulged his grandchildren and yet, over the years, had been asked to deal with monsters and images that no decent human being ever should. When he was in the middle of Operation Alice and coming home after studying those images, hoping to find clues as to who made them so that they could be prosecuted, she never asked him how his day went. Instead, she would let him talk if he wanted to.

That rarely happened, and in all honesty, she was glad. Her husband believed his role was to spare others the trauma of that knowledge and do what he could to reduce the suffering of the innocents who were always the victims.

This was different, of course. But Gil's commitment was no less.

When she'd taken him a last cup of tea at 9pm, he had notebooks and a map spread out on the kitchen table. She saw some scrawled numbers on the notebooks and a couple of circles drawn on the maps. He hadn't even changed out of his shirt and work trousers, but he had the radio playing in the background. A bit of Classic FM as company. Not too intrusive and no vocals.

'Biscuit, *cariad*?' she asked, setting the mug down next to him and a plate of two chocolate digestives. He'd eaten only half his evening meal earlier. Too preoccupied by his project to allow hunger to bother him.

'Now you're talking my kind of language,' Gil said. He looked up at his wife of many years, his expression questioning. 'Should I think about giving this up, Anwen? We could be sitting in a pub garden somewhere, eating pork scratchings and dirty martinis.'

'You hate both of those things,' Anwen said.

'Never too late, is my motto.'

Anwen smiled. But her words in answer were those of a partner in this business that had been their lives for so long. '*Mae'r euog yn ffoi heb neb yn ei erlid.*'

Gil squeezed the hand she'd placed on his shoulder and sipped the tea. The biscuits remained on the plate uneaten still when he went to bed two hours later.

He hadn't needed sugar and flour for sustenance. His wife's words had been enough. He ought to get that framed and set up on the wall. Team motto. He could just imagine Evan's face.

Mae'r euog yn ffoi heb neb yn ei erlid.

The guilty flee with no one to pursue them.

————

RHYS AND GINA nestled on the cosy sofa in their modest flat, their eyes fixed on the exhilarating car chase unfolding on the television screen. Rhys, however, seemed only half-present, his gaze meandering aimlessly over the chaotic visuals. His fingers danced restlessly on a coaster, the bottle of Corona he'd drunk, now empty except for a tiny lime wedge left at its base, coaster-less on the coffee table.

Gina sensed his detachment. She observed the subtle nuances of his restlessness as he fidgeted, the unspoken weight of his thoughts evident in his actions.

Suddenly, he broke the silence, his voice tinged with uncertainty. 'If they asked you to be the FLO, would you do it?'

Gina turned her face to him, her eyes locking onto his. 'What are you talking about?'

'Craig. If Catrin—'

'Oh Rhys, don't say that. Don't even think it.' Her hand reached out to touch his.

Gina, a trained Family Liaison Officer, knew the gravity of the situation. The mere suggestion that she might be called upon to support Craig if the worst happened to Catrin was a dire prospect.

Rhys sighed, his fingers absently running through his dishevelled hair. 'I can't help it, Geen. I can't think about anything else.'

Gina shifted on the sofa, meeting Rhys's gaze with determination. 'Look, I know I suggested we take a break from work, but I can see Fast and Furious isn't providing the distraction you need.'

Rhys nodded, his focus sharpening. 'No, you were right. I couldn't concentrate earlier. Everything was just a blur.'

'But your mind works now, doesn't it?' Gina inquired, a hint of hope in her voice.

'Sort of,' he admitted. 'It's reset. I've got a couple of ideas. Some stuff I read about Hunt on the *Wildscene* site.'

A faint smile touched Gina's lips. 'Then do it. Get back to the laptop.'

'I don't want to leave you alone here…' Rhys hesitated. 'Warlow says we should maintain a clear boundary between work and life.'

Gina shook her head firmly. 'Well, it's not working, Rhys.

Not when it's about Catrin. There are no rules anymore. Go on, get back to your laptop.'

'But what about you?' Rhys asked.

'Much as I'd like to watch Fast and Furious for the twentieth time,' Gina quipped with a mischievous grin. 'Maybe I can help?'

Rhys considered her offer, a sly twinkle in his eye. 'Okay. Can't hurt if I bounce some ideas off you.'

Gina feigned seriousness. 'Perhaps we should do some work first?'

'Keeper,' Rhys muttered with a grin.

'What?'

'Deal. I'll let you help if you make us some decaf tea.'

'Living the dream,' she said as she got up, but then stopped and gave him a coy, over the shoulder grin.

CHAPTER THIRTY-SIX

ANOTHER DAY.

Another troubled night.

Or perhaps it was simply the relentless dehydration that was taking its toll. Catrin lay on the bunk unmoving until the crows' chorus told her it was morning. Thirst clawed at her throat, a relentless tormentor urging her to crack open a morning beer. The thought of such a desperate breakfast made her wince; she could almost see Craig's concerned face, his eyebrow raised in a mix of worry and disapproval. But in this underground prison, with options dwindling, even this unthinkable choice was becoming a grim necessity.

Then she remembered she'd drunk all the beers the day before.

The thought of him, of all her loved ones, brought a surge of emotion to prick her eyes, but she quickly blinked away the tears. Craig would be frantic with worry, just as she was now. The strength she was known for was being tested, and there was a stark difference between strength and despondency.

She hated feeling helpless.

She despised feeling weak.

Her mind spun with bleak scenarios like low-quality film

reels. What would happen when there was nothing left to drink? How much did a body need every day? Could she resort to her own urine, a thought so grim it brought bile to the back of her mouth.

With a heavy heart, she reached for the water bottle and poured some out.

A thimbleful.

The sound it made into the plastic cup, halfway between a clatter and a tinkle, would have brought saliva flooding if she'd had any, and the warm liquid provided wonderful, momentary relief as it slid down her parched throat. She glanced at what remained in the bottle, resolving to ration what was left, though the futility of it threatened to over-whelm her. She needed to stretch out what little she had for as long as possible to maintain that fragile grip on hope.

The internal battle between pragmatism and despair raged on. She clung to the belief that Hunt would return, or that someone would eventually find her. Her determination fuelled her actions as she rose once more, moving from the bottle to clamber up the ladder, and tap against the underside of the shaft door three times with the wrench. She counted to five, then repeated the three taps.

But they were mere shadows of the powerful strokes of before.

And getting feebler every time.

But as with before, only the crows heard and responded to her signal with their cries.

————

WARLOW WAS UP AT SIX. Out with Cadi half an hour later. He left for work before either Jess or Molly had appeared. He had tea today, eschewing his normal morning coffee to avoid the noise the grinder would make and not wake the others.

He stopped at the Tenby Road service station again for a copy of the "ragloid," as Gil had termed it, and flicked through it as he sat in his car, to see if Lane had anything else to say.

He did. He'd made the headline.

Police clueless as huge presence fails to prevent second bombing. Unconfirmed reports suggest the victim was the bomber himself.
Read an analysis from the man who escaped the clutches of bomb-killer Roger Hunt in Geraint Lane's editorial.

Warlow found the page he was looking for, then reached to the cupholder for the Mccoffee he'd grabbed from the Pensarn franchise on his way.

Police Ineptitude revealed as Hunt's Explosive End Shrouded in Questions!
By Geraint Lane.
The chaos surrounding the recent explosive climax in the Hunt-Richards incident unveils an incredible tale of police incompetence. A source close to the inquiry has revealed that the second victim was Roger Hunt himself, a victim of his own explosive device.
At the heart of the action, a bloody attack on a journalist and the abduction of the valiant police officer Catrin Richards unfolded. Yet, instead of a swift resolution, the public has been served a story riddled with ineptitude at all levels of law enforcement.
The ignominious demise of the sinister Hunt, at his own hands, raises more questions than answers. How could a police force supposedly dedicated to public safety allow such a dangerous criminal to operate unhindered for so long? The answer lies in their endemic inability to tackle incompetence within their ranks.
It's not only about the failure to arrest petty criminals; it's about a systemic failure where maddening bureaucracy and

lacklustre investigations normalise such behaviour, leaving all exposed to blatant shoplifters, knife-toting gangs of hooligans, and heinous criminals like Hunt.

The time has come for an overhaul of the policing system, one that no longer sweeps ineptitude under the rug, but takes a hard look in the mirror and commits to protecting the innocent citizens who are left to pay the price.

The scandalous end of Hunt should be the catalyst for genuine change in policing. It's time to turn the page on this shocking saga and demand a safer, more efficient future! #JusticeForRichards

A wave of heat washed over Warlow's face as he processed Lane's words. When his phone buzzed with a notification, he knew it would be Gil. The text message confirmed it.

> #JusticeForRichards? Permission to castrate the pwrs?

Pwrs was a good word. Rude, but very apposite. Warlow texted back:

> You in?

> Yes. So is Rhys.

———

WARLOW MADE HQ BY 8AM. Buchannan met him as he had his hand on the door handle. They exchanged an indignant look which made words unnecessary, but Warlow said them anyway.

'You've read it?'

'I have,' Buchannan said. 'Everyone has. No doubt the powers that be will want a meeting.'

'Don't think I can stand another one. Not until we've had a briefing.'

'Of course.'

'Jess is en route.'

Buchannan nodded. 'The outside world.'

'Give me the nod for when Drinkwater summons you.'

In the Incident Room, the first thing Warlow noticed was the cut out editorial Gil had pasted on the Job Centre.

'What's that doing there?' Warlow asked.

'Not as intel. More an incentive,' Gil replied.

Rhys already had his jacket off and sleeves rolled up. 'Sir, I don't think we've had a formal statement from Geraint Lane since his release from hospital.'

Warlow's lips curled over his teeth in a grin. 'Good point, Rhys. Why don't we invite him in this afternoon?'

'I could get him, sir.'

'Well, if he wriggles, we'll do exactly that.'

The door opened, and Jess walked in. 'I haven't read it myself, but I heard,' she said, eyes straying to the cutting. She walked over and read it. Warlow waited. He watched as Jess, arms folded, shook her head more than once as her eyes followed the words. She still had her arms folded when she turned back.

'We're getting him in for a chat this afternoon,' Warlow said.

'Good. Bagsy being on the other side of the desk.'

'I suggest, for once, tea after the morning debrief.' Warlow walked to the Job Centre and, next to the cutting, wrote, #JusticeForRichards. 'I'm all for that. I suspect none of us slept too well. Gil, how about you go first?'

The DS grabbed a whiteboard marker and walked over to the Job Centre.

'Craig, who is on the way in, spoke directly to the tyre people. As mentioned, they, as part of their processes, mark down mileage and did that on the Mazda on Saturday. The car was not used again until Catrin picked it up Monday morning.'

'Bit of luck, Sarge,' Rhys said.

No one argued. Because they all knew they were due some.

'That mileage reading was 29,687.' Gil wrote the figures on the board. 'When the car was found in Angle, the odometer read 29,851. That's 164 miles, give or take. You with me?'

Everyone was.

'Now, Craig says she didn't use the car on the weekend after it had new tyres in a place in Cross Hands. It's two miles from there to Catrin's house, eleven miles give or take from Catrin's to here. And it's roughly twenty-five miles from here to *Cân-y-barcud* cottage. And it's sixty from the cottage to Angle. That about a hundred miles and leaves 64 miles on the odometer unaccounted for.'

Gil must have slept, or at least his hair had and despite his attempts with a comb, it stuck up at awkward angles making him resemble, in not the best light, Doc Brown from *Back To The Future*, only without a white coat.

'Questions?'

None.

The sergeant moved with purpose to his desk, where he'd spread out an OS map. 'If we assume a there and back journey for Hunt when he had Catrin in the car, if Lane is to be believed, then that gives us an area with a radius of thirty miles centred at *Cân-y-barcud*.' Gil ran his finger over the circle he'd drawn. 'Almost to the coast on the west, but not quite. Into the Black Mountains on the east, Tregaron in the north and to us here in the south.'

'Us and a bit, sarge,' Rhys pointed out.

'Agreed. But it means that according to the mileage, he stayed within this circle.'

'That's good work, Gil,' Warlow said.

'Always the note of surprise.' Gil shook his head.

'Isn't that from Harry Potter, sarge?' Rhys was grinning.

'If it is, they stole it from me.'

Jess leaned in to study the map. Warlow caught a whiff of

her perfume. And lifted his nose, emulating Cadi. 'Still a bloody big area,' Jess said.

'It is, but a damned site smaller than the whole of West Wales. And almost certainly excluding Pembrokeshire.' Warlow put his finger at the centre of Gil's circle. 'So, it's likely Catrin is within this area. That's a start. Rhys, what have you got?'

Rhys's eyes widened. 'Um, I've had a couple of thoughts, sir, but they came to me late last night, so I need to follow them through this morning with a couple of phone calls. To make sure.'

'Okay. Jess?'

'I'm going to see Povey myself this morning. Shake the tree over that phone they have.'

Buchannan's head appeared around the Incident Room door.

'Headmaster's office?' Warlow asked.

'Hope you stuffed newspapers down your trousers to take the sting out.'

Warlow tapped his backside and joined the superintendent for a stroll upstairs.

———

WARLOW ENDURED another dire meeting about bugger all. No one had anything concrete to add to what was already known about Hunt's death. And he was not yet prepared to share the intelligence about the mileage and the car that Gil had brought to their notice.

'The PolSA and his team are widening the area around Angle in a search for Catrin Richards,' Two-Shoes announced.

'She's not in Angle,' Warlow said with a weary edge to his voice. 'It makes no sense. Why would he take her somewhere where he wanted to be invisible?'

'But we have the manpower in situ, as it were,'

Drinkwater said, sounding surprised that Warlow was not pleased at this.

'What makes sense,' Two-Shoes spoke calmly and with venom in the stare she gave Warlow, 'is to at least eliminate fully the possibility that she is on that peninsula.'

The DCI looked away. He saw no point in arguing. Gil's theory had legs. Just not enough meat on the bones to reveal to Drinkwater and Two-Shoes. Still, he decided to throw them a stick to chase. 'We are bringing Lane in for questioning this afternoon.'

'He has an interesting viewpoint on the investigation and the police,' Buchannan said.

'Is this for a detailed statement?' Drinkwater asked.

'Thought it might be a good idea before we read it in the papers, sir.' Warlow's reply was as dry as sandpaper.

'I'll be handling a press conference today. Forensic confirmation of Hunt's death.' Two-Shoes said this in a way that suggested it would make Lane's revelations less caustic. Warlow remained sceptical.

'Povey has confirmed it, then?' Buchannan asked.

'She has.'

Warlow had not heard that. But then, he was off the Hunt case as such, he remembered. As he walked back towards the Incident Room five minutes later with Buchannan, Rhys, doing a full-on impression of Tigger bounding out of the Hundred Aker wood, came to meet them. It was now just after 10am.

'Povey came up with Hunt's number, sir. DI Allanby has contacted the provider. She's speaking with them now.'

'Good.'

Rhys had more bullets to fire, though. 'Never guess who has walked through the front door, sir.'

'Too early for Santa,' Warlow said.

'Geraint Lane plus solicitor. Looks like the ragloids want to protect themselves.'

'Well, well.' Warlow grinned. 'Another pre-emptive strike, eh?'

'Who's interviewing?' Buchannan asked.

'I thought I'd let Gil and Jess have a crack.'

The superintendent smiled. 'I might just come along for the entertainment, then.'

Rhys walked past the two senior men. 'Where are you off to?' Warlow asked.

'Llandeilo, sir. Something I need to check on. I'll be back as soon as I can.'

CHAPTER THIRTY-SEVEN

CHANTELLE BARON, from the way she studied the little interview room before sitting down, had clearly overdressed for the part.

When she took out a napkin from her bag and spread it out on the seat before sitting, the look on Gil's face was priceless. Lane, who had already sat, leveraged his legal advisor's distaste and entitlement with obvious pleasure. His bruises had faded, and his cuts had begun to heal, though he still looked like an RTA victim.

'I want it understood,' Miss Baron said, 'that my client is here voluntarily.'

Jess, completely unfazed by the antics and posturing, smiled. 'We are aware. I'm grateful that Mr Lane feels well enough to attend.'

Jess wore a bit of makeup. The kind you had to look hard to see which, Warlow had decided, made it a thousand times more effective than the trowelled-on layers the solicitor wore. Jess was a good fifteen years older than the lawyer, but unless you knew that, he doubted anyone would have guessed that number. From the observation room, Warlow suddenly realised that Jess would still be attractive when she was ninety. That's what genetics could do that two hours of layered makeup never would.

Gil, ever the professional, pressed the buttons on the recorder, marking the time and date for the record, and ensured everyone introduced themselves. That done, Jess started proceedings.

'How are you getting on, Mr Lane?' she asked, casting a polite glance in his direction.

'I'm getting there, slowly,' Lane replied.

Gil's eyes flicked upwards to meet the journalist's gaze. An unspoken acknowledgement that this meeting held tremendous significance passed between them. However, it was Baron who spoke next, reaching into her elegant shoulder bag to retrieve a stack of A4 sheets in a see-through plastic cover. 'Mr. Lane has prepared a formal statement,' she stated, her tone grave. 'We have tried to include as much detail as possible.'

Gil maintained his composure, his trademark grin never faltering. Baron's stern demeanour barely made a dent.

Jess was ready to engage. 'Great,' she said, her tone full of enthusiasm. 'It's always helpful to see this rather than as a headline.'

Baron's response came back as impassive as ever.

'We have a few questions if you're up for it,' Jess continued.

Lane leaned forward, embracing the role of the brave, wounded soldier seeking justice, striking back at the enemy. Unfortunately for him, the seasoned police officers weren't ready to let his narrative dominate the conversation.

'Just to confirm,' Jess began, 'you've lived at the address you provided in Whitland for over four years?'

Lane's eyes narrowed. 'That is true.'

'Good,' Jess acknowledged. She passed the typed statement to Gil, who scrutinised it, glasses perched delicately on his nose. 'Let's rewind a bit,' Jess said. 'The mugging of a few months ago… your phone was stolen?'

'Yes,' Lane confirmed.

'You replaced that phone with a new phone and a new number?'

'I did,' Lane admitted.

'What relevance does that—' Baron began.

Gil interjected, 'Roger Hunt died. We believe because of a catastrophic error while setting up another bomb.'

Lane nodded solemnly. 'I heard.'

'But, among his possessions,' Jess continued, 'we found a pay-as-you-go phone.'

'Interesting,' Lane replied.

'Wherever he was hiding,' Jess explained, 'he communicated with someone. Not extensively, just cryptic messages, possibly GPS data.'

'Really?' Lane's feigned interest came across as a tad overdone.

Jess nodded. 'The most intriguing part is that he texted only one number, another pay-as-you-go phone. Many of those messages, not all but a substantial number, were received by a phone in and around the Whitland area.'

'Gosh,' Lane said, his eyes wide with astonishment.

'Of course, we have your registered mobile number,' Jess pointed out. 'And that doesn't match the one Hunt texted.'

'Obviously,' Lane replied, still maintaining a forced nonchalance.

'However,' Jess continued, 'a text received from that burner phone number sent to Hunt the day before you were attacked, and Catrin Richards was abducted, intrigues us.' Jess looked down at a printout. 'It reads "CYB tmro".'

'Someone knew our plans,' Lane said, acknowledging the gravity of the situation.

Gil nodded solemnly. 'Someone did, someone who has a lot to answer for.'

Chantelle Baron interjected, her voice oozing authority, 'Have you found the second phone?'

Gil sent her a rueful smile. 'No, and we're unlikely to, given the circumstances. There were no calls made from that phone, and most of the messaging was done via encrypted WhatsApp. But we have received the records from Hunt's phone.'

Baron couldn't hold back her irritation any longer. 'What does any of this have to do with my client?'

'That's an excellent question. Mr. Lane, do you have any knowledge of that second pay-as-you-go phone?' Gil intertwined his fingers on the desk.

Lane's response was concise. 'You're pissing against the wrong wall.'

Jess added a note of reasonableness to the proceedings. 'We certainly hope we are, because it's clear that whoever owned that second phone had advanced knowledge of Catrin Richards's whereabouts on the day of her abduction. That person, even if coerced into it, would be held responsible and charged with conspiracy to kidnap. Given that the abduction ultimately led to Napier's killing, it would also mean conspiracy to murder.'

Jess let all of that sink in and leaned forward. 'Catrin Richards is pregnant. She has been missing for five days, and it will not surprise you to learn that we do not know where she is. I am appealing to you now as a human being. If you know anything, please tell us.'

Lane sat. Arms folded.

'My client is a journalist,' Baron said. 'You realise that if he has any privileged information, he is under no obligation to—'

'He's not a doctor, is he?' Gil asked.

'No.'

'Then protecting his sources is bullshit and the courts will not look kindly on someone not helping in the search for a pregnant officer.'

'Sorry,' Lane said. 'I can't help you. I have no idea where she is.'

Gil held his slippery gaze. 'But was it you who communicated with Hunt?'

Baron turned to Lane. 'I would advise not to comment on anything else you are asked here.' She turned back to Jess. 'May I remind you that my client is here voluntarily?'

'You may.' Gil nodded sagely. 'And may I remind you that

if we find any link between your client and Hunt, whether you believe it to be privileged or otherwise, effluent will hit the fan.'

Baron collected up her things. 'I believe we're finished here.'

'Agreed. For now,' Gil said and turned to Jess. 'I've seen careers ruined over things like this. Even if there is no prosecution. In these days of trial by social media…'

'Is that a threat?' Baron turned on Gil.

'A fact, Miss Baron,' Gil said, meeting her gaze head on.

She smiled, and Warlow was aware of how easy it was to masquerade callous condescension as professionalism in this sordid bloody world they were all shuffling around in. It had become too easy for people to shed their humanity. He also realised that Lane was now on his hit list. Baron, he would never see again, but if he did, he hoped she found some way to come in from the cold.

———

'WASTE OF BLOODY TIME,' Gil said when they convened in the Incident Room a few minutes later. By now it was past midday and a much-needed late cuppa was being consumed. The Human Tissue For Transplant box had been opened and its treasures on display.

'He knows something,' Jess said. 'I can feel it.'

'Well, unless we bring out the thumbscrews, we can forget him,' Warlow said. 'And even if he was in cahoots with Hunt or somehow being coerced, I doubt Hunt would risk giving a slimy eel like Lane any details.'

'Agreed,' Jess said. 'Hunt was too careful.'

Craig had joined them again to observe the interview. 'I could get some of the boys to—'

'No, you couldn't,' Warlow said it quickly, but not in anger.

Craig had lost weight and looked even more in need of sleep than the rest of them.

'Sorry, sir.'

'Don't apologise. I have fantasies, too. Most of them involve driving a stake through a certain vampire's heart.'

'I think Baron had fangs. When she drew her lips back, I caught a glimpse. Lucky, I had that Jalfrezi last night, that's all I can say. I always ask for extra garlic these days. Makes me immune from their vampire charms.' Gil burped gently, and turned his face away.

'And everyone else's,' Warlow muttered.

It brought a smile to Craig's face.

They went back to their phones and computers, but by five, Warlow sensed another day slip-sliding away from him. Appeals had gone out for farmers to check their outbuildings. The PolSA had extended the search parameter towards the vast Brechfa Forest. Though how you searched an area like that, other than with packs of dogs, Warlow dared not think. They were in the middle of vespers. A depressing acknowledgement of their lack of progress. The one bit of new information had come from the Pembrokeshire search coordinator who confirmed no sign of Catrin Richards in their extensive sweep of the Angle Peninsula..

'Tell us something we don't know,' Warlow had muttered. And so, he prepared another little speech to gee them all up.

'We work with what we have. We know about the area he is likely to have driven across.' Warlow nodded at Rhys as he breezed in and whose mobile rang almost immediately. By way of a comedy entrance, his immediate retreat through the door again brought some tired smiles to weary faces.

Warlow pointed to the map now pasted up on the board. 'We know about the phone. Any indication of where he was when he was using it?'

'Towers were pinged at Lampeter, Tregaron, Ammanford. He's been all over,' Jess observed.

'It would fit with his paranoia. He'd not want to use the phone in any one spot just in case it was traced,' Warlow said.

'But Lane said that Hunt had a bike, right?' Gil said.

'Thirty odd miles is nothing on a bike,' Craig said, staring at the map and Gil's circle.

When Rhys came back through the door, he had a glint in his eyes that they'd all seen before. Gil pounced on it. 'I've never seen a detective constable burst, but you'd better tell us before you do.'

'That was Hunt's ex-wife, sir. She was difficult to get hold of. I think she'd turned her phone off. Had to get one of the local Uniforms to visit and ask her to return my call. I've already spoken to the woman he was having an affair with.'

'The teacher.'

'Ex-teacher,' Rhys said. 'That's where I've been. She wasn't answering her phone either. The press have not been too polite in their approaches. So, I had to go myself.'

'For what reason?' Jess got to the point.

Rhys began pacing, teeth chewing at his upper lip. 'Just one second, ma'am.' He hurried to his desk, brought up something on the screen, and printed it off. While the printer clattered and whirred its thing, he tried to explain.

'I saw some photographs on the *Wildscene* website. Hunt had found something. Some kind of rare butterfly. And in that piece he'd written, there were photos of something else. Just some old bits of concrete sticking out of the ground. Now, it so happens that I'd seen something like this on a charity walk over in Abergwesyn. In a field behind the village hall. Two columns of concrete, not very high, one bigger than the other. I had to ask a farmer to explain what they were. But the point is, Hunt had a thing for them. He mentions them more than once on the site, just in passing. But when I spoke to his wife, she told me he would take the kids on expeditions when they were younger to find these things.'

'When are you going to tell us what they are, Rhys?'

'Sorry, ma'am. They are Royal Observer Corps nuclear monitoring bunkers. Built after the Second World War, manned by volunteers. 1,563 were built. Hunt knew about them because his father was a volunteer, so he visited the one his dad helped man when he was a kid. Somewhere in Sussex.

They've been decommissioned and demolished. But not all of them.'

He found another page on the screen that showed the inside of a bunker.

'Hunt's lover, the teacher, also said he'd researched them. He'd even been to the one I'd seen at Abergwesyn.'

Warlow watched as the young officer retrieved the print-out. What he pinned up, filling an A4 sheet in landscape format, was a map of Mid and West Wales and extending across the marches into England. The whole was dotted with red drop pins. Well over a hundred.

'These are the bunkers,' he explained.

'*Iesu*. How many?' Gil asked.

'A lot. But...' Rhys grabbed a red felt tip, measured it roughly and drew a circle. 'If we use *Cân-y-barcud* as a centre point and use your thirty-mile radius, sarge, we have a target area.'

He drew the circle with Kidwelly included at the bottom, Sennybridge to the east, Tregaron to the north, and New Quay in Cardiganshire in the west.

'That's twenty-two,' Craig said, his eyes alight.

'But pretty spread out,' Jess said.

'Doable, though,' Craig added.

'If we split up...' Rhys suggested.

'We could do that,' Warlow said, sensing everyone's need to do something. 'But we know what Hunt is capable of. I don't suggest we do this as individuals.'

'And some of these places have been demolished according to the website,' Rhys admitted.

Warlow didn't let that dampen his enthusiasm. 'We need to inspect every one within the search radius.' He glanced at the wall clock. Ten to five. 'We could start tonight.'

'Might take some finding, sir. They're in fields or over-grown patches of waste ground.'

'Right. Well, let's start properly tomorrow. You and Craig head south and tomorrow go east. Jess and I can call in to the southwest as we go home now, tick one or two off.

In the morning, I'll pick Gil up first thing and do west and north.'

Rhys looked suddenly uncomfortable. 'It's just an idea, sir. I have no proof.'

'It's more idea than we had ten minutes ago, Rhys,' Jess said.

'Doesn't matter if it comes to nothing,' Gil said. 'I'm fed up with sitting here like a garden gnome.'

'Agreed. Good work, DC Harries.' Warlow held the young officer's gaze and got a single nod and an acknowledging smile in return.

That evening, as they set off to their homes, they did so with a glimmer of hope illuminating the oncoming evening's darkness.

CHAPTER THIRTY-EIGHT

Two ROC POSTS fell within Warlow and Jess's reach as they drove back to Pembrokeshire. Or so it appeared on the map. But it took some time to find the first one. Rhys found a website URL built and maintained by a society interested in the study of man-made underground places. Their list was thorough and extensive. There were even photographs taken over a prolonged period, some as far back as 2000. Even so, the Carmarthen post proved elusive, sited on farmland at the northern edge of the town. The address took them along quiet lanes, with no sign of anything obvious.

In the end, Warlow spotted a phone mast on farmland at about the right spot. He did the polite thing and knocked on the nearby farmhouse door. A pleasant, if surprised, young man explained that his dad was out with the cows, but pointed to the masts fifty yards away and, after seeing their warrant cards, invited them to help themselves.

'Nothing to do with us, really,' he explained. 'The masts, I mean. But there was something there before they came. Something low on the ground. A bunker of some sort. We get some money for having the masts on the land, so Dad said yes when they asked if they could use what was there.'

'Any activity lately?'

'Nah. No one's been up there for months.'

Warlow and Jess walked through a field towards a clutch of grey buildings and two thirty-metre masts. Warlow had downloaded images to his phone and found the bunker easily enough. In contrast to the prefabricated buildings that the telecoms companies had erected, the grey concrete of the bunkers, standing no more than a metre or so above the ground just feet away from the communication buildings, looked worn and crumbling. Two weathered, blocky structures protruded from the ground, one more square than the other, with a steel pipe emerging between them. The whole assemblage had an abandoned air.. A heavy steel plate, secured with both a lock and padlock, covered the entrance to the larger underground chamber.

'Must be the shaft,' Warlow said.

A thick cable ran through the louvres of what looked like a second ventilation shaft attached to the larger manmade rectangle.

'This is a bunker?'

Warlow studied the photographs on his phone. 'It is. But according to the website, this one is owned by the telecoms company and has equipment in it.'

'Can we get in?' Jess asked, kneeling at the narrower protruding shaft.

Warlow studied the padlock. 'Not without a key or bolt cutters.'

Jess put her face close to the louvres. 'Hello? Catrin?'

Silence was all she got in reply.

Warlow stood and looked about him. 'He wouldn't have chosen this. It's too close to habitation. The farmer would have seen or heard something.'

Jess stood up. 'At least we know what we're looking for now. Astonishing to think these things were here.'

'Hardly anyone knows.'

The second stop was at Llanboidy, which had just about made it inside Rhys's circle. This one was not as easy to find. They parked up at the entrance to some holiday cottages and

Warlow walked up a lane leading to a farm before finding a path next to the hedge.

'Are you sure this is where it is, Evan?' Jess asked.

'According to—' Warlow stopped talking. They'd skirted the hedge and there it was. Two concrete rectangles, only a couple of feet tall, one narrower than the other and a few feet apart from the larger one that had a more irregular shape. Nothing but overgrown grass between them. It looked like the metal post between the two shafts had also been encased in concrete.

'My God,' Jess said. 'Talk about remote.'

Warlow inspected the steel cover to the main shaft. 'Locked. And the lock is rusted.'

Jess again knelt near the louvres on the narrower shaft and shouted down. 'Hello? Catrin?' She looked up at Warlow. 'I hope no one is watching. They'll think we've gone mad.'

Warlow shrugged. 'Maybe we have. This place is abandoned. No sign of anyone having been here for years.'

'But can you be sure?'

'No. We can't. But if Hunt has picked one of these places to hide out in, no bloody wonder we couldn't find him.'

Dusk was falling now. It had taken much longer to find these two than he'd expected. His phone rang, and Gil's name popped up on the screen.

'Where are you?' Warlow asked.

'Down a deep dark hole a few yards off a minor road in Dryslwyn, I have driven past this spot a hundred times trying to dodge traffic on the A40 as a shortcut. I had no bloody idea.'

'Same here. We're in Llanboidy. But no luck. You?'

'No luck either. I mean, no sign of Catrin, though I have been down into the bunker and taken photos. It's unused. I'll send them along. Getting dark now, though, so I'll see you tomorrow.'

'Is this a wild goose chase, Gil?'

'Who knows? But I have to hand it to Rhys. These places

are ready-made hideouts. And if Hunt knew all about them…'

'Which he did.'

'Then that's your answer. I'll see you tomorrow.'

Warlow stood in the corner of a quiet field, out of sight of the rest of the world, letting Jess inspect the hatches of the post, waiting for Gil's images to come through. The Dryslwyn ROC post had green-painted louvres, but the images from inside were astounding. A white-painted room, a fold-away bench table, a cupboard, cabling on the walls.

'My God,' he whispered.

Jess joined him, and he handed her the phone.

When she looked up, her face in the dying light echoed his shocked disbelief. 'And there are how many of these?'

'Twenty odd within Rhys's catchment area.'

'We need to search them all.'

'I agree.'

Jess handed back the phone. 'But it's mad that the three of us go looking tomorrow. Give me a minute.'

Jess turned away to text, and Warlow's gaze drifted back to the bunker entrances, seen in a new light now that Gil had shown him what was beneath his feet. He tried to imagine what the people who'd manned these posts had been trained for. What would have been the signal? Air raid sirens? Then the observers saying goodbye to loved ones knowing that if there really was a strike, they would never see them again. Sitting in that bunker while the world caught fire…

A harrowing thought. What would they expect to find when they came out days or weeks later? And what would be there for them other than a slow and painful death from radiation sickness or a wild anarchic world?

The sight of this real-life bunker made him shudder, as it brought to life a trope common in films and novels - the chilling reality that authorities had actually planned for nuclear devastation.

Jess looked up from her phone. 'Right, I'm dropping Molly at Neath station tomorrow on her Manchester trip, then I'm picking Gina up while Rhys goes off with Craig. They're doing the south and east. Gina and I could do the western sweep towards the coast, while you and Gil go north. We can meet in the middle.'

Warlow didn't need to think about it. It was definitely the quickest way.

'What time's her train?'

'Eight. I can pick Gina up half an hour later. She's all for it.'

'She would be.' Warlow offered a wry smile. 'I'll take Cadi with me. She'll enjoy the trekking.'

Night was encroaching now, and they needed to get back to their cars. There was no street lighting here and even though the land was dry, hoof-holes left by cows could be damned treacherous and a great way to sprain an ankle.

They walked in silence, concentrating on where they trod. Warlow did not know if what they were attempting would bear fruit. And of those posts they found locked, he would instruct the team to unlock them where they could. His question to Gil echoed in his head.

Is this a wild goose chase?

Perhaps. But it was worth a throw of the dice.

He did not allow himself to think of it as the last throw.

'Remind me to text the others about bolt cutters,' he muttered as they headed down the last lane towards the car.

———

CATRIN STIRRED ON THE COLD, unforgiving chair. Her body ached, and a gnawing sense of exhaustion clung to her. Dehydration parched her throat, and her tongue felt thick and coated in her mouth. Listless and shivery, her watch told her she should sleep, but there was only an inch of water remaining in the bottle. Fear gripped her heart as she contemplated whether it was worth saving for another day.

She placed her hand protectively over her pregnant belly. She couldn't ignore the dire implications of the dwindling water supply on her unborn child. It wasn't just her own survival at stake.

Summoning the last of her strength, she picked through Hunt's belongings again. Amongst the sinister objects scattered about, she'd discovered a bag of fertiliser and a coil of blue plastic water pipe.

She had no idea what the weather was doing above her. But this was Wales. Rain would never be very far away, and desperation bred innovation.

She uncoiled the stiff blue tubing. It wasn't easy and resisted her attempts at laying it out on the bunker floor. This was a desperate gamble, dependent on the chance that rain might fall; a sound she hadn't heard in days, or was it weeks? She studied the cross section of the bunker from the schematic. It wasn't complicated. The air shaft comprised a concrete pipe louvred at the bottom and at the top. She unscrewed the bottom louvre with a screwdriver and fed the stiff water pipe up, using the air shaft wall as a guide until she met resistance. There was no way out. Still, it might capture some moisture if she left it there. She trimmed the bottom end of the pipe with a hacksaw and wedged it in place over an enamel cup.

As the hours dragged on, her anxiety grew, and the moments felt interminable. Sometime during the early hours, she heard it. The patter of rain against the louvres above, and her heart beat a little faster. She pressed her lips against the pipe, praying for the sweet sound of water collecting within.

But all she tasted was the cool night air, redolent with evening pine. The pipe stayed dry as her spirits wilted. She tried to sleep. She tried not to think of that delicious mouthful of water sitting on the shelf.

Tried and failed.

———

CADI KNEW something was different early the next morning. She always could. Either with that resigned but forgiving look she gave him when she knew it meant a drop off with the sitter rather than a walk, or, worse, the accusing look she'd given to his packed luggage when he'd had the temerity to go to Australia without her.

But today was different. Today there was tail wagging anticipation in the air. Warlow had no idea how she knew they were off somewhere, but she did and kept following him from room to room as he got ready. He wrote a brief note for Molly, which simply said, 'Enjoy the weekend,' and included a crisp fifty-pound note.

Well, the kid deserved it. Okay, these days almost everything was cashless. In fact, he could not remember seeing his own children – young adults, the both of them – pay with anything other than a wave of the phone. Still, there was something delicious about having a crisp note in your hand. Christ, he even remembered the days when a fiver felt like you were well off.

He and Jess had hammered out a plan of sorts the night before and then shared it all with the others. She and Gina would aim for the bunkers at Pencader, Newcastle Emlyn, Llandyssul, and New Quay on the coast. Craig and Rhys would tick off Kidwelly, Amman Valley, Resolven, then Sennybridge, and Llanwrtyd Wells on an eastern leg. The last two were very much on the fringes of the catchment area, much as New Quay was in the west. But there was no point being too prescriptive. Pedants never did well in running investigations. One only had to recall the Yorkshire Ripper case, where the investigation was misled by a hoax caller with a Geordie accent, to understand the dangers of being too rigid in police work.

By seven, Warlow and Cadi were on their way east to pick up Gil in Llandeilo. Theirs would be a cross-country trek. Talley, Llandovery, Lampeter, Cam Berwyn and, last, the wilds of Abergwesyn.

Gil was outside the door of his house in Llandeilo as Warlow pulled up. He was dressed in shorts and a polo shirt, as demanded by a forecast of twenty-four degrees after the overnight showers that had done nothing to ease the parched earth. He held a cooler the size of a small baby's crib in his hand.

'I see you've come prepared,' Warlow said.

'Could be a very long day. The Lady Anwen has provided sustenance.'

'Glad to hear that.'

Gil slid the cooler into the gap behind the front seat, then went to the boot, opened it, and greeted a delighted Cadi.

Warlow said nothing. He'd long ago accepted that Cadi had that effect on people.

As soon as Gil climbed into the car, he unfurled a copy of the map Rhys had provided.

'Where to first?' Warlow asked.

'There is a Talley ROC post. That would be close to *Cân-y-barcud*. Logical to start there, I thought. On the website, they say it's been demolished to make way for a bungalow.'

'Best to check, though.'

'My thoughts exactly. Talley Ho!'

Warlow didn't drive off but sent Gil a withering look. 'Is that likely to be the standard of banter I can look forward to?'

'We need something to get us through the day. But I promise to do better.'

'Just as well the bar is set so low, then.' Warlow slid the gear into first and pulled away.

CHAPTER THIRTY-NINE

SATURDAY MORNING DAWNED with the same eerie alarm call; a symphony of cawing crows somewhere above. Three metres beneath the warm earth's surface, Catrin had already drained two-thirds of the last precious drops from her meagre inch of water reserve. Despite that, unbearable thirst gnawed at her as a relentless tormentor.

A pounding headache had plagued her throughout the night, and leg cramps had twisted her limbs into contorted shapes. Dehydration was taking its toll. Her mind, once sharp and focused, now fixated on a single, all-consuming thought: water. The relentless thirst dominated her every moment, eclipsing all other concerns. Trapped in her underground prison, she gingerly touched her parched, cracked lips. With great effort, she held back the tears that threatened to fall, knowing she couldn't afford to lose even that small amount of precious moisture.

Tears were fluid. She could ill afford that. A sense of finality had crept over her in the night. There would be no way out of this tomb. Once all the water had gone, her organs would begin shutting down.

The baby… She squeezed her eyes shut and picked up a pen. With a shaking hand, she wrote Craig a goodbye letter.

———

THE TALLEY ROC WAS A NON-STARTER. Its position on the map was indeed now a bungalow and a neat garden. No sign of ventilation shafts or hatches.

'As described,' Gil quipped, a hint of disbelief in his voice. They didn't even bother getting out of the Jeep.

They were luckier with the Llandovery bunker. Visible from the Cilycwm Road, this site had been looked after. Fenced off and with trees planted on site, Warlow parked up and walked a few yards along a private access road. There was barbed wire, but that was easily negotiated. They left Cadi in the car and climbed into the small compound. Warlow was getting used to the ROC's surface construction. Gil made for the shaft. The hatchway was locked, but he'd read up on this and had brought a variety of hexagonal and other keys, as well as cutters. As it turned out, this one needed only a 'T' bar key.

Gil lifted the hatch, and a cold, musty smell emerged. 'Catrin?' he yelled down.

Nothing in return.

Gil slid a headlight onto his forehead and clambered down the ladder. 'Empty,' he yelled back up, his voice sounding odd from below. Two flashes from the phone camera, and then Gil was coming back up. Ten minutes later, they were back in the car.

'Where next?'

'Lampeter,' Gil said. 'This one is on the University Campus.'

'Interesting,' Warlow said. 'Brings us back full circle to the Denzil Williams case.'

Gil exhaled loudly. '*Esgyrn Dafydd,* I'd almost forgotten about him.'

'Rhys has been on it.'

'Not fair to him.'

'I don't know. Jess says he's got something up his sleeve.'

'A big hairy arm. *Iesu,* that boy's got levers.'

In Lampeter, they found a campus porter, explained what they were after, and were accompanied to the site. It stood in a fenced-off compound east of the accommodation blocks and a business park.

'All locked up,' Gil noted when they got there.

'And way too conspicuous and difficult to get to. The porter said they'd built the fencing in the 1980s because of nuclear protests from the students.'

'Right. Breaking into this place would not be easy. We'll add it to the list of improbables.'

'Agreed,' Gil said.

Cadi, on a long lead, trotted along, enjoying the fresh aromas from each bush and tree. Warlow could not let her off the lead yet. But she did not seem to mind too much when they went back to the Jeep.

'According to this, the one in Tregaron has been demolished,' Gil read from his phone.

'Let's check it out and grab some lunch.'

'Tidy.'

The Tregaron site had indeed been demolished. All that was left was a patch of altered growth in the field where the post had once sat.

Warlow found a spot to park in the shade, and he and Gil ate a sandwich lunch. But then, there were sandwich lunches, and there was a Lady Anwen sandwich lunch. The men sat with windows open, the warm breeze wafting along, creating a refreshing through-draft. Gil had packed some iced water, in preference to tea. There was a time and a place. They checked in with the other pairings and got similar stories. Some sites had been properly decommissioned. A few were accessible but empty and with no sign of occupation.

'Funny place, Tregaron,' Gil said as they sat.

'How so?'

'Well, there's the beast for a start. The Beast of Bont.'

'I thought that was further west.'

'By a couple of miles, yes. But something that could slaughter half a dozen sheep is no joke. And now it's the

Beasts of Bont, plural – and Bont as in Pontrhydfendigaid. Buggers are breeding.'

'All myth, though, right?'

Gil allowed himself a few thoughtful chews before answering. 'You say that, but this place is… well, it's got Cors Caron, the Red Bog of the Teifi to hide in for a start. And then there's the elephant.'

'Of course, there is,' Warlow said without missing a beat. Talking with Gil was like dipping your hand into a bran tub. You never knew what you'd pull out next.

'No, rumour has it that in 1848 an elephant, part of Batty's travelling menagerie, died after drinking contaminated water and was buried behind the Talbot Hotel.'

'Lucky it wasn't in the hotel, or that really would have been an elephant in the room.'

'Scoff all you want,' Gil said between bites of salmon and cucumber. 'But there is occasionally the odd dig.'

'Not a tusk to undertake lightly.'

'Ooh, very good, DCI Warlow. Elephant pun and a hint at unearthing, too. Right, my turn.'

'It's not a comp—'

'No, you're right. Catrin would be cringing at that one.'

'She would.'

'She'd be giving me dirty looks.'

'She would.'

'And I get enough of those at home. I borrowed Anwen's iPad to listen to an audiobook and lost the damned thing.'

'Oh?'

'Yeah.' Gil sounded wistful.

Warlow waited for the punchline.

'Now I'll never hear the end of it.'

Warlow shut his eyes, gave a single nod of acknowledgement for the joke, and started the engine. 'Where next?'

'This next one, Cam Berwyn, is right on the edge, but since we're going past it, I thought we might as well. Halfway between here and the Abergwesyn bunker. On the way to the most remote telephone box in Wales.'

'What's not to like,' Warlow muttered.

It did not take many miles out past Tregaron for the houses to peter out. They were back in the Cambrian Hills, on the Abergwesyn mountain road. As they approached the Diffwys Outdoor Centre, the landscape opened up dramatically. The single-track road wound ahead for miles, flanked by undulating hills, forests, and lakes. To their left, a ribbon of water traced the valley floor, while gentle slopes rose to meet the escarpment.

'*Mawredd*,' Gil muttered in a low, awed voice. 'Not called the "Desert of Wales" for nothing, is it?'

'Five points if you spot a camel.'

'People come here just to drive,' Gil said. 'More likely to spot a caravan.'

Warlow gazed out at the rolling empty landscape. 'If Hunt set up camp up here, no wonder no one found him.'

Gil waited before answering, 'But he was in hiding all winter, don't forget. I doubt he would have wanted to be out in the open for that long.'

Warlow had to agree with the sergeant's logic.

They passed the outdoor centre's house and cabins to climb up and over the next set of hillocks, the still spring green moor grass, and the clusters of forestry huddled on the hillsides like giant caterpillars crawling over the land. Further on, the landscape closed in a little, with the timberline encroaching to within a few yards of the road. A sign announced the Cwm Berwyn forestry area to their right.

'Here?' Warlow asked.

'Take the turning, but it's another half a mile to a rough road in front of a cattle grid.'

Warlow found it easily enough. The gravel road led back to a forestry gate with a lift bar. He let Cadi out, and she immediately relieved herself against a convenient rock.

'This bunker is on a mound. Two hundred yards along the track.'

They were aware of what to look for now. 'The posting on the website suggests it's been decommissioned,' Gil said, eyes peeled for something man-made in this natural wilderness. They walked through a gap in the trees to a clearing, and Gil pointed to the ground. 'Here,' he called out.

Warlow joined him to find the remains of some concrete slabs, the bigger square only a few inches above the ground under the branches of an encroaching tree and half covered by debris. Another smaller pile of partially collapsed concrete and the remains of a small cube stood a few feet away. The bigger block, the access shaft, was filled in with stones and had metal bars where the hinged door would have been.

'Ah well,' Warlow said. 'This one is definitely sealed off.'

Gil stood, hands on hips, and let out a big sigh before saying, 'The next one is in Abergwesyn.'

Gil turned to walk back to the car, but Warlow caught sight of Cadi standing, watching him. He smiled. 'Okay, girl. You've been in the car for a long time.' He turned to Gil. 'How about we give Cadi ten minutes to run about first?'

'Great,' Gil replied. 'Won't do us any harm to stretch our legs.'

The dog ran off as she was wont to do. 'Go on, then, girl,' Warlow sang out. '*Wiwer!*' One word, translated as squirrel, guaranteed to get the dog animated.

———

CATRIN, half asleep most of the time now in her weakened state, shook her head. She thought she'd seen Craig in the toilet doorway once. Had actually called out to him only to realise he wasn't there.

How could he be there?

And so, when she heard these new noises – a shout was that? – she strained her ears for confirmation. And then, like a mirage in the desert of her despair, she heard it again. Definitely a voice. Or were they voices? But she was still wary that these could be phantoms conjured by her agitated mind.

No, no. There were voices. And getting louder, more distinct.

Someone was above. Calling, talking.

She shook her head, wondering if this was some kind of out-of-body experience. Had she died? Were these angels come for her?

She laughed. A brash cackle in a leathery throat followed by a stuttering intake of breath that ended in a half sob.

None of this was funny. Dying was not funny.

Somewhere nearby came the sound of snuffling. An animal? And then a voice called a name she recognised.

'Cadi.'

Cadi?

Catrin's heart raced, a desperate flutter in her weakened chest. Was she hearing things again? Dehydration had already played tricks on her mind. Summoning the last dregs of her strength, she tried to shout, but her parched throat produced only a feeble croak. The vibrant, capable police officer she once was had been reduced to this – a husk, barely able to make a sound.

The ladder to the surface might as well have been Mount Everest; her depleted body might manage the climb, but not quickly. She needed to signal somehow, and fast.

In a desperate attempt, Catrin pressed her cracked lips to the blue plastic water pipe she'd ingeniously threaded up the air shaft. She tried to yell, to scream, to make any noise that might carry. But all that escaped was a pitiful, ghostly wail – more air than sound.

She fell back, desperation enveloping her, clinging to her like a shroud, threatening to snuff out the flicker of hope that flared. She gasped for breath, her vision swimming as the edges of consciousness blurred. A fire? If she lit a fire and the smoke went up the ventilation shaft… but then what if she was wrong? What if she lit a fire and no one saw the smoke? What if the smoke filled the bunker? She'd had a near miss with being trapped in a garage inferno with DI Allanby not that long ago. A fire was simply too dangerous. Too stupid.

And then, from nowhere, her mind sparked with an idea. She fumbled in her pocket, fingers trembling as they closed around the small perfume spray. It was a slender lifeline, an unconventional tool for an unconventional situation.

With trembling hands, she sprayed the fragrance into the tube and blew with every ounce of remaining strength. Another spray, another blow. Twice more before she fell back and tried once more to call out, only to warble ineffectually.

Above her, the scent carried through the air shaft, a faint but unmistakable trace drifting up and into the world above. A world only metres away, but in a different plane of existence.

———

WARLOW WATCHED the dog as she snuffled around a pile of broken branches thirty yards away, dragged into a mound by some forestry worker, no doubt.

'*Dera mlaen, amser I ni find.*'

And indeed, it was time to go. The dog had relieved herself, and Warlow had picked up the spoils. But she didn't want to come away from the piled-up branches.

'Cadi.' Warlow used his lowered voice. The one that was supposed to mean business. The dog looked up, still not keen.

Warlow reverted to putting his hand into the little treat pouch he always carried when they were walking. A signal for the dog to return and usually a good one. It worked this time, too, and Cadi trotted back. She'd gone five yards when she paused and did something that Warlow, and later Gil, once the DCI had explained it, would never forget.

Cadi suddenly froze mid-step. She swivelled her head, lifting her muzzle high into the air. With her neck stretched upward, she inhaled deeply, her sensitive nose twitching as it caught an unexpected scent.

Warlow frowned. What was this? Some other animal's spoor. Something long dead in the forest? But something jangled. A nerve, a thought, an idea.

The dog's response was incongruous. He'd been on many walks with her and other's dog's markings, even dead things on the beach, brought on a low, shoulder-down approach to the smell.

This gesture, snout up, he'd previously only ever seen her do when Jess or Molly was in the vicinity at Ffau'r Blaidd, and then only after they'd perfumed up. In fact, as an early warning system for their approach, Warlow had found it useful to ready himself for their appearance because a few seconds after Cadi caught it, Warlow would catch a heady sniff of Jess or Molly's scent and ready a compliment.

He'd never seen it out in the wild, this little tick of hers. Only indoors and only with perfume.

So, what the hell was she doing it now for?

Had Jess and Gina arrived early?

Warlow walked over to the dog. 'What is it, girl?'

Cadi turned her head, her snout moving up and down as she tested the air. Her head turning inexorably towards the heaped branches.

'Something in there?'

Warlow approached the pile of branches cautiously. As he drew nearer, his eyes focused on the jumble of broken wood and his breath caught in his throat. Within the chaotic tangle of branches, he spotted something that didn't belong - a shape too regular to be natural, huddled amidst the debris.

He turned and yelled over his shoulder, 'Gil? There's something here.'

The sergeant joined him and both men stood, Cadi, now with her head low, sniffing around the bottom of the dense woodpile. Gil shifted his head and took a couple of steps to the side. '*Beth uffern…* is that one of those shaft thingies?' Gil said.

'Another bunker?'

'Looks like it,' Gil said, throwing Warlow a bemused glance.

'The other one's a dummy,' Warlow said, voicing his thoughts, concluding, without hard proof, but trusting his gut, that there was subterfuge here.

His chin went up, testing the air. What breeze there was

today came gently from the east, as so often happened when the weather turned bright in West Wales, bucking the south-westerly trend that brought so much rain. And on that faint breeze, standing next to his dog, Warlow finally caught what she had picked up seconds before. Something as unnatural in this environment as a snowflake in the Sahara.

'Smell that?' Warlow asked Gil.

'No.'

'I do. And so does Cadi. It's perfume.'

Gil looked aghast.

And then, as clear as a mission bell, they heard it.

Three clunks as something metallic and heavy met with something equally metallic and heavier.

'Catrin?' Gil bellowed and began tearing away the branches.

Warlow went to help, but before he did, he reached down and put his hands either side of the dog's neck and rubbed gently. 'Clever girl. You clever, clever girl.'

She responded to the reward with a lick of his hand.

CHAPTER FORTY

It took only a few seconds to reveal what was hidden. 'Christ, it is. It's a shaft,' Gil said, voice straining as he dragged away one of the bigger branches. He reached for another but then paused. 'A thought. What if he's booby trapped this place, too?'

The same thought had struck Warlow. 'It makes no sense. If this is his hideout and he's hidden it and bothered to make a dummy site, he wouldn't want to risk destroying it.'

Flaky logic, yes, but Cadi was leading the way, pushing in towards the ventilation shaft through a gap in the branches.

'We should take it easy, I suppose,' Gil said. 'Eyes peeled and all—'

'Hello?'

The voice muffled and weak, but still a voice, drifted up through the ventilators on the shaft. A poor and weakened copy of someone they knew well.

'Catrin?' Warlow yelled. 'Catrin?'

'It's me,' she croaked. 'I'm here.'

That was the signal for the two men to abandon caution, stripping away the branches with renewed vigour. Within a minute, Gil was kneeling at the shaft with his head next to the lichen-covered concrete louvres.

'Catrin, it's Gil. I'm here with Evan.'

'Gil,' Catrin's voice came up. And was that a laugh or a sob that accompanied it? Either would do, thought Warlow. Because only the living sobbed.

'I'm okay. Well, I'm not okay. I'm very thirsty. Really, really thirsty. I ran out of water yesterday…'

Warlow walked to the other end of the post. Hunt had done a similar job of hiding it with some big and recently felled branches. He dragged them away, revealing a simplified hatch. The plinth, only a few inches above ground level, covered with a shallow tray arrangement with moss and leaves layered into it. They would never have found this on a casual walk through.

Never.

But under the tray that Warlow levered up was a cast iron door held down by a metal bar and two sturdy padlocks.

'I'm off back to the car for water and some tools,' Gil shouted. He didn't ask permission and was up and jogging towards the vehicle parked at the barrier before Warlow answered. The DCI came back to the ventilation shaft. 'Catrin, it's me.'

'Hello, sir.' Her voice was weak.

'Did he hurt you, Catrin? Are you hurt?'

'No, sir. He dumped me here and left. I'm expecting him back. Be careful, sir.'

'He won't be back, Catrin,' Warlow muttered. 'He blew himself up three days ago.'

A long beat of silence ticked by as the implications of that statement sunk in.

'How did you find me, sir?' Catrin asked after a while.

'Rhys had us checking all these nuclear observation posts. Hunt had a thing for them. We've been around the houses.'

'Is Rhys with you now?'

'No. But we've texted him and Craig. They are on their way.' Warlow could see the blue tubing through the vents.

'Good idea. The perfume and the tubing.'

'I heard voices, but I couldn't shout.' Her words sounded

thick, as if her tongue was too big for her mouth. 'Was it you who smelt it, sir?'

Cadi, who had come to sit next to Warlow as he squatted, nuzzled at his hand. 'This close, yes. But it was Cadi who found you.'

'Oh,' a little laugh. Too high pitched for Warlow's liking. A harbinger of tears. 'She's there with you?' Catrin asked with a tremor in her voice.

'She is.' Warlow put a hand on the dog.

'Can I give her a hug when I get out?'

'You can. She is not averse to a hug, this dog.'

Gil was jogging back, carrying the cooler in one hand and a small bag of tools in the other.

Warlow made a face. 'I don't think what you have there will get through those new padlocks,' he mouthed. 'They're shrouded.'

Gil looked at the padlocks and nodded. He joined Warlow at the ventilator shaft.

'Catrin, we'll need better tools for the locks. Rhys and Craig are on that. But we can get some water down to you.' Gil took out a hammer and a thick-looking stone chisel and began hammering at the concrete vents.

'I could do with a drink,' she replied.

'Well, serves you right for winning the hide and seek gold bloody medal. There'll be some noise. Can you get the grill off the shaft below?'

'Already have.'

'Stand back, then.'

Gil hammered a hole big enough to get a half litre bottle of cold water through and let it fall. The men heard the dull thumps as it bounced against the vertical tunnel.

'Get that?'

Catrin answered, short of breath, 'Oh, my God, that is so good.'

'Take it easy. We have tools coming. Meanwhile, I'll see if there are any of the Lady Anwen's sandwiches left. Though Evan ploughed through them like a hungry horse.'

Rhys had texted to say they were twenty minutes out after visiting the Llanwrtyd Wells ROC, with Craig driving his BMW. And that they'd called in with the fire brigade for some proper cutters.

'Will we need an ambulance, Catrin?' Warlow asked.

'No, sir.' She already sounded stronger. 'I'll go in and get things checked out. The baby and all. But I'm okay. I feel it's okay.'

Warlow took a call from Jess. He stepped away to take it, Cadi now off sniffing at another tree.

'I got your text. My God, Evan. Is she okay?' Jess blurted out the words.

'We've spoken to her. Got some water for her. Craig and Rhys are on the way with proper bolt cutters.'

'We're on the way, too.'

'Where are you?'

'Place called Ystrad Aaron. Rhys sent Gina a pin, and we were half an hour away ten minutes ago.'

'You don't need to—'

'Yes, we do.'

Rhys and Craig arrived first. Warlow heard the BMW, driven by a trained police pursuit driver after all, roaring along the narrow roadway, before it pulled up.

Craig carried the bolt cutters. A no-messing tool, three and a half feet long.

'Now, that's what I call a pair of snips,' Gil observed as the younger officers jogged up.

Warlow took Craig over to the main shaft and the two padlocks. He looked flushed. Warlow did not suggest letting anyone else use the tools. Besides, Craig was in traffic and had been to many accidents and seen these tools used by fire and rescue. He had technique, using all of his weight to lean on the cutters' arms. They did the job in seconds.

As they lifted the lid, they found Catrin already ascending the ladder. Craig reached down to help her, while the others watched with broad grins on their faces. She was paler than usual, her skin sallow from the days underground, her hair not its usual lustrous red. She looked thin, too. But otherwise, intact. There were a few tears, and not just from Catrin.

When she broke off from hugging Craig, she turned and addressed her colleagues; Rhys, Warlow, and Gil. 'Right, I'm going to turn around and count to fifty. Your turn to hide.'

'She's back,' Rhys said with a grin.

'Not in the slightest bit funny,' Gil said.

But the laughter that accompanied it was real.

Then she hugged each of the men in turn and finally knelt to Cadi, who had taken notice of her perfume just as the human searchers were about to walk away. She let the dog lick her face and buried her head in her fur.

Warlow overheard Catrin's whispered words of thanks. *'Diolch, cariad. Diolch, diolch.'*

The dog lapped it up.

She was still doing that when Jess and Gina ran through the forest towards them.

Gil looked up. 'Better late than never,' he said. 'I thought this picnic would never bloody start.'

The women ignored him and embraced Catrin in another set of hugs.

Picnic or not, it had turned into a very good day indeed.

———

THE PRUDENT COURSE of action now was to guide the kidnap victim towards a debrief in the morning and get her home for some rest. But this was DS Catrin Richards, and she had endured five long days locked inside a nuclear underground shelter. It was a rare and glorious June day in Britain. No surprise, therefore, that she politely declined Warlow's suggestion to head home and put her feet up. Instead, she sat next to Gina on a weathered, felled trunk, nestled in a sunlit patch. She kept her face upturned into the light, and she took slow sips from her third bottle of water.

The others clustered around the outside of the bunker, scrutinising the exterior and, fifty yards away, the dummy that had been artfully disarranged to mislead casual walkers or bunker hunters. Warlow tried not to think about what might have happened if Cadi had not been with them.

Everyone wanted to get inside the subterranean structure. But everyone also knew that this was now a crime scene. Povey would likely resort to extracting vital organs with the dullest scissors if anyone dared to compromise her domain.

Half an hour after emerging from her subterranean exile, Catrin spoke up, her face still turned towards the warmth of the sun. 'I need to go back inside and get my notebook and coat.'

'That can wait,' Warlow said.

'I spent a lot of time in there, sir. I went through Hunt's belongings. I made a lot of observations. And I found some polaroids.'

'It can wait, Cat.' Craig tried appeasement.

She remained resolute. 'I made notes and kept records. He's been sending numbers. They look like GPS coordinates. Each entry is marked with a symbol. I have to show you and only I can go in there without contaminating the scene.'

'We could discuss it with Alison Povey,' Rhys suggested, attempting to weigh the options.

Catrin dismissed his suggestion. 'Or we could just let me go back down and fetch them.'

'What's on the polaroids?' Jess asked.

'I'm not entirely sure,' Catrin admitted. 'I need to look at them in the light of day since I couldn't think properly down there. I don't want it to have been a complete waste of time.'

'Removing evidence, sarge? Not a brilliant idea,' Rhys said.

'I won't take anything apart from my own notebook. Craig, can you lend me your phone? I can make a video.'

'Are you sure you won't just go home?' Warlow's tone was tinged with exasperation.

'Absolutely sure.'

And so, for the second time in a week, DS Catrin Richards descended into the Cwm Berwyn ROC post, this time with her partner's phone to film every moment. She spent only a few minutes inside the bunker before re-emerging with her purloined notebook, and the letter she had written to Craig, now carefully folded away as unnecessary, her expression a mix of relief and triumph.

Clearly shaken, she quipped, 'Okay, if I ever suggest doing that again, please stop me.'

'That's the potholing holiday in the Brecon Beacons off the agenda, then, Craig,' Rhys said.

'Did they find Lane?' Catrin asked.

'Unfortunately, yes,' Gil said. 'Locked in the boot of his car.'

'Oh, God. Killed and dumped—'

'Whoa there, not killed,' Gil corrected her. 'Had a few slaps but Hunt left him very much alive.'

'But I heard the shots?'

'Sounds like Hunt wanted you to think Lane was dead,' Jess said. 'So that the gun was a viable threat.'

Jess, who had spent ten minutes speaking with Catrin after her emergence, now assumed the role of organiser. 'Right. It's almost three o'clock. You must be starving, Catrin.'

Catrin nodded with a smile. 'Famished.'

That sealed it. 'All right, then,' Jess said. 'There's room at the George in Lampeter. I suggest a celebratory tea.'

'Do they take dogs?' Catrin asked.

'They certainly do. That was my first question,' Jess said..

Catrin smiled. 'Good, because I'm buying Cadi a steak.' She went to the dog and once more knelt next to her.

Warlow shrugged. 'Why not? But it's my treat. It's not every day you witness a real-life Lazarus re-enactment.'

'No need for you to pay, sir,' Craig said.

'No. It's all good. My ex's probate has just been executed. Might as well celebrate the living with a present from the dead.'

CHAPTER FORTY-ONE

LESS A TEA, more an early supper.

They ate with the gusto of people whose appetites had been blunted of late by the anxiety of a lost colleague. There was drink, too. But not in excess. A half pint only for the drivers and more cool, delicious water for Catrin. There was a necessary frivolity and several bad jokes. Gil's toast put a tin hat on it even if it revisited his quip of earlier.

'I got it wrong. Here's to the silver medallist in the world hide and seek championships, DS Catrin Richards.'

Of course, it was Rhys who provided the lead into the joke when he asked, 'Why runner-up, sarge? Who's the world champion?'

'No idea. They haven't found the bugger yet.'

Catrin's jotted thoughts proved to be of most interest, and the polaroids, or at least her video of them, eventually proved to be the key. She'd found the images at the bottom of a pile of Hunt's clothes. The snaps may have fallen out of his pockets, and one of them looked the worse for wear, stained and curly from water damage.

She sent copies to everyone's phone via their WhatsApp group, and they identified one easily enough. *Cân-y-barcud* taken from a vantage point at the rear of the building. The second depicted Lane's vehicle inside the dilapidated feed shed where Hunt left the journalist bruised and beaten on the day he kidnapped Catrin.

'*Aide-mémoire*?' Jess said.

'In case he needed to go back, you mean?' Rhys asked.

'Maybe.' Warlow hadn't quite made his mind up.

However, the third polaroid turned out to be the mysterious one. It was faded from sunlight and damp. But a seascape image with the top edge showing a quarter of the rear window of a car in fading light.

It was Craig who put the pieces together. 'I know where this is.' He peered at the image blown up on his phone. 'This is Kidwelly Quay, and that's Lane's car in the foreground. I recognise the sticker.'

'*Mam fach*, from the time he was mugged?' Gil was halfway through a sticky toffee pudding with custard when the penny dropped.

Rhys sat up. 'Craig's right. This spot is close to where we stood waiting for the coastguard to bring in the boat that got abandoned when that surgeon was killed in Laugharne.'

Catrin nodded slowly, seeing it now for what it was.

'We'd need to check the exact positioning, but I'd put good money on this being the same spot where Lane's car was parked when he was supposedly mugged and the mugger drove him to the Quay and locked him in the boot,' Craig continued. 'So, Hunt was on the scene then, too. And knew who Lane was.'

'Hunt was the mugger?' Gina asked.

'If there ever was a mugging,' Warlow said, his face betraying what they were all thinking.

Catrin opened her notebook again. 'These are the scribbles that Hunt drew next to the GPS coordinates.' She held the book up. What she showed them was her copy of what Hunt had drawn. Half a dozen strokes of different lengths in a bucket shape.

'He was into wildlife,' Craig pointed out.

'Look like tufts of reeds or grass to me,' Rhys said.

'Grass,' Warlow muttered with a tiny snort.

'As in… grass?' Gil added, confused.

'As in an informant.' Warlow's expression hardened into distaste.

'Lane?' Craig asked.

'Might be hard to prove, but it looks like that to me. If we can find evidence linking Lane to Hunt—'

'I'll be happy to take lead on that, sir,' Catrin said. She'd gone pale again at the idea that all the while, her involvement with Lane had been leading to that one moment. The moment she'd not refuted his suggestion that Napier had a home in Angle. Or at least not refuted it enough with Hunt listening in.

'I'll help you with that,' Gil said.

'We all will,' Jess added, a bitter smile on her lips.

Rhys grinned. There was a touch of the manic about it.

'Why are you grinning?' Gil asked.

'This is like the Lord of the Rings, sarge. A quest. Like the fellowship.'

'Don't get carried away, Rhys.'

'No, he's right.' Gil surprised everyone by supporting Rhys's suggestion. 'But Lane is no evil genius. He's one of the filthy orcs. A bloody abomination.'

———

ONCE THE RELIEF and celebration of finding one of their own unscathed after a brush with a killer was over, Warlow found time to take stock.

Mundane reality impinged in the form of other cases, the small matter of Denise's will and all the frayed ends forming the tapestry of his life that needed tying off. Or at least trimmed, so that they did not form an untidy fringe that might trip him up. He refused point blank to be drawn into the media frenzy that blew up around the Hunt/Richards case. He left Two-Shoes and Drinkwater to handle the press. And, as was becoming increasingly obvious to him and to others, to watch Two-Shoes, like some oily masseuse, manipulate Drinkwater.

On the grubby, grease-stained pole that those who craved power had to scrabble up, Two-Shoes, knees clamped together, had a tight hold she would not easily relinquish. Warlow respected her only as much as any potential victim respected a predator who had survived in hostile environments. And the Police Force had won no awards for the way it treated women, and especially not women with political aspirations.

Warlow had no idea how Two-Shoes identified herself otherwise, personally, sexually, or in the pronoun Grand National. He knew she was single, and had some insight as to why, if not by choice. Her personality was so abrasive that it would take an extraordinarily patient person to consider a relationship with her. Anyone who did would likely feel trapped, as if caught in a spider's web.

And frankly, he cared about as much as an owl duet.

'Two hoots,' Gil explained to Rhys on hearing Warlow use this idiom.

What Warlow did care about was how her machinations had affected his team. So far, like a slow leak from an oil tanker, it had only resulted in pollution and regret. Everyone's except hers, of course. But as he watched her calmly and icily respond to the press grilling, carefully cultivating the narrative to ensure Dyfed Powys came out smelling of roses and using the personal pronoun at every opportunity to avoid the mention of anyone else, he had to admire her skill.

No, not admire. Wonder was a better word. You hardly ever admired a mudslide as it engulfed a village, but you did wonder at it. Human nature was an unpredictable beast.

They had not yet called Lane to book. But they would. Putting the journalist in the frame for conspiracy would need time and a lot of sifting through the fragments of information from Hunt's belongings in the underground shelter as well as what had not been damaged beyond repair from the mess in the generator shed in Angle.

But a case is what they would build, and Warlow wanted it watertight.

'DDS?' As Gil so aptly put it. 'Tight as Daffy Duck's sphincter.'

Amidst the media frenzy over the Hunt/Richards case, Warlow couldn't ignore other pressing matters, particularly the seemingly minor but conscience-nagging matter of Denzil Williams. The innocent shop worker who'd died in pursuit of a thieving miscreant, gone but not forgotten.

Certainly not by Rhys.

―――――

A FEW DAYS after Catrin had climbed out of the bunker, the team, Catrin included – Warlow had given up telling her to stay home by then – listened as Rhys, at Jess's behest, outlined his findings.

And very interesting they were, too. They'd cleared the boards of Hunt, leaving a space for Lane, and Rhys had a blank area of whiteboard underneath the pasted-up image of the dead shop assistant, Williams.

This morning, he gave them a quick summary. 'Denzil Williams died of a ruptured brain aneurysm. The post-mortem found he had multiple such deformities in the vessels inside his head, any of which could have burst at any moment. The pathologist's interpretation of events is that, though it is possible the heightened activity and stress of pursuit may have contributed, the aneurysm could as easily have burst if Denzil Williams had been constipated.'

'You'll need to explain that one a bit, Rhys,' Gil said.

'Straining at stool is the term he used. Puts your blood pressure up. Way up, apparently. For the few seconds it takes.'

'I find kimchee oils the wheels,' Gil said.

'No need to be smug,' Catrin muttered.

'Oh, I've got a hit list of propulsion fuel, with varying degrees of effort reduction implied. We're not talking bran flakes here. I'm talking about cast iron guarantees. Though, if it's got to the stage where it's as hard as cast iron, the risk of a tear is significant—'

Warlow shut him up with a glare.

'As you were saying, Rhys?'

'The pathologist also said that the head injury occurred from Williams hitting the ground, probably after unconsciousness resulting from the aneurysm rupturing. Not vice versa.'

'So, he wasn't struck.'

'No, sir. But what bothers me, as you remember, is the discrepancy between witnesses.' Rhys wrote up two names on the board. 'Kaylee Morris, the witness standing next to the thief, described him as older, early forties. The shop assistant, Libby, said he was much younger. DI Allanby rightly pointed out description and identification are highly subjective. So, I looked for more objective evidence.'

For once, no one commented. That is, Gil kept quiet.

'The CCTV evidence was the camera above the till and not that helpful. We see the thief and what he's holding, but under a baseball cap which shields his face, plus the fact that he was wearing flesh-coloured gloves. There is no CCTV in the car park where the "incident" took place. Then I went back to the footage within the shop.'

Rhys had set up a monitor on a mobile stand next to the boards. He ran the video again, this time using his trusty laser pointer. He circled the purchases Kaylee Morris had placed from her basket onto the area, ready for scanning, but which were never bought and simply returned to the shelves following the incident.

'It's an unusual collection. Four big bottles. Two of cola, one fizzy water, and one cordial. The water and cordial are expensive, not the cheaper own-label variety. Black bin bags and rubber gloves. Mega bag of crisps, again the fancy type, not the cheap ones. There are two bottles of cooking oil. One an origin olive oil. Pasta and pasta sauce. Well known brands, not the own-label cheapies. It took me a while, but what links them is that they are all taken from the first and second aisle as you walk into the store.'

'Not the best of diets,' Catrin said.

'No,' Rhys agreed. 'And not the cheapest either. Remember that Kaylee is a single mother with three kids.'

'What conclusion have you drawn, Rhys?' Warlow was enjoying the DC's presentation.

'I think Kaylee Morris had no intention of buying these items. I think she grabbed them off the shelves willy-nilly. They are nothing but props to fill the basket.'

'So, you think she was in on it?' Gil asked.

Rhys nodded. 'I asked Semple, the store owner, to go through all of his inventory. The only things unaccounted for are three toys. One a remote-controlled car worth £30. Kaylee spent some time in the cards and toy alcove before the incident happened. There's no cctv coverage there. I think she may have taken the toys, and they were most likely in her backpack when I interviewed her at the scene. When I visited her at her temporary accommodation, she introduced me to a friend. A tallish woman in her late twenties. About the same height as the lager thief.'

'But didn't the teller describe the thief as having stubble?' Catrin asked.

'You can get stubble makeup, sarge. Very popular these days, too. Some people use it to bolster their identities.'

Gil wisely kept quiet on hearing that one.

'And when I visited Kaylee, one of her children was looking for his "mote". Which could have been reference to a remote control.'

'Bloody hell, Rhys,' Catrin said. 'I ought to get kidnapped more often.'

Warlow's shocked glower triggered a little shrug from an unrepentant Catrin. 'Too soon, sir?'

'Too bloody right,' Warlow growled.

Catrin grinned, delighted by her triggering.

'So, do we get a warrant for Francis's temporary accommodation?' Gil asked.

'Not my decision, sarge,' Rhys replied.

Warlow picked up on the reluctance. 'Isn't that the right thing to do?'

Rhys's mouth worked as he formulated his answer. 'There is a lot of conjecture in my theory, sir. I'm not sure the CPS will buy it.'

'Fair point,' Gil said. 'But a crime has been committed.'

Rhys looked unhappy. 'It's tough for them, sir. In the shelter. One room for the four of them. Kaylee Francis, I mean. I know it's not up to us to make judgements.'

'But we have to,' Warlow said. 'Every day. And intent is not the same as accident, but it's the difference between murder and possible manslaughter. I will talk to the CPS and tell them what we have. What we could need to take it further. I suspect if we did get a warrant, that remote-controlled car would be nowhere near now. Still, I have to admit, you did well there, Rhys. Very impressive.'

Gil was silently clapping. Jess smiled. Catrin simply nodded with her eyebrows raised.

Rhys, though, remained contrite. 'If I was honest, sir, if it wasn't for Denzil Williams and his daughter needing some form of justice, I'd offer to pay for the toys and forget the whole thing.'

'A step too far on a slippery slope there, Rhys,' Warlow said. 'But we know what you mean.'

CHAPTER FORTY-TWO

WARLOW TOOK the Williams case to the Crown Prosecution Service, and, as Rhys feared – and secretly hoped – they opted not to prosecute based on lack of evidence. They interviewed Abby, Kaylee's neighbour, but she claimed to have been elsewhere at the time of the robbery and said nothing more on the advice of her solicitor. When Libby, the shop assistant, was shown Abby's photograph in amongst a group of others, she did not pick it out. Indeed, she asked why she was being shown images of women – Abby being not the only one – when the robber had clearly been a bloke, stubble included.

'We're all about inclusivity and diversity,' Gil had said, which almost made Catrin choke on her coffee on hearing it in the observation room.

Despite all of that, Warlow spoke to Denzil Williams's daughter after the inquest, which returned a verdict of death by misadventure.

'I suppose it's good that it happened like that. Quick, I mean. He might have had a stroke and lingered.'

They stood outside the coroner's court on a bright day, offset by Nicola Sheedy's black clothes.

Warlow agreed, 'There is that. Probably the best way of

looking at it. When my turn comes, I'd take that if I ever get a choice.'

And so, the dust settled.

To an extent.

Warlow dug out the letter from Denise's solicitor and read it all again.

Read about the enigmatic Fern once more.

But unlike Quasimodo, it rang no bells.

Not yet.

Molly, freed from exam shackles, took on the role of Cadi-day-care, and girl and dog became water-sports experts in the period before Molly's post-exam trip abroad. Those weeks were as much Cadi's reward as the Molly's.

And Cadi deserved it for doing a 'bloody Lassie,' in Gil's words. 'Shame that bunker wasn't a well.'

The Hunt-Napier-Richards case had far-reaching consequences, much like the nuclear threats the observation post was built to monitor. The investigation's aftermath spread widely, affecting many people within the police force and beyond and there seemed to be no way to contain its impact.

An internal inquiry was announced and Warlow did his utmost not to be in the same room as Two-Shoes until such time she could be questioned as to the wisdom of placing a vulnerable officer like Catrin Richards in the journalistic spotlight. Because that, as a cause for Hunt's interest in her, became the accepted narrative.

For now.

That would change once Catrin dug up enough evidence to have Lane prosecuted. The GPS coordinates provided by Hunt were already yielding promising leads. The team had initiated ANPR searches in the areas indicated by those coordinates, focusing on the specific dates and times mentioned in Hunt's journal. They'd struck lucky and found two with Lane, via his expensive cycle, in the vicinity. The more the merrier, Warlow insisted. He did not want to give the vampire any opportunity to retreat into the shadows by shining a light on him too early.

But they would. A big, shiny, bright one.

The half way mark of the year had come and gone, which meant, as the naysayers always loved to point out, a drawing in of the nights and a descent into cold, dark winter.

Christ, living in the UK could be fun-filled. But deep down, Warlow knew that, though the Brits liked to complain – and he was sure a couple of universities offered courses on how to do just that these days – they had bugger all to complain about compared with other people. Nevern wasn't in the Crimea or the Gaza Strip. There'd be light and warmth and food for everyone come winter.

It could be very much worse.

At least Warlow had the chance to read Denise's will properly and to search his memory banks – and the PNC – for anyone by the name of Fern. He'd had no luck... so far.

And despite Napier no longer being around to answer Gil's questions, they would get access to his records once a decent enough time of mourning for his widow passed. They'd couch the search in terms of needing to examine records to better understand Hunt's motivation. What little Catrin had gleaned from interacting with the killer had only reinforced Gil's determination to stare into the dark heart of whatever had been going on with Napier and Royston Moyles, the serial Peeping Tom.

CHAPTER FORTY-THREE

AND JUST TO ADD TO the frivolity, much to Warlow's chagrin, Jess had not forgotten about her "friend" from Manchester and the invitation to meet up for a drink. Warlow envied her openness, and she was finally making friends locally through fitness classes and Pilates. He'd always admired the ease with which women developed friendships. Gyms were a prime example of where like minds met. He understood but did not buy in to it, much preferring his little home-made weights room and walks with the dog to keep him fit.

Molly found a job in a café on the beach at Newport and did either eight until three or eleven until six shifts. Her mood, despite the forthcoming trip abroad with friends, had not been the best this last week or so as Jess had found a more promising property to rent.

And so, on a warm July Friday evening, with the sun still a long way from setting, Warlow parked the Jeep and walked through the garden of the Fundle Arms in Stackpole. Hugely popular with locals and visitors alike, it served good seafood and had rooms. Luckily, school holidays had yet to begin. When they did, there would be no chance of grabbing a random table as Jess had done this evening at 7.30. He'd left Cadi at home, and as Warlow walked through, Jess waved to him from a bench-style table under an umbrella. There were kids around of course; It was a summer's evening, and the sun was out. In a lot of pubs up and down the country, gardens like this would have been filling up with both casual and committed drinkers. It was hot enough to feel uncomfortable in the sun. But no one in the Fundle Arms had taken off their tops.

It wasn't that kind of pub.

Jess, all smiles, introduced a man, aged somewhere in his mid to late forties. Fit looking, hair greying a little, and a woman of about the same age, tanned, and toned, who looked like a runner. His name was Mark Naismith, hers, Penny Naismith. They greeted Warlow with the same Manchester accent that Jess had. It went some way to explain their connection to her, which she elaborated upon as Warlow slid into a seat. Penny's sister had been a colleague of Jess's in the GMP and had been at the birthday party she'd recently attended. It was here that Jess had run into Mark again.

Warlow listened to all of this with a fixed grin and the realisation that he'd grasped the wrong end of the stick with both hands. For a while, as the Naismiths made all the social running, naturally and without effort, he ran a mental comb through the knots of his misconceptions and realised he'd been a complete idiot because he'd interpreted Jess's invitation as her way of telling him she was moving on.

Where exactly she was moving on from was another existential debate he was yet to have, but even so, he almost laughed out loud at his own hubris. But Jess's insistence at the meeting had daunted him. Only after she and Penny went to the little outside bar area servicing the garden did the true agenda surface. And when it did, he was too surprised to be offended.

'What's it like being Jess's boss, then?' Mark delivered the question with a grin.

'Easy. She can do my job, and often does, without turning a hair.'

'Always been very capable, has Jess. She tells me we have something in common, though.'

'Are you in the job, too, Mark?' A reasonable assumption since a lot of Jess's friends up north were ex-colleagues.

'God, no. Having Penny's sister keeping her beady eye on me is enough. Haven't been near the back of a lorry since she joined up.'

Warlow ejected a little huff of surprised laughter.

'No, I mean, the virus,' Mark said, his smile not slipping an inch.

Warlow's smile faded quickly, replaced by a frown. He managed to keep his jaw from dropping open, but only just.

Mark saw it and explained, 'I'm a haemophiliac. Diagnosed aged four. They started treating me with factor V111 when I was ten. I got the imported stuff from the States. You could sell your blood over there. Prisoners and drug addicts were top of the menu. So, I got HIV for no extra charge.'

Warlow blinked. It was rare that he was lost for words, but this statement had so much loaded within it that he needed to unpack it before answering. For a start, it meant that Jess had spoken to Mark about him and his own HIV status. Not that Warlow considered his medical situation a secret. Not anymore. But still.

'Me and my brother were both haemophiliacs.'

Warlow picked up on the past tense.

'He was younger than me. We both got the double whammy, like you. Hepatitis C and HIV. When they started treating us in the 70s, the NHS knew about the likely transmission of viruses, but they didn't do any testing in the USA.'

'But you look well,' Warlow said. Tom, his doctor son, would have been proud of that blandishment.

'Yeah. My liver isn't brilliant, but there's no cirrhosis. They monitor it. And the antiretrovirals keep a lid on the HIV. My brother wasn't so lucky. He died when he was twenty-five. From AIDS.'

'I'm sorry to hear that,' Warlow said.

Mark nodded. 'Yeah. Theresa May might have failed her GCSE negotiation technique exam and went the way of all unelected PMs because of it, but to give her credit, she set up a full inquiry into the imported contaminated blood scandal. We got them to admit their failures, though there were some Ministers of Health who still couldn't summon enough guts to admit they'd done anything wrong. It was a shit show back then. I hope they all spontaneously combust in their own beds.'

Warlow's brows crumpled.

'Sorry,' Mark said. 'I'll never be over it. But look at me. I have survivor guilt. Because I'm one of the lucky ones. I hear you are, too. Different circumstances, obviously. But my titres are negligible. We have two kids, Penny and me. She's the one that helped me come to terms with it and made me think I could actually live a normal life. I thought I'd never have kids. Should have taken shares out in condom companies. But Penny said stuff that struck home. In situations like this, it isn't the patients who are the heroes. It's the people around them. The docs said I was safe, and I am. How's your titre?'

How's your titre?

Not a phrase you heard every day in the Fundle Arms, Warlow was willing to bet. But a valid question nevertheless in the midst of all this volunteered information. A question shared only by a select few. Victims of happenstance and the worst luck. Mark's, and tragically his brother's, due to lousy diligence and ministers delivering BS fed by civil servants who failed to check facts and up-to-date research. Warlow's, courtesy of a vindictive junkie intent on passing on her own misery by hiding contaminated needles in her clothes and hair. She'd found a target in Warlow who, in doing his job, had received his own postmodern Snow-White style curse.

"By the pricking of my thumbs", indeed.

Disarmed by Mark's frankness, Warlow found himself opening up and chatting as if he were in the irritatingly chirpy haematology consultant's office for his six-monthly check-up. Sharing views on drug side effects and dosages. The overwhelming impression Warlow got was that Mark was hugely grateful for what he had. By implication, Warlow was reminded that he should be too.

He glanced up at Jess standing in the queue, made longer by the good weather, sharing a joke with Penny. For a second, even after the exchange with Mark, he toyed with allowing himself to be irritated by this set up.

Or was it an intervention? Jess's way of hammering home the message that he was being a fool to himself and to others.

Warlow the sullied. Warlow the tainted.

For some time after separating from Denise, he'd felt destined to be alone. Or rather, felt unready to be anything else but alone, even if he'd let his imagination wander into the deep and uncharted waters of proper companionship. He'd had a little taste of this with Molly and Jess staying with him. But this had been very much the small plate taster menu, not the main course. And, knowing that it was coming to an end, he'd begun to brace himself for going hungry again.

Jess had not so much led him into a trap here as brought him face-to-face with a mirror and made him look into it.

He had a choice now.

Walk away and sulk, return to the cottage and watch his life slide back into the old patterns with everyone at arm's-length. Somewhere he could cultivate his curmudgeonly existence with irritation at the world at large as fertiliser. But Jess would simply say he was using the HIV as a psychological barbed wire to keep visitors at bay.

Yes, it was easy to maintain a professional distance within the cut and thrust of work. Not so simple when it came to the merry dance that was social interaction. Like in the Fundle Arms. Because here, you had to be yourself and not try and work out how much the scrote opposite you was saying was true. Mark was no scrote. He was a pleasant, open man with a shared life experience. And Jess's motivation was nothing more than her wanting to show Warlow that there was a life, a normal life, there for the taking.

Warlow's anger dissipated then like smoke from a jar.

He glanced up at the bar, and saw her half turn to look over her shoulder, an eyebrow raised in his direction. An all-encompassing expression that included exasperation at the queue, but also a question in the upturned corner of her mouth.

Are you okay with this?

That was what he read.

As well as the usual astonishment at how she looked so bloody good simply standing in the line-up to order drinks. The summer sun had turned her olive complexion a little darker, and she'd done something with her hair to clip it up away from her face.

He sent back the briefest of smiles. One that also softened her eyes. She turned away as Penny spoke to her.

At the same time, Mark asked Warlow another question.

'Jess said you have a place down here?"

'I do.'

'Lovely part of the world. We come down every year. Hard to believe there is any crime at all. But Jess says there's enough to keep you both busy.'

'More than enough.'

'She likes it here. Doesn't stop blabbing about it. Penny is happy for her. I mean, we all think she deserves a bit of luck after Ricky. Bloody fool that he is. Penny and her sister want Jess to come back to Manchester now that Molly will be in uni.'

'Oh?' Warlow had no right to feel anxious about that, but his physiology betrayed him with a little twinge in his gut.

'But no way, hoze A.' Mark grinned. 'They've been staying with you while they look for a new place, I hear, so I don't need to tell you how much they've been smitten.'

Jess had previously told Warlow she had no intention of returning to Manchester. But it was good to hear corroboration. Something he needed to hear. He picked up his phone and glanced at it. A ruse he often used to great effect to break away from a conversation.

He sent Mark a perfunctory smile. 'I need to answer this.' Warlow walked away towards a corner of the garden and sent a text to Jess:

> We need to talk.

She texted back:

> Sorry if I've offended you.

> You haven't. But we need to talk.

He hesitated before sending that last sentence, struck by how bloody ridiculous texting was when the woman he was texting stood only a few yards away. It must have struck Jess too, because, a moment later, she came across the garden with a tight expression.

'Evan, I—'

She never got to finish as a voice came through the crowd.

'There you are, Mum. I thought you were at the bar.' An exasperated Molly Allanby approached.

'Penny's at the bar. She's about to order.'

'Good. I could murder half a cider. Where exactly is she?'

Jess made eyes at Warlow. Molly was not high maintenance, but she had a teenager's approach to expecting the adults to move when she said jump. She lowered her voice to address Warlow. 'I really didn't mean to offend you. Mark is so great. But if I have, I wouldn't blame you if you left. There, I've said it.' She turned to follow her daughter.

Warlow put his hand on her arm. 'I'm not leaving,' he said. 'But there is something I needed to say.'

'Mind my own business, I get it. It's just that Mark is here on holiday and—'

'Will you be quiet, DI Allanby? What I want is for you to please stop looking for somewhere else to live.'

Jess's eyes narrowed, and then crinkled into a smile that made her look like her daughter's twin. She sighed. 'Rick has agreed to buy me out of the house in Manchester. It should be my round. It means I might be able to buy a place of my own instead of renting.'

'Wow,' Warlow said. 'That's tremendous news.' It wasn't, but he thought he got away with it.

'I'll need some help looking. You know the area well. It's expensive down here but I'm not averse to buying something that needs a bit of work.'

'Good idea,' Warlow said, trying to suppress the crushing disappointment he felt. A disappointment he had no right to feel.

Jess gave him a toothless smile. 'But it seems stupid to move twice. If you'll have us, we could stay a bit longer. I can move into Mol's room once her term starts. You won't have to stay in your man cave much longer.'

The disappointment ebbed away.

'Where would Molly sleep when she comes back?'

'Maybe by then we'll have worked something out. Who knows?'

Warlow frowned. 'Yes, but—'

From the bar area serving the garden, Molly called out, 'Penny is at the bar, and she needs a hand.'

Jess gave a mini eye roll and turned towards Molly. 'Coming, love.'

He watched them hurry away to fetch drinks, still unsure about what the implications of that little exchange were. But in truth, buying a property could take months. That gave him a little time to… what?

Had he just been nudged? First by Mark and now by Jess? Or, if you looked under the hood, all by Jess.

He looked at his phone. No more text exchanges. He glanced back at Mark who was here as living proof that the barriers Warlow had arranged around himself were paper thin.

Before he returned to chat to Mark, he lifted his face to the sun and let its warmth bathe him, hoping that one of the gods looking down might give him some inspiration. Instead, high above, the seagulls circled, waiting, no doubt for someone to leave leftovers on a table. Their cries were a lament for the ever hopeful of this world.

Like him.

Evan Warlow, you are an idiot.

And, as he turned back towards the garden, for once, he allowed himself a little smile. No gods would help. If things needed working out, he bloody well ought to get a pencil and sharpen it. He had no more excuses. Make-your-mind-up time. And he was crap at it. What if he was reading this all wrong?

The bugling of the gulls followed him as he walked through the garden. Whether they were laughing at him or cheering him on, he couldn't tell.

But there was only one way to find out.

ACKNOWLEDGMENTS

Here's the text reduced by approximately 33% while retaining key details:

This novel's existence depends on me, the author, and others who turn an idea into reality. Thanks to my wife Eleri, Sian Phillips, Tim Barber, and other proofers and ARC readers for their help. Special mention to Ela the dog who drags me from the writing cave for walks, though she avoids rain.

My biggest thanks go to you, lovely reader, for joining me on this roller-coaster ride with Evan and the team.

If you enjoyed it, could you spare a moment to **leave a review or rating?** A few words on my Amazon page would help others discover the book and support authors you like.

A FREE BOOK FOR YOU

Visit my website and join up to the Rhys Dylan VIP Reader's Club and get a FREE novella, *The Wolf Hunts Alone,* by visiting the website at: **rhysdylan.com**

The Wolf Hunts Alone.

One man and his dog... will track you down.

DCI Evan Warlow is at a crossroads in his life. Living alone, contending with the bad hand fate has dealt him, he finds solace in simple things like walking his neighbour's dog.

But even that is not as safe as it was. Dogs are going missing from a country park. And not only one, now three have disappeared. When he takes it upon himself to root out the cause of the lost animals, Warlow faces ridicule and a thuggish enemy.

But are these simply dog thefts? Or is there a more sinister malevolence at work? One with its sights on bigger, two legged prey.
A FREE eBOOK FOR YOU (Available in digital format)

Only one thing is for certain; Warlow will not rest until he finds out.

———

By joining the club, you will also be the first to hear about new releases via the few but fun emails I'll send you. This includes a no spam promise from me, and you can unsubscribe at any time.

AUTHOR'S NOTE

As I write this series, I find myself inventing, and then having to tie off, threads as I go along. This book ties together more than one. For one thing, it brings to an end Roger Hunt's existence. A figure that has haunted more than one book. In addition, it has allowed me to bring, I hope seamlessly, one of my favourite characters to the heart of the matter. When I announced the title, The Last Throw, and had Cadi on the cover, it rattled a lot of readers. I hope now that most of you will have calmed down and know that I am not that type of author. But this book is about change and renewal with one of the team now having given birth. That gives me scope to explore more and different dynamics in future stories.

Oh, and the Royal Observer Corps bunkers mentioned in this book are not a fabrication. Well, the location of one of them is, but the rest are very real… I bet you've driven past one without even noticing. It's a strange, sometimes frightening, but also wonderful world we live, and my job is to take you to the lesser known corners of this amazing part of Britain.

Not everyone here is a murderer. Not everyone… Cue tense music!

All the best, and see you all soon, Rhys.

And do not forget that for those of you who are interested, there is a glossary on the website to help with those pesky pronunciations.

READY FOR MORE?

DCI Evan Warlow and the team are back in…

Dragon's Breath

A man wanders lost on a filthy night in the Black mountains of Wales. Despite the valiant efforts of the rescue Services, he does not survive.

Forensic evidence suggests he was drugged and abandoned. A deliberate act of malevolence and a vicious crime to boot.

DCI Warlow and team are drawn into a mystery that soon spirals into more deaths and a poisonous trade. The Dragon's breath threatens everyone it touches and the community at large. A devious killer is abroad. One that cares for nothing other than their own twisted greed. And no one is safe from its deadly reach.

Made in United States
North Haven, CT
21 November 2024

60729519R00188